BAD LAND

BAD LAND

CORINNA CHONG

A Novel

ARSENAL PULP PRESS
VANCOUVER

ARSENAL PULP PRESS
Suite 202 – 211 East Georgia St.
Vancouver, BC V6A 1Z6
Canada
arsenalpulp.com

The publisher gratefully acknowledges the support of the Canada Council for the Arts
and the British Columbia Arts Council for its publishing program and the Government
of Canada and the Government of British Columbia (through the Book Publishing
Tax Credit Program) for its publishing activities.

Arsenal Pulp Press acknowledges the xʷməθkʷəy̓əm (Musqueam), Sḵwx̱wú7mesh
(Squamish), and səlilwətaɬ (Tsleil-Waututh) Nations, custodians of the traditional,
ancestral, and unceded territories where our office is located. We pay respect to their
histories, traditions, and continuous living cultures and commit to accountability,
respectful relations, and friendship.

This is a work of fiction. Any resemblance of characters to persons either living
or deceased is purely coincidental.

Cover design and interior typesetting by Jazmin Welch
Text design by Jasmin Linton
Front cover art by Alfred Stieglitz, *Georgia O'Keeffe—Hands and Horse Skull*, 1931,
 7 9/16″ × 9 7/16″, gelatin silver print
Back cover photograph by Jake Warren (@jakewarrenphotography) via Unsplash
Edited by Catharine Chen
Proofread by Alison Strobel

Printed and bound in Canada

Library and Archives Canada Cataloguing in Publication:
Title: Bad land : a novel / Corinna Chong.
Names: Chong, Corinna, author.
Identifiers: Canadiana (print) 20240317246 | Canadiana (ebook) 20240317254 |
  ISBN 9781551529592 (softcover) | ISBN 9781551529608 (EPUB)
Subjects: LCGFT: Novels.
Classification: LCC PS8605.H654 B33 2024 | DDC C813/.6—dc23

For my mummy,
then and now

... the ridges, the pinnacles, the hoodoos, were not only worn by water but shaped by wind too, cut by the sky; there was no wind now, this morning, yet he, Web, in the stillness of dawn heard the endless nagging of the wind, the nagging sky that had worn his face almost black, his mustache almost white: time. It was over. Past. No. There was no past, never.

—ROBERT KROETSCH, *Badlands*

Violante in the pantry
Gnawing at a mutton bone
How she gnawed it
How she clawed it
When she felt herself alone.

Girls are cruelest to themselves.
Someone like Emily Brontë,
who remained a girl all her life despite her body as a woman,

had cruelty drifted up in all the cracks of her like spring snow.

—ANNE CARSON, "The Glass Essay"

LAYER

Layers of sediment cover the bones,
burying them deeper and deeper over time.

1

I OFTEN IMAGINE how Jez would have seen it.

There she is, Ricky's passenger in the rust-pocked Buick as it speeds down the 9 and veers north, tracing the ridgeline that scars the golden pelt of the prairies. She watches the land become a dry crust, the beige of dead skin, sprouting tufts of sagebrush and stray grasses combed flat by the wind. Then the puckered hills begin to swell out of the earth, growing higher, wider, baring their stripes of ancient rock and clay and ash, layer upon layer. As the Buick sinks into the valley, the hills knit together behind them, closing them in.

Welcome to Dinosaur Country, says the sign at the edge of town. It is not unusual here to see a velociraptor or a T. Rex riding in the bed of a truck. You might even see one with a saddle. Reins, even. Dinosaurs, especially carnivorous ones, sell things here. But for me, it will always be the city of bones, since bones are, truth be told, all that's left of what once was.

My brother always called this a "fake" town, which was why it so perplexed me to see him back. When Ricky was a boy, someone at school got him onto the word *fake*. Our Mutti's bosom as she bent down to hand us our lunch pails, like antiques compared to the plastic sacks of our classmates.

"Did you know your mom's boobies are fake?" the other boy said to him. He was a very pale child, all freckled up and down his skinny arms.

"Fake?" Ricky said. Mutti never used the word, but he knew it was not a kind thing to say. "So?" he shot back.

Mutti's breasts, of course, were not fake. They were merely large, and very round and glossy, like fishbowls. She wore blouses with scooped, ruffled necklines to fringe their roundness.

I didn't think the incident had fazed Ricky; he was always good at masking how much he took things to heart. But the word came up again soon after, when we were strung along on the requisite sightseeing trip with Mutti's aunt Regina, straight from Dresden—my namesake, as you might guess. Her annual visits always involved a trip to see the World's Largest Dinosaur, during which all of us would pretend it wasn't exactly the same as the year before. I see Tante Regina always as just a large head detached from its body, cat-eyed with thick black liner, with a wide, grinning mouth and an auburn beehive staked on top. A large head signalled a large intellect, according to Mutti.

Ricky and I trailed behind Tante Regina through the parking lot, the tail to her kite. The wind was surging that day, whipping tree branches and shaking leaves loose. Tante Regina held her hair up with both hands, as though balancing a vase. She came upon the towering concrete T. Rex and sat herself on its giant yellow toenail. Her gaze travelled upward, and her mouth opened, teeth parting.

"Guck mal, wie riesig," she muttered. *Look how big.* The T. Rex stood inert, fixed in mock stride against the living valley beyond. The hills in the distance churned in the wind, their tangled grasses writhing.

"It's only fake," Ricky replied in English. "It's not even to scale. *Tyrannosaurus rex* was only an average of twelve metres long."

He knew that Tante Regina could not understand him. She simply smiled, pointed up at the creature's collection of thorny teeth.

"He eat you, maybe?" she said, grinning.

Ricky's face then, his expression, turned sore in the jaw, as though he'd been chewing on a piece of toffee that had proven too much work.

I remember it still, dozens of years later. The expression that showed Ricky understood then how the world was full of fake, and there was nothing he could do to change it. The T. Rex was everything he hated about Drumheller. His fear of being eaten up by it captured in that face. I recognized it immediately when it met me again, on the day Ricky finally returned.

It was the end of summer. The Never-Ending Summer, they were calling it, for the stubborn heat had been pressing its fist down on us since May, suffocating the life out of the land. I was walking, for the first time in nearly two weeks; I'd finally given up on waiting for the heat to relent. But something else was different that day. It sounds foolish to say, but I could feel it in the air—cracker dry, laced with a kind of delicate rawness, like an open wound. I looked up at the barren sky, the sunspots in my vision making inky clouds over the blue.

Perhaps it was because of that feeling, how it stalked me all the way down the block and back to my house, that I felt spooked, hackles raised like a prey animal, when I caught sight of someone sitting in my front yard, cloaked in the shade of the oak tree. Not just one person, but two. My steps slowed, arcing around them. They'd already become part of the landscape, their suitcases stacked under their bottoms. Ricky and a miniature person—a girl; two round faces, an orange and a mandarin, both baring that same expression, rotating in unison to follow my steps.

I hadn't seen Ricky in seven years. I'd never seen the girl. In fact, I hadn't even known of her existence.

"Have you been watching the news?" were Ricky's first words. Then, seeing my blank face, he added, "CNN's calling this a heat dome. Covers the whole western half of North America."

Puffing air in and out of my lungs, I said, "I'll decide for myself when the world's going to end." I took a deep, slow breath to calm my heart.

"You haven't changed, I see," he said. If I'd seen only his eyes, I'd never have known it was him, for they had a queer shine at the centre that I'd never seen before. But the rest of him—the round face, the buzzard-like posture—was just the same. Sweat dotted his forehead like a smattering of tiny blisters. "Here's Jez," he said, standing with his hand on the girl's arm so that she stood too. "My daughter. Ours."

When he said "ours," he meant his and Carla's, of course. Ricky never liked to refer to relations by their names; we were always "her" or "she," and he trusted us, his family, to know him well enough to make sense of his talk. Carla was a stick of a thing with a small, upturned nose. Everything about her was sharp, even her hair, gelled up in spikes like crocodile teeth. She always seemed to be sticking her elbows out, hands on hips, making herself into a perfect triangle. I hadn't seen her since the wedding.

The girl, Jez, peered up at me, then fixed her eyes on my heaving belly. She drew her lips in, held them between her teeth.

"Hello," I said. I clasped my hands behind my back so I would not offer to shake her hand or pat her on the head.

"Please to make your acquaintance," she said softly.

"Pleased," Ricky quickly said. "It's 'pleeze-duh,' not 'pleeze.'"

The girl said nothing.

"She's shy," Ricky said, waving at the air above her head. "It's normal for girls her age."

"What age is that?" I asked.

"Six." He slid his hands into his pockets. The pants looked tight, strained and wrinkled in angry slashes around his crotch. "Should we go in?" he continued.

"With those?" I pointed to the suitcases. There were eight of them altogether. Four were piled next to the oak's trunk, hiding in the shade, where I hadn't seen them earlier. They bulged, teetered. But Ricky didn't bother to wait for an answer. He was already staggering up the front steps, a suitcase in each hand.

Jez took the edges of her thin cotton skirt in her hands, as if to mimic her father. She climbed the steps—one foot up, touch the other, one foot up, touch the other—like a flower girl in a wedding procession. Her skirt was decorated with small holes, and the light shone pinhole beams through them, making constellations on the pavement.

I didn't ask Ricky what he was doing here, where Carla was at. He would be embarrassed, to be sure. His ring was a fixture on his

14

finger, the skin ballooning around it where weight had gathered since his wedding.

He piled the other suitcases at the foot of the stairs, then went about fixing cheese and pickle sandwiches for himself and Jez. The kitchen was greyed over, the curtains drawn to keep the heat out. Ricky's darkened form moving through the kitchen, checking the fridge door closed with his hip, rooting around in the drawer for the butter spreader with the wooden handle—it prickled, made me itchy. Nothing had changed, was what he said without saying. As if he'd never left, we'd never grown beyond childhood, this house had never become mine.

"I broke it," I said to him, as I watched him dig among clattering knives. I switched on the light. "The wood was old. It cracked, split right down the centre." I used my finger to draw a line to the ceiling. Ricky stopped his burrowing and peered at me, at the spot on my head where the hair is fine and sticks up straight.

"Well, what have you done with it? I could fix it, you know."

"It was old," I said. "I gave it up."

A sigh then, heavy as a sunken boat. He retrieved a regular butter knife and went about his business. I did not tell him that I'd taken to making sure I didn't dip my knife twice, so as not to smear crumbs into the butter. I watched him scrape the excess on the edge of the dish, leaving a speckled clot that would be abandoned there, dodged until the dish was empty, then washed down the sink.

With Jez, I began with sidewalk chalk. She was crouched over the front step, her dark hair curtaining her face, playing with a small narwhal toy that Ricky had called her "beanie." Though it had no legs, she made it walk on the step, tapping the butt of its tail along the cement. Its horn, a spiralled cone of metallic-looking fabric, poked to the sky. I learned by listening to her soft talking that its name was Earl.

"Okay, we found the top of the mountain," she whispered to herself. "Now we hafta find the graveyard."

I placed the old bucket of chalk next to her. The pieces had long ago been scraped and broken into so many chiselled chunks.

"Your papa says you like to draw," I said.

Without a pause, she grabbed at a chunk of pink chalk and began scraping it along the edge of the step, Earl still clutched in her other hand.

"This is the edge of the mountain," she said. "Don't fall."

"What happens if he falls?" I asked.

"He gets bloody," she said. "The blood pours out of his eyes." Her fingers splayed in a spraying motion.

"Well," I said. "We wouldn't want that."

She looked up at me, twisted those pink lips of hers. It was clear she was not accustomed to such matter-of-fact answers.

"What's your name?" she said.

"Regina," I replied. "But I'm your aunt. So you can call me Auntie Reg."

"That sounds like a boy's name. I never heard a name like that before."

"Your oma—do you know what it means, 'oma'?"

She shook her head, making her wispy hair shake about her ears.

"It means 'grandma' in German. You have a grandma. An oma. She is German. And she gave me my name. It's German too."

"What's a German?" she said.

"Germany is a country. All the way on the other side of the ocean."

"With the bat train?"

"The what?"

"The train, the one like a bat," she repeated.

"Yes," I nodded. "The upside-down train." So Ricky had spoken of Mutti. He'd told Jez about the place where our mother was born, famed for the suspended train that snakes through the city. The passenger cars hang from giant iron wheels orange with age. People board at floating stations that meet the flanks of the cars as they glide along their route. Mutti always called it a magical city.

"It's named Wuppertal," I told Jez. "Your papa probably told you stories about it."

"He doesn't like stories," she said. "They're not real. Only fake."

Fake. I clucked my tongue at that. "Some stories are real," I said. "Like the one about the narwhal named Earl and the brown bunny named Waldo."

"What bunny?" she said in a whisper.

"There was a bunny named Waldo. He lost his mother, and he was very tiny and cold. He stayed under that oak, the one right over there, waiting for his mother for a whole day. But just as the cold night was about to come and freeze his bones, Auntie Reg rescued him and became his new mother. And then, sometime later, he met a narwhal named Earl, and they became best friends forever. The end." It was a crudely abridged version of the story, but Jez seemed satisfied.

"I never knew a bunny before," she said.

"Would you like to meet him?"

She nodded, a smile spreading across her face. It is true that every child loves a bunny. Perhaps because of a childhood memory, I have a soft spot for brown bunnies. In this memory, it was not my bunny, but one belonging to the girl who lived in the house on the corner. She found the wisp of a thing on a golf course, so she said to all the neighbourhood girls who had gathered to ogle it. But it was so tiny and waiflike that we assumed some older, more careful parent had rescued it on her behalf. Abandoned by its mother, she said. She held the bunny up above her head to give us a glimpse of its underside. The umbilical cord, a black ashy curl, like a long-dead and shrivelled worm. I held the thing, and the dried-up cord scraped across my palm as it shuffled about. It would have been rude to recoil; I imagined myself a kind of nurse, putting on a stone face so as not to embarrass the patient or show my own squeamishness.

"It will fall off soon," the girl said. I forget her name. But I remember that I asked if she would keep the umbilical cord when it fell off.

"What for?" she asked, crinkling her nose.

I had pictured it preserved in a tiny glass ball, but I knew enough at that age to just shrug, let her forget.

Many years later I acquired a brown bunny of my own, quite by fate, it seemed. He arrived precisely on the anniversary of Mutti's departure. It seemed only right to give him her maiden name, Grünewald. But I kept tripping over the word, choking on my attempts to roll a German "*rrrr.*" So I called him Waldo for short, even though you're meant to pronounce the *W* as a *V* in German.

When I introduced Waldo to Jez, he was wearing his red ribbon around his neck, making him look like a furry present.

"Ooooh," Jez cooed. She peered into the hutch, her tiny fingers like larvae pressed to the edge of the gate. Then she poked Earl's horn through a gap in the wire grate that seemed perfectly sized for it and let him hang there. "Can I pet him?"

"Yes," I said, prying the gate open. "But be gentle."

Her arms shot out like bullets from a gun, fingers snatching fur. It happened so quickly that I hadn't any time to stop it.

Waldo made a small, horrible noise—the sharpest, tiniest of yowls—something I'd never heard before, like all the wind was being squeezed from his lungs at once.

I slapped the girl hard on the forearm. Her fingers unclenched, dropped Waldo. Like flicking a switch. She didn't cry. She only peered up at me with the very same expression she'd given me the first moment we met.

"Gently," I hissed, my finger held up. "He's only a small creature, you know. His bones are so thin, like little twigs. If you're too rough, they'll snap, just snap and break and he'll be as good as dead because you can't repair a broken spine on a bunny." I breathed in deeply. It was more words, all in one string, than I'd said out loud in a long time.

"Let's go in now," I said to fill the silence. I pushed the gate closed, shoved it in tight. Waldo hopped about as if nothing had happened. My hands shook.

The house was Mutti's old house, and it still showed. All dark, shiny wood and heavy drapes wafting ancient cigarette smoke. The floorboards purred under my feet. I slept in the same room I had as a child—an alcove in the roof, sloped ceiling on both sides. The walls were the pink of a womb. A single window, round as a planet, looked out onto the street. It was the only uncovered window in the house. I lay beneath it at night, knowing that the moonlight shining into the grooves of my hands was the spell to make me sleep.

I hadn't any sense of the dinginess of the place until I led Jez up the stairs to my room and saw a mummified spider in the corner of one of the steps. It had turned on its back, its legs drawn into its belly, its tattered web making a shroud over its body. It had surely been there a long time, but only now, as I saw things through Jez's eyes, was every detail suddenly magnified. When I opened the door, the pink carpet was patchy with stains, the linens on the bed were threadbare, and the smell of sleep seemed to emanate from the walls. I saw the crack that one of Mutti's men had put in the drywall with a baseball bat years ago, and the missing knobs on my dresser. Jez peered around, her eyes finally settling on the window.

"This one's your room?" she asked.

"Yes," I said. "It was painted this colour when I was as young as you. Before that it was a normal colour. Taupe, or maybe even white. It wasn't always so pink."

She didn't appear to be interested in my excuses. Instead, she tip-toed to the bed, pulled back the covers, and climbed inside. "This is you," she said, staring up at the ceiling. "Let's say I'm you and you're me."

I sat on the end of the bed, and the mattress tossed her small body. "I'm you?" I said. "How could I be you?"

"It's easy," she said. "You pretend. Pretend you're me, okay?" She sat up and looked at me expectantly.

"All right then," I said. I cleared my throat. "My name is Jez," I said in a squeaky voice, "and I'm a little girl. A very pretty little girl."

She flopped back onto the bed. "I'm an auntie," she said, making a starfish. "Look how big I am."

"You're enormous," I said. "Big as the moon."

"Yeah," she said. "Big ol' bitch."

"Uh-oh," I said automatically, sounding just like Mutti.

Ricky's voice interrupted then. "How're you getting on?" He came through the door. "What do you think?" he said, looking around the room. Jez scrambled under the covers. The word had stung the air and now seemed to hang there, invisible to Ricky. I stood and brushed off my dress as a way of busying myself.

"Cozy, isn't it?" Ricky continued. Jez wriggled under the covers, giggling breathily to herself. She knew the word was a bad one, and it seemed to have given her a surge of energy to use it.

"Not a bad place to live for a while," Ricky said. "Just you, me, and your aunt."

This was Ricky's way of asking to stay, and from the look in his eye I surmised that he had no clue as to how long it would be. I bit my lip to stifle a snort of protest. He still considered it his house too. His home. And now Jez's as well.

"Jez," I said to him. "It's an unusual name, isn't it?"

"It's short for Jesmin," he explained. "Like Jasmine, but, you know, different. She picked it."

I nodded. Of course Carla had picked it.

"I'll get some groceries," Ricky said, and lumbered back down the stairs.

"Can I come?" Jez said, and hopped out of the bed, bounding after him.

At dinner, Ricky asked if Jez could have my room. Had she asked for it, I wondered, or was this Ricky's idea? Jez was a silent witness to our conversation, attention focused only on her food and on swinging her little legs.

"It's a child's room," Ricky tried to reason. Ever since he was young, he's tried to use his words to best me. I've always been larger. "It's really too small for you," he continued. "For anyone. Adult-sized, that is. Think of the stairs, how narrow. What if you lost your footing?"

I'd tumble. A boulder down a canyon, chunks of rock flying in all directions. My crash at the bottom would splinter the foundation, open a vein that would travel all the way up the walls, crack the house in half like an egg. I'd imagined it many times.

"I've never stumbled, not once," I told Ricky, lifting my foot as if to prove its reliability. I was wearing my green Crocs. I rested my heel on the edge of the dining table, my toes flickering in the holes. "And I've got good grip."

"We're having dinner," Ricky said, eyeing Jez as she smeared butter onto her splayed potato with her index finger. The effort was requiring all her attention, to Ricky's relief. I knew I would hear more about my impropriety later, once Jez was tucked away in Mutti's old room. As it turned out, I received a stern lecture, complete with finger wagging, about how careful Carla was about bringing Jez up right, how manners were a thing that got a person somewhere in life, how I should take care not to undo what had been done for her.

Afterward, Ricky took his old room, even though the master bed was a queen and his was a single with a rubber mattress.

Things are different, I wanted to say, as I helped him carry his suitcases into the room. *It may not seem so on the outside, but inside they are.* I wanted to say it, but I got that feeling again, the prickly heat beneath my skin, at the thought of speaking so plainly to him. So instead, I left the room and retrieved my sandals. He came into the front hall and watched me lower my bottom to the chair and let the sandals clap to the floor. I went about bending myself between my legs and strapping the sandals to my feet. He looked at me queerly.

"I'm trying to 'get healthy," I said, borrowing Dr. Snider's words. Ricky's eyebrows perked, but he did not say anything as I went out the door.

It's not because I want to be thin, I should have added.

It had all begun long before, nearly a year ago. I'd gone to see Dr. Snider for a sinister-looking mole, all ragged around the edges like a ruined pie. Sitting on the exam table in a gown that was just large enough to stretch across my front, the ties like limp noodles at my armpits, I leaned on my right buttock, hand under my thigh, pulling up the flesh and rolling it over, like turning a pig on a spit. Dr. Snider gasped a little, not at the mole but at my ability to move parts of myself in this way.

"I don't like the look of those edges," he declared. "Has it grown? Was it always this large?"

"Not always, I think," I said. "The size of a dime when I first noticed it. It's a loonic now, I think. Maybe a toonie?"

"Let's get you in for a biopsy," he said, flipping through his chart. "Did the nurse take your weight?" he added, as if it were a necessary sidenote.

"Yes," I said, raising my arms in some impulse to make myself appear even larger. I let my hands fall to the nape of my neck and willed myself not to shiver against the cool air blowing on my bare back.

"I'm sure I don't need to tell you that your weight is a concern," he said. "Try walking. Just a few blocks every day, at least. Get healthy. Okay?"

I half-expected him to chuck me under the chin, the way he smiled, breezing me with the swift open and close of the door on his way out. But I liked the way he said it, *Get healthy*, as though I could pop down to the drugstore and pick up a bottle of Healthy that afternoon. The word, the breath of it, letting tongue touch teeth.

I had dressed myself and left without bothering to schedule the test. But I did walk, like he said. I started with once a day. To the end of Styracosaurus Street and back. The neighbourhood was rotten—broken windows, crabgrass everywhere, rusty Chevies scattered across lawns. In winter, one house had a Santa-hatted T. Rex figurine on the roof, with a long tube of yellow lights dangling from his crotch down into the snow. The owners kept him up for almost half the year, November to March. I used him as a landmark. *Make it to the pissing T. Rex*, I used to say to myself. *Just make it there and you can turn around.* My chin dripped sweat.

For the first few months, a layer of trampled snow covered the side-walk, too many slick spots and mini moguls to dodge. I would trundle over them as though I were filled to the brim with liquid, not a drop of which could be spilled. But there was one day I remember when the snow and ice had melted. It was March, one of those days that feels like an open front door letting in the frigid air and flushing out all the stale furnace heat. There was nothing between me and the T. Rex but concrete. Flat grey squares lined up in a path like a Monopoly board—move ahead five spaces, stop to breathe, roll the dice, see how far your luck gets you. An old man with a toy poodle leashed in one hand and a cane in the other passed me on the left. He chose the soggy lawn, making a wide half circle around me. The dog sniffed my toes, and the man stole a glance at my sandalled feet as he passed. *Sandals are easier*, I wanted to tell him. The sound of the jangling leash cut through the cold silence.

I paused in front of number 32, the house with the yellow door, not realizing that someone was crouched there, below me, working the flower beds that ran along the walkway leading up to the porch.

"Afternoon," a voice said, and I must have jumped a little, because it quickly followed with, "Down here, m'dear."

I looked down at a grey, curly head, which rolled back to reveal a toothy grin. "Lovely day, isn't it?" Her hands wore canvas gloves printed with camellias, the fingers coated in grey dirt. She returned to her task, head bobbing.

"Yes," I said. I was panting and didn't want to talk, but her smile had flashed in my mind and stuck there, emerging more clearly by the second, like a Polaroid. She'd lived in the house for as long as I could remember, but I'd never learned her name. Once, she'd come to our front door to give a box of split iris bulbs to Mutti, who'd scoffed at the gesture. "What is she trying to say, giving us her dirty leftovers?" Mutti had said, dumping the bulbs in the trash.

"A bit early for planting, isn't it?" I asked the woman, wanting to be friendly, wanting to see her smile again, all lips and gums, pink as cotton candy.

"You're right," she said, eyes fixed on her hands. She sighed then and sat back, clapped her hands on her thighs.

I stood. Silent. Moments passed. A gust of wind flew by, making an empty little plastic pot roll on its side across her lawn, skipping on snow patches. She took no notice.

"But I'm only pulling the weeds," she announced, hoisting herself up again. With one gloved fist, she yanked at a clump of grass sprouting from the crack between one slab and the next. A sound like cotton ripping. And I could see then that between each of the first four slabs there was a vacant seam, while all the remaining squares were bordered with tangles of half-dead grass and weeds waiting to be cleaned up.

For some reason, I was terrified. I had no knowledge of why in that precise moment, but I knew that I had seen something. A kind of premonition, one that predicted not the future, but some alternate universe. I left without saying goodbye and trucked back toward my house faster than I would normally care to move.

What I had seen was how that sidewalk came apart at the seams. The pieces fell away into the mud. The mud bubbled up and pooled, then dried and baked, a mud desert like the ones you see on *National Geographic*, glazed with a fine layer of swirling sand. And I imagined my own bones trapped just below the surface, sprouting weeds, stitched together with roots. My mass tied to each filament, pulled up and out of the body, balls of dirt hugging precious bulbs at the centre. A pair of tiny hands clutched them.

2

THERE WAS A TIME, as a child, when one season seemed like a lifetime. Particularly summer, when the ten-week vacation from school seemed to stretch out like an accordion. One summer, when I was seven or eight, I found a little frog in Michichi Creek and brought it home to keep as a pet. It was only about the size of my thumb, and I captured it inside a soft-drink cup along with a clump of moss, which I was convinced would make a delicious treat. I managed to keep the frog secret for two days, spritzing it with water every couple of hours to keep its skin moist. Eventually, though, I was no longer content to let the frog be and began to experiment, first by prodding its backside with a stick. It was alive, its dewlap steadily ballooning, but it didn't react. I realize now it was probably frozen with fear. I poured it out onto my palm, and it tumbled onto its back, so I poked it with my finger to turn it back over. Nothing. I pinched its sides between my thumb and forefinger. Still nothing. So I squeezed. Gently at first, and then not so gently. Its insides squirted out into my hand like a blob of mustard.

I didn't know what to do; I knew I had done a bad thing, and it seemed wrong, criminal, even, to simply discard the corpse in the garbage or the toilet and wipe away the mess. So I shoved my fist into my pocket and walked around like that for the rest of the day, willing myself to ignore the warm slime that oozed inside my hand, until Mutti finally noticed and forced me to show her what I was hiding. By then the body had almost entirely liquefied, soaking through the lining of my pocket and infusing its swampy stench into the fabric. At first Mutti yelled at me for making such a mess, but her face turned grave when I told her what it was.

"What is wrong with you?" she said. "That's cruelty, Regina. That was an innocent living creature. And you destroyed it."

The entirety of that memory spans only three days, and yet I was changed in that time. It was as if I could feel myself getting older, minute by minute. Not long after, the new school year arrived, and by then I'd truly become a new self, in a new grade, among a new group of classmates, with a new vision of myself as someone who would always be askew in the world, as if living a kind of incorporeal existence.

I once said to Mutti that time moved too quickly, and she nodded proudly, as if I'd just solved a tricky riddle. "We are but a blip in time to this earth," she said, and picked up a fossil that was sitting on the windowsill. "The rocks don't care," she added.

And so, recalling how the rocks would not care, I struggled to think of something to tell Ricky about when he said, "So. What's new?"

"What's new," I repeated. My mind shot back to his wedding—the last time I had seen him. Carla pressing red velvet cake into his face, smearing his cheeks with colour deep as blood. Him sputtering a bit with the force of it but laughing anyway. He hadn't yet known the trouble I'd caused. I'd caught a taxi back to the airport before he found out, and slept sitting up at the terminal, fitfully, until I was finally called to board. The time between then and the present was a gaping hole.

"You're still at Fossil Land," Ricky said, although he already knew this. "And you've taken up walking."

"Yes," I said. "I've been walking. I go at least once a day, sometimes twice." Saying the words out loud made my endeavour seem much less momentous than I'd thought.

26

"That's nice," Ricky said. "Fresh air is good for the lungs." He reached into his shirt pocket and pulled out a cigar, chewed the end, and spat it over the porch railing. It was a clear night, still thick with the warmth of the day, and Jez had been asleep for hours. Ricky seemed to have claimed my wicker bench for himself, so I sat on the front step, my mind scanning the years for something, anything, that was important enough to speak of.

"Big news at the museum," I piped up.

"Oh?"

"We're getting animatronic dinosaurs," I said. "An ankylosaurus and an oviraptor ... and two others, I think."

"So ... they move around? Waggle their tails and such?"

"Something like that," I said. "They're state of the art, I'm told. Very lifelike."

Ricky was trying to suppress a smile. His lips pressed together in a tight line, but I could see it in the glint of his eyes. He puffed on his cigar to contain it.

"You think it's silly," I said.

He breathed out smoke slowly, watching it curl and dissipate. "Not silly," he said. "Just ... odd."

"The thing is, people are interested in experiences," I said, sounding just like my boss, Darrell. "They want to know what it would have been like to *see* dinosaurs."

"Then they could go see an alligator," Ricky said. "Go to the zoo. An alligator would be more lifelike than a robotic dinosaur."

I had nothing to say to that. Even after seven years away, Ricky knew me too well to believe that any kind of machine could enchant me. Just minutes earlier, when he'd taken out his cellphone to poke the tiny buttons, my face must have betrayed something of my repugnance, for his head shook ever so slightly, a trace of ridicule.

But I had been trying to feed off the excitement of Darrell and my other co-workers at Fossil Land, who had begun starting every conversation with phrases like "Two more weeks to launch!" or "Ready for the big shakeup?" The higher-ups were projecting a 30 percent increase in visitor traffic. Darrell had gathered all the attendant and security staff to sit around his laptop and watch a video of the animatronic dinosaurs produced by the company that made them. The video showed a T. Rex—their most popular model, as the flashing banner at the bottom of the screen proclaimed—cocking its head and moving its twiggy arms up and down like a Broadway act. Bruce and Marilyn, the two full-time attendants for the exhibits, oohed and aahed.

"The skin is amazing," Marilyn said. "Look at the texturing. Very impressive."

"And they've got the updated physiology," Bruce added. "See the feathers on the crest of the back?"

"Oh, yes," Marilyn said, putting her face right up to the screen. "How wonderful. Are those real feathers?"

"Ostrich feathers," said Darrell, beaming like a proud father.

I nodded and smiled along with my co-workers, pushing my cynicism down into my gut. On the robot, the feathers looked like an absurd afterthought, a way to dress up the animal, as if to give it a costume. I had a very difficult time believing this fact was true and not some paleontologist's bad joke.

Marilyn herself had said that paleontologists had no sense of humour. She had been involved with one for a few weeks a year prior. Then one day she arrived at work with her hair in disarray and her eyes puffy, and that was the end of that. She stopped wearing high heels and doing her hair in a forties victory roll, and began instead wearing a baby-blue cardigan that drowned her curves.

Marilyn tried for a while to set up a romance between me and Bruce by scheming with Darrell to schedule our lunch breaks together. It was not a wise strategy, since watching a person eat is not, in my mind, the optimum scenario for seduction. Not that I know a thing about seduction. On the first day of the lunch date, my meal was a sandwich with cucumber slices that kept falling out and slapping on the cellophane that I'd unfolded to make myself a kind of plate. Bruce sat across from me, chewing his neat little ham sandwich, contemplating its edges as he turned it round and round in his hands.

"Ham and jam," he said to me, lifting the sandwich like a prize.

"Jam?" I said. "And ham? I've never heard that combination." Truth be told, the idea of it caused my stomach to churn.

"It's good," he said. "It's just like turkey and cranberry sauce. Salty and sweet."

I nodded politely. Salty and sweet, just like Bruce, in a way. It was his look—his scruffy jaw and severely pointed eyebrows paired with a rosebud mouth and a band of cotton-fluff hair that framed the balding globe of his head. He was nice, to be sure, but I was content to know only his surface and not what was underneath.

I returned to my cucumbers, unpeeling the bread of my sandwich to lay them back inside. I licked the mayonnaise from my fingers and caught Bruce looking. There was something in his gaze, a slight widening of the eyes. It was revolting to him, I realized, to see me deconstructing my food in this way, half eaten, spoiled with my bite marks. But my impulse in that moment was to repel him further. I squashed the sandwich into my face, letting the mayonnaise smear across my cheeks, and then grinned at him, mouth full, like a ravenous chipmunk.

Bruce avoided the lunchroom after that day and began taking his meals out instead.

Marilyn then took it upon herself to arrange for me a blind date. Most men, I see as versions of Ricky—a bit helpless, but desperate to deny it. But I was open to the prospect. Marilyn said we had a great deal in common. In Marilyn's mind, a large woman needed a large man, and that would be enough to bond them.

Over the telephone, before the date, Roy had asked if I would like to go to a movie, to which I replied no, I didn't like movies, though really I did not relish the idea of having to wedge myself next to him in the narrow theatre seats.

"I'll surprise you, then," he insisted. It seemed a kind gesture, so I did not protest. But when he arrived on my doorstep, he was not the trimly dressed man that his soft voice suggested. He was wearing a T-shirt that said NIRVANA across the chest, with a picture of three stringy-haired boys sitting against a brick wall, knees poking through the holes in their jeans. Their faces were faded and stretched against

Roy's flesh beneath. I studied the T-shirt more closely than I studied Roy's face, and I suspect now that he took my staring as a criticism of his barrel-like midsection and the way the indent of his navel made a shallow crater in the fabric, which then travelled under the lip of his belly. His hand found the edge of the shirt and yanked it down, prompting me to stop my staring and retrieve my coat.

From what I'd seen in movies, I'd expected at first to be brought to a fancy restaurant with French food and violin players serenading the couples at each table, but now I'd no idea what to expect. Roy parked us in his blue Mazda at the back of a concrete building in a parkade. It took me a moment to realize that this was the back of a strip mall, at the front side of which was the entrance to the Brick and a few other desolate shops. The only entrance here was a single glass door that appeared to lead to the basement.

I admit I felt a tingle of fear seeing how secluded and empty the space was. Just two other vehicles sat in the lot, looking as though they'd been abandoned there for months. I let Roy lead me to the mysterious door, telling myself that his arms looked soft, and I was larger than he. But I saw his plan as we got closer to the door and the small white letters stuck to its surface came into view: BOWLING.

I pretended not to see the sign. I needed time to manifest an appropriate reaction. A polite one. This was meant to be fun, I reasoned with myself. He thought it would be fun. But I could not ignore that I was wearing a dress, and that the dress I'd chosen had a tendency to ride up at the back, especially with excessive bending. That and I wasn't any good at bowling and had been asked to leave the alley in high school gym class after I threw the ball at the pins with so much force that it put a crack in the varnish where it landed halfway down the lane. And the fact that countless moist feet before mine had likely turned the leather bowling shoes putrid, putting me at risk of catching some kind of foot rot, if I could even get them on.

"Ta-dah!" Roy cried when we reached the bottom of the stairs. It was dark, and his teeth shone purple in the black light.

"Well," I said. "Look at this." It was all I could manage. The lint glowing all over his body made him look like a speckled egg.

"You like bowling?" he asked.

"I haven't played much," I said. It was the truth.

"I'll teach you," he said, hands on hips. "Don't worry. I'm something of a Fred Flintstone myself."

"Oh," I said. "Good. I suppose I'm more like Dino." Then, seeing the way his eyebrows fell, I said, "Or even the ribs, the rack of ribs. You know, the ribs that make the car topple over?"

He laughed a tinny laugh and avoided my eyes. I considered confessing that I wasn't very good at making jokes, but decided not to risk creating even more awkwardness between us.

"I'll get your shoes," he said, pointing at the desk by the back wall. "What size?"

"I'm not sure," I said. "I can do it. I may need to see. I might need to look at them."

"That's fine," he said. "You can choose the lane we want. Make it a lucky one. I'll get you a couple of pairs. What size?" His body was already pointed at the desk and his feet were moving toward it, so I yelled out, "Twelve. If they have it."

He nodded and glanced at my feet on his way, no doubt checking to see if they were, in fact, as large as they sounded. The shoes would not fit me, I knew.

I chose the lane at the very end. A few empty cups and nacho remnants sat on the table, but it seemed the most private space and the one farthest away from the overhead speakers booming dance music and the family playing a game at the other end—two sweater-vested adults and two sullen-looking teenage girls chewing mouthfuls of hot dog. Roy returned with a stack of shoes, one pair for himself and sizes ten and eleven for me. He refrained from admitting that a size twelve for women was too gargantuan to possibly exist in a bowling alley. He couldn't have known that I would've taken the opportunity to heartily agree. I humoured him, slipping my foot into a size eleven shoe as far as it would go, which was only halfway.

"I can watch you do the bowling," I said, holding up my foot for him to see.

"Damn," he said. "That's too bad. That's really too bad." He marched back to the desk and spoke briefly to the attendant, who only shook her head.

"Crazy," he said when he returned. "They really don't have any bigger sizes. Jeez."

Roy was kind enough, I suppose, but all I could think about that night as I sat in the fibreglass booth—watching Roy's scores collect on the screen overhead, his three-bounce dance when he made a strike, the way he chewed on the end of the straw stuck into his Coke, turning its end into a little flag—was how his T-shirt seemed more real and more alive than he did. Perhaps it was the way the smirks on the boys' faces glowed in the neon light, but Roy's face was like a sheep's in comparison—all one colour, the eyes empty enough to blend in imperceptibly with the rest. That night as I lay in bed, I thought briefly about what it might be like to have Roy's hands on my neck, pressing, those empty eyes on mine. The hands squeezing, tighter and tighter, forcing the breath out of my throat. Then my own hands rising up, a single finger extending to shuck one of the eyes out. I saw the finger sink in behind the eyeball, all the way to the second knuckle, and twist. I imagined the pop it would make, how his head would bobble on his neck. It made me feel a bit guilty, but it was a harmless indulgence of imagination, like a scene out of *Ren & Stimpy*, which, I surmised, was a probably a show that Roy enjoyed.

The next day, when Marilyn asked, "So, how was it?" I said it was fine, and it had been. Roy had even tried to give me a chaste kiss at the end of the night, which was not at all offensive but felt like two pieces of plastic pressing against one another—his dutifully pursed lips and my unyielding cheek. I knew I was only doing both of us a favour when he asked if he could call me again and I said, "No, I think you'd rather not."

Of course, I told none of this to Ricky. He would not have been interested. We sat there on the porch, him concentrating on his cigar and me observing the trickle of cars passing by on the street, the mosquitoes hovering, searching the breeze for the scent of our blood. It must have been the better part of an hour, and through all that time, I was working myself up to speak, to tell Ricky about the one thing that really did matter. I sat on the steps for what seemed like eons, breathing in the billows of roasty smoke he exhaled, knowing it was sticking to my clothes and wishing with all my might that I could simply say it and be done. Finally, I gritted my teeth, opened my mouth, and said the words.

"I got a letter," I said. I could not look at him, but I could feel his eyes on the back on my head.

"Oh?" he said. He did not sound at all surprised. "From who?"

He knew, of course, but I played along.

"From Mutti," I said. I turned and looked at him then to gauge his reaction. He puffed on the cigar and held the smoke in his lungs. He'd taken one of Mutti's crystal bowls to use as an ashtray, and he cast his eyes down to the little pile he'd made as he blew out the smoke.

"It was two years ago now," I continued. "Maybe three."

Ricky set the cigar down and rubbed his fingers together as though sprinkling salt on an invisible meal. In the quiet of the night, his callused fingertips made a shearing sound against one another, like ice being carved.

"The ol' bitch managed to pick up a pen, did she?" Ricky finally said.

"It was typed," I said, as if it mattered.

"Figures," Ricky said, rising from his seat. He stubbed out the cigar, bull's-eye in the centre of the dish. The screen door whacked shut behind him.

I'd meant to tell him that Mutti had asked me to donate all of her carbonized plant fossils to the Tyrrell Museum, and I tried, but half of them they would not take. As it turned out, the ones of real value were those that had made perfect impressions in the rock, clear and unbroken, each leaf of every frond intact, the discovered pieces of some long-gone life story. The rejects, however, were the ones that Mutti had most prized, displaying them on bookshelves and windowsills in place of the trinkets and houseplants that an ordinary mother would have. Ghosted images that seemed to fade in and out of the rock, as though the plant itself had been caught in time midway through some alchemic transformation. I'd found new places for each of them around the house, believing in some silly way that this would renew them, make them feel like mine, though they never did.

If it were up to Ricky, I suspect he would have tossed them all in the river.

3

THE NEVER-ENDING SUMMER was a kind of limbo for the land. The hills, crisped to kindling on the outside but alive on the inside; the roots, lying dormant under the earth, longing for a few drops of rain. Not quite living, but not quite dying. Inside the house, it felt much the same. The three of us—Ricky, Jez, and I—hovering on the edge of something none of us could yet name.

Four whole days passed before anyone even mentioned Carla. Jez found me in the bathroom in the morning just as I was pointing the barrel of a hair dryer at my face, poised to flick the switch.

"Is that my mummy's hair dryer?" she asked.

"Maybe," I said, lowering the hair dryer as if I'd been caught. I had found it lying on my bed, its cord wrapped tightly around its handle. I'd never had one before; blow-drying had always seemed like an unnecessary chore, since my hair dried perfectly well in the open air. But knowing that this had been Carla's, I felt impelled to try it. Jez's little marble eyes watched me unravel the cord and plug it in. Then I took out my comb and laid it next to the sink. I met her gaze in the mirror. Held it there for a moment. I didn't want her to watch me, though

I didn't know why. Drying my hair was not a private act. But I felt exposed.

"Will you blow me?" she said in a quiet voice.

"What?" I said, my face turning crimson in the mirror.

"You know," she said, "*shhhew ...*" She ran her fingers along her cheeks, ruffled the stringy ends of her hair.

"Does your mother do that?" I said, aiming the hair dryer at her face. "*Shhhew,*" I echoed.

"No," Jez said. She took the dangling cord in her hands and wrapped one loop around her wrist, contemplating it like a bracelet. And then, abruptly, she let go, turned around, and skipped out of the room.

"Attachment issues," Ricky said when I told him.

"Don't you mean detachment issues?" I asked him.

"No," he said. "Because she's still attached. That's the whole problem."

I pictured an invisible string looped around Jez's wrist like the hair dryer cord, weaving its way through the rooms of the house, up and down the stairs, knotted in the banister, under chairs, scooping under doors, hung up in tree branches, swinging across streets like a limp power line, jigging in the air, a kite string stretching up into the clouds. Somewhere off the map, Carla on the other end, a matching blue line encircling her wrist. I held the image in my mind, writing a small speech in my memory, a way to tell Jez that she would always have a mother, even if she could not see her. But like most things, it became silly as I thought about it, and I let it dissolve.

The house had already begun to morph when I wasn't watching. In the kitchen, I'd opened the pantry door to find that one of the shelves had been adjusted to a lower position, and my brown sugar and flour had been relocated to make way for boxes of fruit snacks, bags of chips, and a stack of tuna cans. Then, a toaster oven had appeared on the counter, its door left open like a mouth. In the bathroom, I'd stubbed my toe on a plastic stepstool emblazoned with *Sesame Street* characters that was parked in front of the sink. The next day, it even happened in the unfinished basement, a place that had always seemed tomblike to me. I found the clothesline, which I had strung from the ceiling, now detached on one side, my hanging undergarments in a wrinkled pile on the floor. A miniature wooden train set occupied the space instead, the tracks all laid out in a winding network of routes, with tiny traffic lights and trees and buildings and even a little roundhouse placed along them. Everything looked new and shiny and untouched and seemed to be the work of magic.

"Is she not afraid of the dark?" I asked Ricky, as I mounted the last of the stairs. I had my wrinkled laundry in my arms and promptly began folding it and smoothing it in front of him in hopes that he might acknowledge his imposition.

"No," Ricky said, "she's fine. She's a strong girl. Nothing much bothers her." He could see I was annoyed as I snapped my undershirts back into shape, folding them sharply and laying them on the kitchen table alongside his breakfast plate. It was time for him to give me something. A bone, some fragment of explanation. Ricky knew it too. He sighed.

"She's out of the picture, you know," he confessed. He stuffed a forkful of scrambled eggs in his mouth, leaving a line of ketchup on his chin.

"I see." I waited for him to continue. He began to chew ferociously, breathing through his nose in small whiffs. Perhaps he wanted me to interject, I considered. When we were young, Ricky had always preferred to play guessing games when it came to venting his feelings.

"Is she at her mother's? In Phoenix?"

"Don't know," Ricky said. "We were stopped at a gas station in Taber. I was filling up. Then, *piff*." His hand made a sweeping motion, like the swift wing of a bird.

"She left? At the gas station?"

Ricky went on chewing, eyes on his plate.

"Where did she go?" I asked.

"Don't know. Jumped in a truck, maybe?"

I imagined Carla springing like a deer, eyes flashing white, soaring through the open door of a semi. "There's only so many places she could go," I said. "At a gas station."

Ricky only nodded.

"Perhaps she was taken?" I ventured. "Abducted?"

"No," Ricky said. "Not that. For sure not that." He tugged a napkin out of the stack in front of him and dabbed at the corners of his lips as if to seal his certainty. "She was having a hard time …" he began, then stopped. I decided it best not to press.

"Took us four days to drive up here," he went on, herding the last of his eggs to the edge of his plate. "No air conditioning in the Buick. We had to take breaks midday, find a mall or something to cool off in."

"It's her first time in Canada? Jez?"

"I suppose it is." He eyed the ceiling in the place where Jez had made her room above. "I haven't really told her it's a different country. Does she know Canada, I wonder? Do they teach that in kindergarten? Maybe not in Arizona." He stood and began rinsing his plate. "You should ask her," he said on his way out.

"What about school?" I hollered at him.

He poked his head back in the doorway. "School? What about it?"

Years ago I had used to pinch his nipples when he was being obnoxious, and I wished I could return to those days. Jez had been doing nothing but ride in the car with Ricky as he ran errands around town. What did any ordinary child do during the day but go to school?

"Have you signed her up for one?" I said instead. "I imagine it's the sort of thing you want to do in advance."

"She needs some time, I think," he said, drumming his fingers on the door frame. "It's a big adjustment. New country, new house." He shrugged and went on his way. What Jez needed was not time, I wanted to say. She clearly needed a mother.

≈

Mutti and I moved to this country before Ricky was born. I was only a baby, not yet one year old. Mutti had been studying geology at the Freie Universität Berlin, and I was born when she was still living in the dorms. I was too young to remember anything about moving from Berlin to Drumheller. My earliest memory is of the Red Deer River, seeing it from inside a canoe. I was about three years old and sitting between Mutti and a man whose name I do not recall. His beard was black as coal and scraggly and untrimmed, like a billy goat's. There was the cold river and the little whirlpools that the man's paddle made in the water, and there was the rocky riverbank that we followed, looking for fossils poking out of the bluffs. I found a shard of bone, thin and curved as a shell, and the man told me it was part of a human skull. I'm still not sure if he was trying to trick me, but Mutti did not correct him. Someone gave me peanuts, and I threw up in the canoe, even though the water would have been a much more sensible choice. It seemed too clean somehow, and I was afraid to ruin it. Funny, which moments stick in one's mind.

At one point the man undressed and jumped into the cold water. He swam alongside the canoe on his back, his dark privates skimming the water like an eel. We floated past a herd of cows grazing on a butte, and an enormous bull stood at the edge, staring us down. I remember thinking we shouldn't be there. That nature did not want us. That the man's nakedness must be a mortal sin in this place, in the eyes of the bull, wild as it was.

Looking back on my childhood, it seems I went everywhere with Mutti, and I learned far more from our outings than I ever learned at school. I knew how to spot the difference between sedimentary and igneous rocks before I learned to spell. At the time I thought that all mothers gave such lessons, but now I wonder if it wasn't one of the many reasons I was friendless and why Mutti was often told that I made the other children "uncomfortable."

But I'd made improvements since then in my ability to connect with children, thanks in large part to Waldo. The neighbourhood children had invented a game of spotting me; when I passed by their yards on my walks, they'd call out, "It's the Big Bunny Lady!" whether or not Waldo was with me, their little fingers pointing. Sometimes I'd make an ape face, puffing my cheeks and bugging my eyes out, or I'd bare my teeth at them like a mischievous wolf, and they'd stare and stare in wonder. Sometimes, if a suspicious parent wasn't around, I'd even sit with them for a while to let them play with Waldo and feed him a carrot or two. I could tell by the rhythm of Waldo's nose, how it twitched a tiny bit faster, that he adored children. Perhaps it was because human attention of such glee and fervour was a novelty to him, since he was a wild bunny when I found him.

Grünewald means "green forest." I like to imagine that he came from one—a lush, enchanted forest like the ones in fairy tales. But the real story isn't quite so charming. Waldo was one of many bunnies who had spontaneously overtaken my neighbourhood one spring. An epidemic, they were calling it. Too many foolish people had let their pet bunnies loose in backyards, on camping trips, in flimsy outdoor hutches overnight. And against the odds, the escaped bunnies were surviving, spending their winters on golf courses, peppering the pristine snow with trails of shiny fecal beads. Not just surviving, but thriving. Multiplying. Breeding like … well.

I call them bunnies because they are not rabbits. Rabbits are lean and large, with ears that stick to the sky. They move like insects, darting in blink-fast zigzags. Bunnies, on the other hand, are round and downy, like a basket of feathers, with saddle flaps for ears. Their hops are slow and lazy. They are the kind you see circling glass cases in Petland, while children on footstools reach their hands in for a chance to touch. It is strange to see bunnies roaming the wild. Three of them arrived on my front lawn and hopped about there all morning, as if on a play date. I assumed a neighbour would arrive eventually to collect them. By noon, one of the bunnies had migrated two doors down and was chewing the new tulip buds. By midafternoon, the black one had disappeared. I could not abide the thought of the smallest bunny spending the cold night outside. I spied him from my bedroom window, still hopping aimlessly beneath the oak—sniff, hop, sniff sniff, hop. And there was that first pang of love, a feeling that would hit me again each time I went out onto the porch and saw him hopping around his hutch, anxious to roam free.

I'd taken to bringing Waldo with me on my walk every Saturday, although I'd broken this routine a few weeks prior on account of a sore ankle and hadn't since gotten back on track. I'd buckle Waldo into his harness—red, his favourite colour—and stuff carrot sticks in my sock in case he needed a snack. If you've ever tried to walk a bunny, you'll know that they are blind to the guiding influence of a walking path. They drift always to the grass and are pleased to mill about in one spot, nibbling without pattern or thought of hunger. It's not that they are unintelligent; they simply have no concept of destination, or future. Their lives are a constant present. I strive to remind myself of this philosophy when my human brain tricks me into speculating on what could have been. There is no such thing, of course, as what could have been—only what is.

And so, with Waldo, I'd wrap him up in a cloth like a baby and swaddle him to my chest. On chilly days, I'd even put his little red toque on his head, which I'd knitted to fit him perfectly, complete with a miniature pompom on top and two holes on the sides for his ears to come through. He'd ride in his swaddle quite happily, soaking in the heat from my body. I'd take him like this to a park and leash him to a tree so he could wander his ten-yard radius, watching the children play, and I could sit on a bench and enjoy the sun on my face.

But now, after the sore ankle and then Ricky and Jez's arrival, poor Waldo had been spending hours alone in his hutch through the days, and my motherly guilt was beginning to set in. I was resolved to take him out that afternoon.

Jez watched me prepare for our outing. I had asked her to hold on to Waldo while I got the bolt of cloth around my back. She sat on the floor on her knees, hands wrapped under Waldo's belly like I'd shown her. His feet kicked, his toenails scratching against the bare skin at the edge of her shorts.

"Where're you taking him?" she asked.

"To the park," I said. I held out the hammock I'd created for him and gestured for Jez to place Waldo inside.

"He doesn't want to go," she said, petting his head. Waldo's feet continued to kick, but Jez's grip remained steady.

"Nonsense," I said, taking him from her. I placed him inside his nest, and he squirmed about to find comfort. Then I tucked a carrot under his nose. He settled immediately and pressed the carrot to the cloth so as to pin it for his mouth to work away. Jez watched all of this as though in a trance.

"See?" I said. "He hasn't been out in weeks. He needs an outing."

Jez sucked on her bottom lip, seemingly unconvinced. It occurred to me then that no one had taken her to the park, not once, since she'd arrived. I'd always thought that children and bunnies were remarkably alike, and now here was the evidence.

"Would you like to come?" I asked.

She nodded.

I'm not sure why I hadn't thought of it sooner. This was an opportunity for Waldo and Jez to become friends.

"Find your shoes, then," I said, and she was off like a rocket to the back door. She came back moments later carrying Earl and wearing her winter boots. The rings of white fuzzy fur round their tops were nearly the same colour as her bare legs, making it look as though the fur were sprouting from her ankles inside.

"You're going to wear those?" I said.

She looked down at her feet. "Yes," she said.

"Expecting it to snow, are you?" It hadn't snowed for almost six months, since the end of March. Though it was the last day of August, the Never-Ending Summer was holding strong; the sun was already baking the land and creating a haze on the horizon. But Jez skipped out the door in her boots, and so I followed behind.

For a very small person, Jez could walk remarkably quickly, and I found myself puffing like a dragon to keep up. Poor Waldo was being bucked about in his wrap, and I had to keep adjusting his carrots for him.

"Does your papa like to take you to the park?"

She seemed to know the way as she marched ahead. "No," she said. "He said I'm not allowed."

They had surely driven past this park many times on their errand runs. It surprised me to hear how cruel Ricky could be.

"Why?" I asked. "Why does he say you're not allowed?"

"Dangerous," she said. How ironic that Ricky had always moaned about Mutti's shrieking whenever he got too close to the water, to the edge of the cliff, to the road, to the homeless man, to the little dog tied to a fire hydrant outside the supermarket. *Richard, come*, she would bark, and Ricky would purposefully move farther away until Mutti's voice became shrill enough to cause heads to turn.

Now Jez was stopped and bending down to look at a crack in the sidewalk. She positioned Earl to look as well, pointing his horn straight down. "Ants," she said. They were swarming on the body of a dying worm. The worm twisted and writhed. We took a few silent moments to watch the scene.

There again was that awful vision: the sidewalk coming apart, opening into a chasm, swallowing the worm. The earth turning inside out, and now, rising up out of the dirt, a bone, sheared off to a sharpened point—

"I can see the park," Jez said, jumping up.

I took a breath, and my mind cleared. "There's the slide," I said.

She tucked Earl into my hand and ran ahead, her boots kicking up clouds of gravel dust.

I found a bench off to the side and latched Waldo's harness to his retractable leash. He seemed pleased with the patch of deep-green grass I'd chosen for him and slowly pinwheeled on that spot, sampling the smatterings of clover buried in the grass. It was my turn to settle in and use the handkerchief in my pocket to collect the little waterfall that had sprung from my brow. I sat and kicked off my Crocs, wiggling my sweaty toes.

Meanwhile, Jez had already found a playmate—a boy who looked a year or two younger than her. His blond spray of hair floated up all over his head as though it had been rubbed by a balloon. At the other side of the park, his mother surveyed, arms folded. A cigarette chopsticked between her fingers stuck out at her elbow, the plume of smoke snaking into the air. Her eyes briefly met mine, and she tossed me a smile so quick it could have been a twitch.

A few yards away, a little girl who lived down the block from me was wailing in her mother's arms, apparently devastated to be torn away from the spring-loaded stegosaurus she'd been bouncing on. "Shush, Mila," her mother said. "It's time to go." The way the mother eyed me when she said it made her reasons obvious. She hadn't forgotten about how I'd once talked to Mila and made the mistake of telling her about Mrs. Nakamura, the woman who used to live in the little white house that Mila now shared with her mother. I told her that ever since English ivy had suffocated Mrs. Nakamura's garden years ago, I'd thought of the house as haunted by an evil spirit. I never learned her mother's name, because when she came out of the house, Mila ran straight to her and her eyes began to pour like a tap, and the mother looked at me as if I were a bear who'd nearly mauled her precious child. Now, she glared in my direction even while wrangling the girl, who arched backward and kicked her legs. I stuck my tongue out at the mother, and she scurried off.

Clearly, however, I was not actually so frightening, as Jez and her new friend were now bounding over to me, breathless.

"There," Jez said to the boy. She pointed a finger at Waldo.

"What's his name?" said the boy, getting down on his hands and knees to thrust his face into Waldo's. Jez yanked at the neck of his T-shirt and he pulled back. *Good girl*, I thought to myself. Waldo simply hopped in the opposite direction and continued his clover hunting. The boy's hand reached out and grazed Waldo's back.

"That's nice," I said. "He likes a nice back rub."

The boy's finger touched the top of Waldo's head, as if to anoint him. The boy tested the downy hairs there and around Waldo's ears.

"What is your friend's name?" I asked Jez.

"Turtle," she said.

"My name's not Turtle," the boy said, grinning. "It's Stuart."

"Stuart," I said, "you make a good friend to a bunny. That's very gentle."

"I got a lizard at home," he said. "It's my brother's. Archie."

"Archie's his name?" I replied, and Stuart nodded.

Jez got down on her knees next to Stuart, her shoulder right up against his. She began making a very faint sound, a kind of *heeeeee, heeeee* that came from between her clenched teeth, like a steaming kettle. She had her nose nearly in the grass.

"Are you being a bunny?" I said. She went on with her noises and Stuart went on petting. Their hips shifted against each other, bums wriggling in their eager pursuit of Waldo.

"I'm the wolf," she said quietly to Stuart.

"I'm a wolf," he parroted. "*Ow! Awooo!*"

"I like to eat rabbits," Jez whispered. Her voice was a kind of thin hiss, like the voice one might make for a ghost in a storybook. "They're so delicious," she continued. "Yummy, yummy." She waggled her head toward Stuart's, nearly touching her nose to his, and *slurp-slurp-slurped*.

Stuart turned onto his bottom and placed a hand in the grass, scanning the park for his mother. She was sitting on a bench now, behind the swings. She waved at him and tapped her cigarette ash into the gravel.

"Let's go on the swings now," he said to Jez. She chased after him.

Were all children like this, I wondered. So morbid. Mutti was so squeamish when we were children that we were never permitted to speak of vomit or bodily fluids of any kind. Even when Ricky tried to tell us about a nosebleed at school, Mutti would stop him before he could finish. "Oh mein Gott," she would cry, clapping her hands to her ears. "Hil-fe!" Strangely, however, she had not seemed shaken by gushing blood, broken limbs, flesh torn ragged when they were right in front of her eyes.

But I sensed that Stuart too was unsure about Jez, even if he didn't know his own feelings. They were lying with their stomachs on the swings, their feet skittering in the gravel to push themselves higher. Jez shook her hair out as she swung, making it dangle and sweep across her eyes. There was something unaffected about her—the way she carried herself as though she could see only one inch in front. Her world seemed to be only one dimension while everyone else's was three. In comparing the two children, I could perceive it. Stuart kept glancing up to see if his mother was watching him, and copying the little tricks Jez did with her feet in the gravel.

I looped Waldo's leash around the bench to secure him and moved around the perimeter of the park, close enough to hear the children on the swings. Jez was giving instructions.

"You do a swaffle, like this," she said, shimmying her boots in the gravel so that it covered her toes. "Then you do a spink!" She pulled up her feet, making the gravel scatter. Even when she spoke to Stuart, Jez seemed to be speaking to herself.

4

LATER THAT WEEK, I went into the basement and stumbled over something in the dark. The crack it made, and the warm, gooey spray across my bare calf, put a picture in my mind of a lobster cracked backward, juices squirting. I hobbled to the light switch and saw blood. My own, oozing from a split at the end of my big toe. I'd tripped over the toy train set and snapped the end off of one of the tracks, which had also been spritzed with blood. The amount of blood was rather shocking. I found a dishtowel in the laundry and wrapped the end of my foot to stop it from dripping everywhere.

Making a show of my annoyance, I pried all the other tracks apart and collected them in my skirt, along with the trains and miniature trees and signposts. I carried the jumble up the stairs, limping thunderously on my lame foot, then dumped the lot on the floor of Jez's room. The pieces clacked against the hardwood. A little blue engine tumbled and came to a rest propped up against the pile, its smiley face pointing straight at me.

"What happened?" came Jez's voice from behind me. She had Waldo cradled in her arms, and though his hind legs were pumping against her belly, she held him tight.

"Well," I said, taking Waldo and setting him on the floor, "aren't these your trains?"

She nodded.

"Are they meant to be booby traps, then? Or are they meant for play?" I'd thought it was a rhetorical question, but she stared at me as though it had not occurred to her that this was a thing intended for play.

"Look," she said, pointing at my foot. The blood had begun to soak through the cloth. "Does it hurt?" Her eyes were bright, as though excited by the prospect.

"No," I said. "Not really. But it's quite deep."

She crouched down and put her face right up to my foot, touching her finger to the bloom of red. "Does it hurt now?" she said.

"Never mind," I said, going down on my knees too. "Here. You make a track. Like this." She sat on her haunches beside me and we worked together, attaching the pieces in a long, meandering line. There was a bridge, which we discovered had a little tunnel underneath that was just the right width for another track to run underneath, and so we went about building a second route branching off the first.

I confess, I began to enjoy myself. When I was a child, I would have loved such a toy. Trains have always been rather fascinating to me. Mutti left a whole album of pictures of the Schwebebahn in Wuppertal, which I used to flip through from time to time. The trains in the pictures are, in fact, just like Jez's little toy cars, each one with its own candy colour—blue, red, yellow, and so on—and a particular character in the design, except their wheels are not on their undersides but rather running along their backs like a spine. The tracks on which their wheels glide make a web over the city. I often picture it from above, all of Wuppertal laid out like a child's toy set, the Schwebebahn as the centrepiece, each house and church tower and tree and road placed just so.

And yet, there is also something very brutal to me about the Schwebebahn. Its power, perhaps, which comes not from the force with which it moves but rather, from the way it looms over the city, propped up on hundreds of massive iron arms, like a giant robotic centipede. It strikes me that at the turn of the century, when it was born, it must have seemed so alien with those arms, their steep angles slicing the sky into geometric patterns and spearing down through the brush and the trees. It must have looked unreal and out of place, an intrusion on the plainness of the landscape.

"Look at that," I said now to Jez. "Waldo thinks he's a train." He was hopping along the tracks, sniffing their wood-chip smell. Jez stood and watched carefully, sucking her finger.

"Have you ever been on a train?" I asked her, and she shook her head. "Well," I said. "How would you like to ride this one?" I held up a red car, then placed it on the tracks and trucked it along.

"Is it going to my oma?" she said.

"In that case," I said, "we'd have to turn it upside down." I raised the car in the air. "Like this."

"Then where does it go?" she asked, her eyes following the floating train as it meandered through the air.

"Wherever it wants. You can imagine it. Imagine there are tracks up in the sky, miles and miles of them. It's like flying." I made the car swerve and dip. Jez joined in, taking the green engine from its little storage garage and making it fly and careen.

"Like this," she said, and held up her arm to press the wheels to its underside, rolling the engine up under her armpit and to her neck, under her chin, over her face. The wheels traced a set of faint red lines, following each other in parallel across her skin.

"Oh," I said, "that must be the mountain." She let the engine rest on the very top of her head, her hair now floating about with static.

"This is the Arctic Arpilego," she said.

"The Arctic Archipelago?" I repeated. "Is it not too chilly up there for your train?"

She thought about this for a moment, taking the engine into her palm and examining its features, its smooth green sides, and the tiny smiling face that looked out from its front end. Her lips began to move ever so slightly, and I realized as I watched her that she was having a private conversation. She held the train closer and closer to her lips, speaking to it without making a sound. I turned my attention back to Waldo to give her the privacy that somehow seemed appropriate, even though she showed no awareness of my presence.

When she was finished, she knelt next to me and did the same to Waldo, touching him nose to nose, moving her lips soundlessly. She sat back on her heels.

"He misses his mummy," she eventually said.

"How can that be?" I said. "I'm his mother, after all."

"Nooo," she said. "The other mummy. The one who went to the Arctic."

"She did, did she. Why did she go there?"

"The Arctic is the other place. Our place is very hot, and the Arctic is very cold. That's where narwhals make babies."

"That's right," I said. "It's very, very cold. I don't know if a bunny would fit in with all those narwhals. And polar bears."

"She doesn't have to," Jez said. "She can live by herself. She wants her own house, and she doesn't want to feel so big anymore."

"So big?" I asked.

Jez shrugged. "He got too big," she said, wrapping her hands around Waldo's belly. "Growed up. She couldn't fit him inside her anymore."

"Because he was too big."

"It was his heart," Jez said. Waldo wriggled, and she picked him up, holding him to her chest. "His heart was too big and hers was too small. She said, 'I can't take care of you anymore.' And she kissed him like this, she was crying." Jez buried her face in Waldo's fur and peppered him with little kisses.

"I see," I said. "Was she sad?"

"Uh-huh." It was the most sincere look I'd seen on Jez's face. Her eyes looked down at her chest, her mouth drooped.

"What about the papa bunny?" I said. "What did he do?"

She looked up at me with a quizzical expression, as though I should already have known the answer. "He tried to gobble her up," she said.

Looking back, I wonder at which point I knew, truly knew in my bones, that Ricky was hiding a terrible secret. Something different from the secrets he normally kept—something he feared enough that pretending it was not real was the only option. There were signs all along; I see that now. His interminable restlessness, like a mosquito trapped inside a jar, which had never been a trait of his before, was a clear warning on its own. But I was as much a fool as he at the time, determined to go on living as if everything were fine. As if nothing would have to change.

Another sign: I found an ice cube tray in the freezer one day, full of frozen insects. A worm, a caterpillar, a grasshopper, a sprinkling of ants, and even a little white butterfly, each floating at the top of a cube of ice, suspended in its final pose of suffering. I'd initially thought it to be evidence of Jez's inquisitive and analytical mind and showed it to Ricky, assuming he'd see it the same way. But instead, he looked at the tray like it was a bomb ready to explode. He snatched it from my hands and took it out to the yard, where he dumped the cubes out into the side garden under the hostas. Then he scrubbed out the tray without a word and refilled it with clean water.

Later, Ricky approached me in the living room, wringing his hands. I saw that his nails had been bitten down to the quick. "I have an idea," he said, sitting himself on the footstool in front of me. I was drinking my tea and knitting a tiny sock for Waldo. Although the house was still warm from the heat of the day, I had it in my mind that the frigid temperatures of fall were bound to arrive abruptly, as they always did, at which point Waldo might need some slippers for our walking excursions. It seemed to me that a bunny's bare paws, finely furred as they are, must be just as tender as a person's feet, and walking on frozen earth and even snow could therefore make him vulnerable to frostbite.

"An idea," I repeated, eyes on my knitting.

"For this little problem of ours," Ricky said.

I held my breath, readying myself for something. An explanation. A confession. Ricky seemed to be holding his too. We looked each other in the eye for a long moment, until Ricky turned away.

"I would get a job, see," he began, "but then there's Jez. Someone needs to look after her."

So it was the money problem. I let out my breath and returned to my knitting. I should have known it was coming. Ricky never was a good saver. He used to spend his pocket money on gummy candies from the gas station, and as he grew older his vices evolved from Pepsi and Snickers bars to cigarettes and beer to cigars and whiskey. I wondered about the house in Phoenix, a stuccoed bungalow painted peach, nearly identical to the one Carla's parents owned. I saw it sitting empty, hot and stale with its windows sealed up, a few scuffs and nicks on the walls the only evidence that a family once lived there. Then I remembered that Carla had purchased the house before she met Ricky, and thus she alone owned it. Thinking about that gave me an alternate vision of the house, with Carla inside. My mind's eye peered through the window, where I saw her wearing a gown like a sparkling sheath and eating dinner at a pristine glass dining table, a Humphrey Bogart type seated across from her in a tailored suit. Inevitably, they would be sipping champagne, clinking their crystal glasses.

"What about school?" I said.

"I've told you," Ricky said. "Not an option." His cheeks were ruddy, and he had his hands balled up in little fists, so I could tell he was gearing up for something, already in defence mode.

"Is that not against the law?" I said.

"Jesus." Ricky tossed his hands in the air. "They won't know, for god's sake. And anyway, I'm her father. Her *father*." This was Ricky's way of asserting that I was not her mother and therefore had no say in the matter.

"All right," I said. "So what's your idea, then?"

"Well. Here's the thing." He sat on the edge of the chair across from me and set his elbows on his knees. "We don't need all this space for just three people."

"It was always three people in this house," I said. "Three bedrooms."

"The master is too much for Jez," Ricky said.

"It's no bigger than my room," I said.

"Yes, but she's small. A child. Better for her to have a room suited to her size. It's like a cave in there for her."

"She seems quite cozy," I said. "The way she sleeps with her arms and legs spread out. I think she needs the space."

"She had a nightmare last night," Ricky said. "You must've heard her wailing."

I shrugged. "Children have nightmares all the time."

Ricky ran his hands through his hair. "Could be the heat. It's bloody hot in here. There's no circulation. And the roof needs replacing, you know. The shingles are coming loose."

"Is that so?" I said. I stretched my completed sock over two fingers, judging its size. "You've done a roof before, haven't you?"

"I don't have the tools, Regina. It requires special tools. And with my bad knees I shouldn't be clambering up on ladders."

"Jez is quite the climber. Master of the monkey bars. I brought her to the park the other day. That's what we called her, master of the monkey bars."

"Park?" Ricky said, standing now. "What park?"

"The one on the corner," I said. "She was aching to go. Parks are built for children, you know."

The room went dead then. Ricky was silent, standing rigid but full of air, like a balloon poised to be pricked.

"A park?" he said again, quietly. "With other children?"

"Of course," I said, shrugging. "Jez had a fine time playing with a little boy. Stuart was his name."

"You don't know what you're doing," Ricky said. His voice was deep, the words measured.

"What I'm doing," I said, "is living my life."

"Look," Ricky said, advancing toward me with his finger pointed at my face. "You don't get to be Queen of Sheba Supreme around here. This house is as much mine as it is yours."

Without giving it a thought, I stuck Waldo's sock over the end of his finger. It seemed at the time a way to defuse him, make him realize how petulant and rash he was being. But as I sat there, watching his eyes on the sock, seeing behind them the workings of his brain as he tried to understand what I'd just done, I recognized my mistake. What Ricky hated more than anything was being shushed, and it was as though I'd put a cap on his argument, sealing it up and dismissing it as banally as I would a tube of toothpaste.

"You're insane," he said, flicking the sock from his finger. "You've lost it now. Just like our mother."

I had no response for that. Instead I picked up the sock that was lying at my feet and fiddled with it. Ricky was practically snorting, breathing heavy as a bull, his whole body vibrating. My mind flashed back to a fight we'd had as children, when he pinned my arm behind my back and pulled it from its socket. When he let me go the arm dangled like a marionette's, and I could only look at it, waggle it, and picture it as some kind of alien that had suckered itself to my body.

"This is my house," I finally said. "You left. You chose to leave here. I stayed."

"You had no choice," he said. And as he stormed out of the room, he added under his breath, "You had nowhere to go."

"Just get a job," I yelled after him. "A job is a job is a job."

≈

A job is a job is a job. One of Mutti's old sayings. For years she worked at the Final Cut, a store that converted Super 8 film to VHS tapes. *Preserve your precious memories,* said the sandwich board that sat on the sidewalk outside. Back when we were not yet old enough to care for ourselves, Ricky and I would sometimes go with her on her Saturday shifts. We watched countless home movies of strangers in their backyards, kids running through sprinklers, dads flipping burgers. It seemed that all the people from the past were having a backyard barbecue. That or getting married. I found a white linen bag one day and looped the handles around my ears, then glided across the threshold between the storefront and the backroom, picturing myself a bride crossing into a church full of gasping spectators.

What did Mutti do all day? I can only recall her stationed behind the big Formica counter at the front, chewing her nails and waiting for customers to vex her. The store I remember vividly. Film canisters stacked one on top of the other like giant cartoon coins lined the narrow hallway that led to the backroom. There, Mutti's boss, whose grey beard was as thick and long as a full head of hair, loaded film reels onto a machine that gulped them in, frame by frame. A mess of wires connected the machine to a video recorder, which fed into a television that blared the new recording. Elmo, it was called. The machine, not the boss. He called it Elmo and referred to it always as though it were a flesh-and-blood person. "Elmo needs a little break," he'd say to Mutti. "He's been slogging away all morning on this bar mitzvah."

The boss was always "Sir" to Mutti, so I never learned his real name. Sir wore a green felt beret atop his bald head, but the shine of it still seemed to glint from underneath. With his attention always on Elmo— which, Ricky and I joked, was his one true love—he needed Mutti to deal with the dribble of customers who wandered in, often by accident. Their questions were an imposition on Mutti, who hated speaking to strangers. "It is Serd Avenue," she would repeat again and again, to the vacant expressions of the customers looking for the movie theatre on Third Avenue. "Where?" they would say. "Serd," she'd reply. "Ss-herd."

I have one very clear memory of Mutti in the store. Once, a man came in with a canvas backpack full of loose film. He shook the ringlets of film out onto the counter, and they made a sound like tiny seashells.

"What's this?" Mutti said, whisking the pile with the tips of her fingers. Ricky and I were playing a game of Life on the carpet behind the counter. I was winning and had a family of six people plugged into my little red car, and Ricky had been yelling about how it wasn't fair. But something in the air between the man and Mutti caused us to stop everything and emerge from behind the counter to watch.

The man smiled. His teeth were very white, and he had the hair of a movie star, held in perfect waves that rippled across his crown. He winked at Ricky.

"Hey darlin'," he said to Mutti, and she grunted. He pulled a can of soda pop from his jacket pocket and cracked it open, taking a long sip before turning back to her.

"I was hoping you'd do me a solid and convert this to a tape. You can do that, right?"

"Mmm," Mutti replied, inspecting the film. "That is what we do here."

"You do it yourself?" he asked, leaning on the counter with his elbow.

"We have a machine," Mutti said. "It's a mechanical process. My boss can do it for you when he gets back." She glanced at her watch. "After lunch. He knows this machine."

"Beautiful," said the man. His eyes trained themselves on Mutti's face, studying it in the same way Mutti studied the film strip. Mutti didn't seem to notice.

"Your film is dirty," Mutti said. "Very dirty. See?" She held one of the loops up to the light.

"Yeah, well," he said, pausing to take another long drink. "I like dirty."

Mutti's face turned red and spotty in the silence that followed. She looked straight at the man, and he looked back. I felt my own cheeks fill with heat. I looked at Ricky. He was sitting on the floor again, cross-legged, head bent to hide his face. He had the look of a half-open clamshell.

"Hey, kids," the man said, peering over the counter at Ricky. "I saw one of those kiddie rides just outside. A dinosaur one."

We said nothing. Ricky took his little blue car from the game board and began fiddling with the people.

The man reached into his pocket and pulled out some change. He thumbed out six quarters in his hand and offered them to me. "How'd you like to go ride the dino? You and your brother?" he said.

I was about ten years old and Ricky was seven—much too big for the kiddie rides—but I knew that if I wanted to be a good girl, I should oblige. So I took Ricky's hand and the quarters, warm and moist, in the other and led him out of the store. He rode the dinosaur six times, his legs dangling almost to the ground, while I kept my eye on the blue car in the parking lot, waiting to see if someone got in, although I knew it belonged to the man. It had a rabbit's foot hanging from the rear-view mirror, and I stared at that foot, wondering how it had become a foot severed from the rest of the body. A meat cleaver, with one clean cut.

The dinosaur was meant to be a sauropod of some sort, shiny purple with a green saddle, and Ricky rode it with a kind of gait in his shoulders, as though he was imagining himself a cowboy ambling through the wilderness. His small head turned this way and that, his expression stern. After a while I sat down on the curb and looked out at the badlands in the distance, their layers of white ash bright as bone. I pictured Ricky riding his horse on the mushroomed top of a hill, stirring up clouds of dust. Then I pictured Mutti's skin like that, beige and plump and rough to the touch, marked by rills like shadowy pathways under her breasts, between her legs.

When the sixth quarter ran out, Ricky climbed down and sat with me on the curb. I noticed the smell first. I could see that his pants were wet, but I purposefully looked at them askance, as I knew it would only embarrass him to know that I knew. He'd recently begun collecting his own bedsheets on some mornings and balling them up in a pile atop the washing machine for Mutti to find.

Then, out of nowhere, Ricky screamed. His mouth opened wide, and out came a sharp, high-pitched scream. I covered my ears.

"What was that for?" I said.

He shrugged. "That's what the girls do," he said. "That's what they do at school when the bell rings at the end of recess."

Just then the man emerged from the building, carrying his unzipped, empty bag and empty soda can. He tossed the can toward the garbage bin and missed but kept walking anyway. Ricky and I watched as he got into the blue car and drove away.

I remember this as though it were one of the home movies that Elmo had preserved forever on vhs tape. Jez is almost the same age as Ricky was at the time, and her expressions are copies of his—the same stern brow and hard eyes that give nothing away. I remember the imprint of Ricky's wet bottom on the curb. I remember the little puddle on the pavement under the kiddie dinosaur, seeing it as we went back inside, but not knowing what to do, so doing nothing. Pretending. Mutti cluck-clucked when she saw us. She got Ricky out of the pants and his underwear and fashioned a kind of skirt for him out of her scarf.

"Silly boy," was all she said.

Mutti worked at that job for four years, until everything was VHS, and film had become a relic. She was not sad to leave it behind, as far as I could tell. Within a week, she was working a new job at a thrift store a few blocks down. *A job is a job is a job.*

It seems that I took that saying to heart. I took the first job that presented itself to me, and it also happened to be behind a counter. Not many jobs, after all, have such a marked off-season that you can sit and read your books on weekday afternoons, interrupted only a few times an hour to sell tickets to visitors. I felt cozy in my little booth, which was only just large enough for me and so cocooned me perfectly. There were essentially three phrases in my workday vocabulary: "Welcome to Fossil Land Discovery Museum"; "That comes to" (followed by the total cost); and "Thank you, and enjoy your visit." Using the computer to issue tickets turned out to be fairly simple once I got the hang of moving the mouse with the lightest touch, and became even easier when we switched to touch screens and I only had to punch my finger to one of four floating boxes—*child*, *adult*, *senior*, *family*—and let the customer do the rest. I wore a collared white shirt and a shiny black vest embroidered with the museum logo. My uniform had to be custom made when I began the job, so for the first two weeks when I worked the floor, I wore my own dress with a Fossil Land sticker on my chest, which seemed to scandalize the visitors. They slowed their pace as they approached me to ask for directions to the washroom, looking around for someone who appeared to belong to the museum. Darrell, who wore a navy suit and dinosaur tie every day, had taken it upon himself to hover nearby, pretending to polish the information plaques, and apologize to each approaching visitor before I'd given them an answer.

"We have a trainee working with us today," he said, his hands clasped behind his back like a butler. "Please bear with us." And then he ushered them away, as if they might be too frightened to face a very large, un-uniformed woman alone. I was just twenty-one at the time, still with a teenager's modesty. I didn't tell anyone when the white shirt split at the seam in the back only a few weeks later and the fabric under the armpits turned a sickly yellow. I wore my vest always and kept my arms at my sides. Eventually, I learned to sew with Mutti's old Singer and mended the shirt myself. I bleached it out so many times that it turned transparent, but rather than ask for a new one, I made one for myself. It is not easy to make a tailored dress shirt—I did it by taking apart all the pieces of the old one and using them as my pattern— but back then it was easier to suffer through a laborious task than to suffer embarrassment.

After some time I became invisible to Darrell. He'd say hello to me in the morning, and I'd comment on his tie—"Triceratops today, is it?" or "That pterodactyl doesn't come out too often." He'd give a little chuckle and then go on his way, unlocking doors and buffing smudged glass with a little cloth he kept in his coat pocket. Once I accidentally caught him and his wife in the staff lunchroom, having a spat. I walked in just as she threw a basket of plastic forks at him. The forks scattered like fireworks and made a chorus of clicking against the linoleum that seemed to amplify the awkward moment, with me in the doorway and Darrell's wife frozen in place, seeing me there as witness to the scene. Her glasses had slid down her nose, and her hair was falling out of her bun. She looked as though she had just come off a roller-coaster ride, whipped and winded. Darrell appeared not to see me at all. His solemn expression betrayed not a hint of shame, and he began picking up the forks one by one, silently placing them back in the basket as though this were an everyday chore. His wife began to cry, and I took that as my cue to leave, closing the door very softly behind me.

It was the first time I realized that my size was a kind of power. While in one way it made me a spectacle, in another I could use it to make myself disappear. Darrel and others like him didn't care what I thought, what secrets I might know. They saw largeness as a different category of existence, as if large people had no significance at all in the world of regular-sized people.

I learned a great deal about people in my fifteen years at the museum. The way they spoke to a stranger, the way they handled their money, and mostly the state of their hands—clean or dirty, chapped knuckles or fingers glistening with freshly applied hand cream—said so much about who they were under the skin. I even learned some words in other languages—Mandarin, French, Norwegian—simply by listening. But I did not, oddly enough, learn very much at all about dinosaurs. Even though Mutti was gone, I could feel her shadow standing at the entrance, telling me to let the past be. "Schnee von Gestern," she would say when I asked her questions about her life before I was born. *Snow from yesterday.*

And then there was Ricky, whose seven years away remained in shadow. He was living by the same code. I wish I had realized then, when all the signs began to emerge, that Ricky and I were still our child selves underneath, both of us suspended in our own little cubes of ice, unable to see how trapped we really were.

5

RICKY WAS CRACKLING the next morning, alight with a new kind of energy that I felt in the air as soon as I awoke. At breakfast Jez insisted that Earl be given his own little bowl of oatmeal, and Ricky obliged cheerfully, even floating two squares of white chocolate on top and calling them ice floes. She finished both bowls in minutes, using her finger like a spatula for the remnants.

It seemed the Arctic was something of an obsession for Jez. Ricky said she'd seen a documentary film about narwhals and couldn't stop fussing over it since.

"Jez," he said, eager to show me the evidence. "What does a narwhal do?"

Without missing a beat, she collapsed her chin, opened her mouth, and emitted a guttural croaking sound. The sound was alarmingly unhuman, like a squeaky hinge on an old door.

Ricky chuckled and gave a single clap. "When they're about to attack," he explained. "That's what they sound like."

"Why do you like the Arctic so much?" I asked Jez.

"Narwhals," she said, looking at Ricky, who nodded his approval. She stroked Earl, who was pinned beneath her arm. I knew this was not the only reason, but Jez skipped out of the room, having performed her trick.

"Have you ever thought of moving there?" I asked Ricky. "To the Arctic?" I smiled to signal that I was only joking, but Ricky had his face turned away.

"I need you to look after her today," he said. "I have things to do. Important things."

"Me too. I have work," I said.

"You could bring her along," he said. "She's very quiet. She won't be any trouble—she always manages to busy herself."

"If only Mrs. Nakamura still lived on the corner," I said.

"What? Who?" Ricky said.

"Mrs. Nakamura, remember? She looked after us when Mutti was at work."

"Oh. I forgot all about it." He was scratching his hair and feeling his pocket for keys. I scanned his eyes to see if he was truly serious.

"You did not," I said. "You did not forget."

"Why are you so ornery?"

"You couldn't have forgotten. And I'm not ornery."

"Will you take her or not?" Ricky said, jumbling his keys in his hand. "She likes you. She told me so."

Ricky knew this would soften me. What aunt does not long to be liked by her niece? He saw it in my eyes, and a little smile of triumph formed on his lips. "It won't be all day," he said. "I'll come get her just after lunch." His hand gave a quick wave as he stepped out of the kitchen, calling Jez's name.

She appeared a moment later, spying on me from behind the door frame with a single eye.

"It seems you're coming with me to Fossil Land today," I said to her. "Do you know what a fossil is?"

"An animal," she said, coming into the kitchen. "With furry legs."

"Close," I said. "It was once an animal. Or a plant. But it died a long time ago. And over the years the dead body of the animal turned into a rock."

"It can't turn into a rock," she said.

"Yes, it can too," I said. "Even you could turn into a rock." Jez did not respond to that idea, but as I cleared up the dishes she stood there pinching her lips between her fingers, clearly contemplating the possibility.

I retrieved one of Mutti's favourite treasures, a chipped albertosaurus tooth, from the windowsill and set it on the table in front of Jez. "There's one," I said. "A dinosaur tooth."

She held it between her thumb and finger, turning it around to inspect it from all sides before holding it up to her own mouth and sliding it against her eye tooth.

"Be careful," I said. "Your oma was quite proud of that one."

I'd been with Mutti when she found it. Back when I was young, Drumheller was positively teeming with fossils. Mutti said it was the quality of the sediments, their fine clay structure, that so efficiently preserved ancient creatures in their rock coffins. As a child I naively believed the fossils were the animals themselves. I suppose I was too young to understand the concept completely—that an animal's flesh and bones could dissolve away but still leave a vestige of its existence. What you were seeing, Mutti explained, was not the animal's self but rather an imposter. Imagine, she said: you could step out of your skin but it would still hold the shape of your body. That was what a fossil was—a kind of empty shell filled up with minerals to become a perfect imitation of the original.

"You'll see more like that at the museum today," I told Jez, setting the tooth back in its place. I began to whip up a collection of snacks for Jez from the things Ricky had stocked in the pantry, all of it sugary and garishly dyed. She seemed neither distressed nor excited by the prospect of spending the day with me. She got her little turtle-shell backpack with Earl packed inside and held it out for me to add the snacks.

"What's a museum?" she said as I zipped it shut.

"A museum," I began, "is a home for old and precious things. There are different kinds of museums. Some of them are for art. The one we are going to is for fossils. And dinosaurs."

Jez contemplated this, her eyes drifting off into space. I offered the straps of her backpack and she slid her arms in, clearly having committed this drill to muscle memory.

"We get to see the dinosaurs?" she said.

"Yes, you'll get to see them. My friend Marilyn will give you a special tour."

She brightened at that idea, lifting her chest and giving a little "yip!" as she ran out to the garage.

I took the turn onto Centre Street on our way to the museum. It was a slight detour, but I had it in my mind that I might as well show Jez some of the sights on our way, since I doubted that Ricky had bothered. We rolled past the old tap house, Jurassic Laser Tag, the nail salon, the thrift store. Several boarded-up shops with faded FOR LEASE signs languished along the strip—more than I had remembered. There was the bus bench with the green triceratops statue sitting on one side, smiling and holding a dripping ice cream cone, with little pink bows on her horns. On the adjacent corner stood a little knee-height T. Rex dressed as Batman, whose eyes in the holes of his mask had been spray-painted over with red since I'd last seen him. There was the shop where the Final Cut had used to be, but which was now a frozen yogurt chain where I had frequently seen a lineup of tourists snaking out the door two summers ago. It was deserted now and looked to have somehow gone out of business. I thought about pointing out to Jez that Mutti had once worked there, but I quickly realized that would have no meaning to her at all. None of it, in fact, seemed to interest her; in the rear-view mirror I could see that she was gazing at the roof with her mouth hanging open and busying herself with switching her tongue back and forth. It dawned on me then that she had come from Phoenix, a big city, and therefore this place, with its four-block downtown strip, would appear to be only a paltry little town in her eyes.

It was the water tower, of all things, that got her attention.

"What's that huge robot?" she said. Atop thin metal legs squatted the tower's white drum body. A collection of antennas stuck out of its top.

"It does look like a robot, doesn't it?" I said. "It's meant for hold-ing water. I don't think it's used for that anymore, though." I was a bit ashamed that I did not know this for sure.

"What's it used for now?"

I shrugged. "Decoration," I said, feeling even more foolish. "Here's something exciting," I said, pointing out the window on the opposite side. "Look over there. That's the World's Largest Dinosaur."

"Whoa," she said.

"It's a bit scary, isn't it?" I said. It was, in truth, quite comical looking in that moment, with its bulging yellow eyes and stunted arms forking at the air.

Her head turned to look at it as we passed. "But it's not real," she said. Ricky had taught her well.

I shrugged off her disenchanted response, assuring myself that the dinosaurs at the museum would be far more exciting for her. The day was already warm, buzzing with energy; clouds of gnats churned in the ditches along the highway, and all around us the crusty hills of the badlands were baking like great loaves of bread. It happened to be the big day at Fossil Land—the unveiling of the new animatronic dino-saurs. The day before, we'd had to suffer Darrell's high-strung employee safety orientation, through which he had sweated so profusely that the pits of his blue dress shirt were soaked down to his waist by the time he was finished. "We can't be too careful, people," was his man-tra; I counted it twelve times, making a kind of game of anticipating the next repetition instead of listening to Darrell's rambling. What I knew by the time he was finished was that people, especially children, were expressly forbidden from touching, climbing on, or approaching the dinosaurs within breathing distance. He had set up a perimeter of velvet ropes to delineate where the visitors were permitted to stand and watch the dinosaurs in action, and he stationed two attendants in the room to ensure their compliance. All of the employees, myself included, had already received a sneak preview of the spectacle, and it put me in mind of the old fortune-telling kiosks at the carnival, the ones that rose to life like marionettes when you put a coin in the slot. Darrell flicked a switch, and the dinosaurs twitched and jerked, and all of us obediently clapped and cheered. I looked into the beady eye of the oviraptor and it blinked craftily, the eyelid clicking back into place with an eerie precision.

I admit I had not expected to be impressed by the dinosaurs, but I was, perhaps for the wrong reasons. They did not appear particularly realistic to me per se, though how to judge the realism of a thing that no one has ever seen in reality is beyond me. I was intrigued instead by their ferocity as machines. The mechanisms rolling beneath their skin made them look like straitjackets for whatever was alive inside. I imagined little people trapped beneath, doomed to play in a bizarre, unending charade.

What seemed even stranger was that the dinosaurs could not walk. I suppose my expectations were too lofty in imagining them as they appeared in the movies. While their upper bodies moved, their feet were fixed in place, and so all three stood together in the room, making a triangle that seemed to signal some kind of association, while their bodies remained isolated, untouching. They were glued to the spot, each performing its own little dance.

I asked Darrell why they couldn't walk, and he scoffed. "Really, Regina. We're not yet *that* advanced," he said. "And anyway, think of the liability issues. You can't control a walking dinosaur. They'd be bumping into walls, knocking over the other exhibits. Chaos." He spoke of them as if they had a will of their own, which I think he might have believed on some level.

Darrell was expecting hordes of visitors on opening day, and so he was none too pleased to see me walk in with Jez that morning. But as soon as she curtsied and batted those long eyelashes of hers, Darrell relented. He gave her a stack of programs and set her to task handing them out to the visitors as they left the admission booths.

"Enjoy your visit to Fossil Land's interactive dinosaur experience!" he coached her to say, and she enunciated carefully, as her parents had taught her to do, sounding very adultlike. Of course, it made the visitors laugh every time, much to Darrell's glee. One man who came with his teenage son asked Jez what her favourite dinosaur was, and she made a very convincing case for the blue-footed babbylosaurus from the Arctic Archipelago. Tragically, the man believed it was a real dinosaur and asked me to direct him to the exhibit about it for more information. I hadn't the heart to expose his foolhardiness in front of his son, so I told him it was in the very last fossil case, hoping he would forget by then. But Jez had told him the babbylosaurus was her favourite because it had toenails like razor blades, which was perhaps a detail too sinister not to be believed, especially coming from a pigtailed six-year-old girl. She leered and fanned her fingers out against her cheek as if imitating Freddy Krueger when she described it.

When it was time for my break, I took Jez to the lunchroom, and she sighed like a regular working stiff when I placed a cup of juice in front of her. She peeled open a package of penguin-shaped fruit snacks and chewed away.

"A little tired?" I asked her.

"Nope," she said, looking in a daze.

"Are you having fun?"

"When do we get to see them?" she replied.

"Well, you've been working hard this morning," I said. "I'll see if Darrell will let you visit them for a while."

Marilyn came into the room then, as if on cue.

"Well, hello there!" she said in a chipmunky voice. Jez glanced up at her, narrowing her eyes. "I heard there's a little monkey in the museum today," Marilyn continued. She must have expected Jez to respond in some way, to show her gratefulness for this patronizing game, because Marilyn stood in the doorway, mouth open in a crazy grin, her hands spread out as if ready to catch a giant beach ball. But Jez did not respond and made an effort to concentrate instead on the far more interesting task of freeing her fruit snacks from the package. Inside I was proud. It may have been the first time I felt a kind of ownership over Jez, a blood link that made all of her actions reflect back on me.

In the absence of any acknowledgment from Jez, Marilyn tried a different tactic. She crept around Jez's chair and poked her head around Jez's shoulder in an attempt to surprise her. Jez simply rotated her head slowly and peered at Marilyn.

"Are you Jez?" Marilyn said in a syrupy voice. "What a pretty name," she added. "Is it Chinese?" When Jez only blinked, Marilyn quickly said, "My name is Marilyn, but you can call me Mary. Or Mare. Whatever's easier!" She giggled. "Wanna come with me to see the brand new cool dinosaurs?" She held out her hand.

Jez looked at me, and I nodded. Just by making eye contact I knew she understood what I was telling her—that Marilyn was harmless, if a little dotty, and that humouring her was really best for all involved. Jez obliged and climbed off her chair, tucking it back into the table before toddling off alongside Marilyn, whose outstretched hand went unheld.

When I got back to Admissions, Darrell was checking the numbers on the computer.

"Can you believe this?" he said. I shook my head, though the charts on the screen were all gobbledygook to me anyway.

"We're barely above average for a Saturday," he said.

"Well," I said, "perhaps it's too early. It's not yet noon. Going to a museum is more of an afternoon activity, no?"

"The marketing people really dropped the ball on this one," Darrell replied. Then, perking up, he said, "Onward and upward!" and pointed his finger to the sky, marching away.

It was not five minutes later that I heard the scream. At first I didn't think it was a human sound; it was shrill, unbroken like a fire alarm, and indeed my first thought was that one of the dinosaurs had short-circuited and sparked a little blaze. I was in the middle of printing tickets for an elderly couple, and when the sound went off, we all jumped, and the woman cried, "Goodness!" clutching the brim of her Tilley hat. Her husband patted her on the back and looked to me for an explanation.

"I wonder what that was all about," was all I could think to say as I passed them their tickets. Thankfully this seemed to assure them, and they went on their way.

I expected Jez to come running out immediately, but a long time passed, perhaps even half an hour, with me sitting in my booth, one eye on the queue and the other on the big fortress-like double doors to the exhibits. I began to worry that Ricky would show up any minute and I would have no child to give him. But the thought of it, getting Ricky riled up, also gave me a tiny bit of pleasure. My tolerance for his feigned disaffection had begun to wear thin. Now, as I worked through a surge of tour bus customers, passing out tickets on autopilot, the scream still ringing in my mind, I thought back to Mrs. Nakamura and what Ricky had said earlier, that he'd forgotten all about her. That was a pure lie. Her garden, in itself, had been enchanting enough to be remembered forever. It was a Japanese-style garden filled with exotic perennials that should not have been possible to grow in Drumheller, which she tended and pruned with religious devotion. And beyond the garden was that fact that Ricky had loved Mrs. Nakamura like a mother. She had no children of her own but clearly wanted them; she happily babysat me and Ricky at least twice a week after school, and each time Mutti thanked her she would insist that we were the most wonderful, sweetest children—which I knew could not be true—and that we fed her soul. Whenever we went to her house, she offered us flawlessly round homemade mochi balls in rainbow colours that magically melted as soon as they touched the roof of your mouth. I was fond of her, to be sure, but Ricky adored her. His face changed whenever he saw her; his eyes lit with a kind of bright obedience, like a dog's upon his master's return. I suppose it was because Mrs. Nakamura was everything that Mutti was not: quiet, reserved, delicate, someone who approached every small task and even every movement of her body with the same care and precision she gave to her garden. Even her smile, the thinnest pink crescent, seemed cultivated to perfection. She taught us to make origami animals and to fold clothes into neat little packages, and though these were not normally activities that would interest Ricky, he would follow her steps without hesitation, soaking in the praise he received with every perfect fold.

Mrs. Nakamura was married, but she'd kept her maiden name, which was unusual for the times, and even more so given what kind of man her husband was. He worked at a bank and was rarely home when we were there, but if he was, Ricky and I knew to make ourselves scarce. He had the look of an army general with his blond brush cut, his starched, buttoned-up shirts, and his pin-straight posture, and the stolid expression on his face was so constant that I was convinced for a long time there must be something wrong with his face, as if he were physically incapable of moving the muscles, until once I saw him cough and briefly grimace with the strain of it. He barely said a word to us or his wife, and she would present him with plates of food arranged like mosaics, bowing as she placed them ever so gently, without a sound, on the table before him. The way she held her breath whenever he was around made me think that if Ricky and I weren't there, he'd probably have transformed into some kind of vicious beast and ravenously gobbled up the food and anything else in his way.

Still, no one, least of all me and Ricky, ever expected that Mrs. Nakamura would, seemingly out of nowhere, lose her mind. She began to wander out at night in some sort of trance, ending up in neighbours' garden sheds or garages, and would scream incantations in Japanese when she was found. Then, one day, she disappeared. Mutti told us later that she'd been sent to Ponoka. The mental hospital.

Ricky had been devastated, though of course he didn't show it. He kept making origami animals for years afterward, but only in the privacy of his room. His creations became quite advanced; once he made a black dragon, and another time a little Yoda, and he lined them all up on his windowsill like his own private memorial, collecting dust as the years passed. I wondered now what had happened to them. If he'd kept them, or if he'd thrown them away when he moved.

I checked my watch. It had been nearly forty-five minutes since I'd heard the scream. The big doors swung open then, and the elderly couple came out, the woman making a beeline for me and poking her head into my booth. "I thought you should know," she said, "there's a child running about. Lost her mother, maybe?" I thanked her and assured her I would sort it all out, and she went off to join her husband in the gift shop.

I could see the end of the line of customers. I rushed them through and finally got enough of a lull to be able to leave my booth. I hurried toward the doors to the exhibits, but before I could even get to them, Jez came striding out. I say striding because she was swinging her legs and planting her feet as though imagining herself a giant crushing a village. She stopped when she saw me. Her face was calm and expectant.

"Everything all right?" I said. She nodded and ran to me, clinging to my legs. I bent down and hugged her. But her grasp was stiff rather than tender, and she slid down to her bottom.

"Were they scary?" I asked her. "Did the dinosaurs frighten you?"

"Yes," she said, in that way of hers that was too automatic to be believable. She nuzzled her nose into my leg.

"Where is Marilyn?" I said. "Did she take good care of you?"

Jez jumped to her feet, apparently having remembered her job, and grabbed the stack of programs from my booth. "She has a dead kid," she said. She held the programs in two hands, shuffling them to line up their edges.

"What?" I said. Surely I'd misheard her.

"Her kid," Jez said. "He died. A long time ago. And they put him in the museum for old and precious things."

"Really," I said, catching on to her game. "What was his name?"

This took her a moment to invent. "Grinky," she said, pressing a finger to her lips.

"I see," I said. "Was Grinky a dinosaur?"

She got that faraway look in her eyes again and nodded slowly.

"Is that why you screamed?" I said.

Marilyn came bursting from the doors. "There you are," she cried, upon seeing Jez. "I was just answering someone's question and next thing I knew, she had vanished!" Marilyn mimed a cartoonish brow-wiping action. "Like a little dog, she is," she said. "She can smell her way home."

I did not know how to respond, since it seemed an insult to compare a child to a dog. But I saw that Marilyn quickly recognized her mistake, as her eyes went back and forth, replaying the words in her mind. It was important to a person like Marilyn to keep her judgments on the inside.

"Do you have a doggie at home?" she blurted. Jez ignored her. Marilyn turned her attention back to me.

"She's a quiet one, isn't she? A little doll with those dark eyes." She folded her hands together, shaking her head. "And gosh, she's a listener." Then, in low tones behind her hand, "Better than my therapist!" She laughed her tin-can laugh, and I forced a smile.

"I was just nattering on and on about Jamie," she continued. "Couldn't help myself. He's home in two weeks, you know. Gosh, I'm sure I've told you that already."

I smiled again because she had, dozens of times.

"Just wait 'til she grows up," she went on. "She'll break your heart, leaving you behind."

We stood there watching Jez tiptoe between the floor tiles, and I tried to picture her grown up, a woman. But she was only an enlarged version of herself, that round, doe-eyed face blank as ever, and in my mind she kept growing and growing until she was tall as a skyscraper. Would it be different, I wondered, if I were her mother? Would I see her grown-up self as some incarnation of me? Eventually Marilyn got tired of my silence and announced that she had better get back to the grindstone.

Over my years at the museum, I'd observed many a child run away, gleeful to commit some act of defiance to mortify their parents, like tossing handfuls of sand from the Discovery Dig into the air, sending showers raining all over the guests, or attempting to swing from the tusks of the woolly mammoth skeleton. It seemed fairly normal, there-fore, that Jez would see this as a place to test her boundaries. But it was clear that Marilyn had been unsettled by Jez. There was a distance between them, like a force field that Marilyn would not dare to cross, even though she was one of those women who could kiss and cuddle a baby within seconds of meeting it. But no, it was not even that, not just a physical distance. It was something deeper, some gut instinct of repellence, perhaps, which was visible on Marilyn's face even though she thought she'd been able to keep it shrouded below the surface. I recognized it, of course, because I'd grown accustomed to receiving that look myself.

Ricky arrived to retrieve Jez only minutes later, seeming quite chuffed with himself over whatever he'd been up to. "It all worked out, didn't it?" he said to me, and swept Jez away without waiting for an answer.

I was eager for the day to settle back into its usual pattern, but when the elderly couple was leaving the gift shop, they made a point to return to the entrance.

"Did you find the little girl?" the woman asked. "I tried to help her but she was a bit—agitated."

"The little brat bit her," the man cut in. "Grabbed her arm and tried to take a bite out of it!"

"Dennis," the woman said, bracing his arm, "it's all right. She was just scared."

"Thank you for letting me know," I said. "We've found her mother and everything is just fine."

"Oh, thank goodness," the woman said.

Luckily Darrell was not around to overhear this, but he must have gotten word of it by some other means. He told me at the end of my shift that if I tried to bring my niece to work again, he would have to let me go. It was an easy way for him to account for the flop of the new dinosaurs' debut. They were too precious a commodity to the museum, to Darrell. It was impossible for him to accept that no one else gave a damn about them.

6

THE SECOND WEEK of September was the hottest and driest of all the weeks in the Never-Ending Summer. Fires had begun popping up all over northern Alberta, and though we could not see the smoke, the smell of burning wood hung in the air. I envisioned the road leading into town and a single match, thrown from the window of a car, lighting up the grassy ditch in the blink of an eye. The flames spreading, clambering up the slopes of the valley. Columns of fire shooting from the tops of the buttes like erupting volcanoes. And the bones buried beneath, burning away, layer by layer. Ash falling down on us like snow.

We sat out on the shaded lawn beneath the oak because the house had become an oven. School had surely begun by now; the streets were quiet, no other children to be seen. Ricky put out a small paddling pool for Jez, but she seemed more interested in throwing rocks into it than swimming. There was not a bead of sweat on her body, and when I asked Ricky if she needed to wear a hat, he reminded me that this was the norm in Phoenix. I'd only been there once, for Ricky's wedding. At the time I hadn't known that I would never return, that it would be the last day I'd see him for seven years.

The day of the wedding had been a blaze of orange, like being inside a flame. It was mid-July in Phoenix—Carla's hometown—and the ceremony took place in her parents' backyard on a plane of pristinely mown grass. The heat seemed to scream, burning through the straw hat that I had purchased specially for the occasion. It was the breathability of the straw that had drawn me to the hat, but under the sun it seemed reasonable to think it could in fact be a fire hazard. I thought for certain that the hairs on the top of my head would be singed and blackened by the time the ceremony was over. Perhaps then I would have fit in with the quilt of black heads that surrounded me. How unperturbed they seemed, despite the heat, was a mystery.

Seeing as I was the only family member on Ricky's side and about six times the size of Carla's tiny relatives, I was given a whole row to myself at the very front. I sat on a white plastic chair in my blue flower-print dress, cradling a little river of sweat between my thighs.

Carla had chosen bright orange for her bridesmaids' dresses, the bouquet, and her earrings and necklace, and Ricky and his best man wore orange satin vests to match, with tiger lilies tucked in their lapels. More lilies spilled from bouquets affixed to the ends of each row in the audience, and from giant fountain-like arrangements in tall orange vases that flanked Ricky and Carla as they stood with the minister. Orange bows and sashes were pinned to the sides of each chair. Even the air was orange in the afternoon light. Carla's black sheaf of hair seemed to carve out a hole against all of it, like the eye of a jack-o'-lantern.

When the time came for the "I dos," Carla's voice quavered, and from my spot in the front row I could see her eyes turn glassy. She was smiling, and though I barely knew her, I couldn't recall having ever seen her smile before. Ricky was flushed and shiny, though more from the heat than the excitement, since his face had none of the brightness of Carla's. He looked the same as always; the same face he'd had as a baby he kept into his adulthood, which was one of the things Mutti always said about him when we were growing up. "Richard still has the face of a baby," she would say when giving her regular updates to Tante Regina over the phone. Mutti would have despised the wedding, the colour, the flowers, watching her boy get married to someone like Carla. She would have wanted him to end up with someone more like herself—industrious, earthy, round faced, and built with hips for child-bearing.

Carla was a corporate lawyer who worked for one of the companies intending to drill for oil just outside of Drumheller. She met Ricky while he was working on springtime road repair, and I assume that she must have approached him, as Ricky has always been lamblike around girls, particularly ones like Carla. He invited her over for dinner shortly after they met. I made boiled potatoes with creamed spinach and my famous meatloaf—Mutti's secret hackbraten recipe. The trick is to mash a slice of stale bread into the meat to create the glue. "Mit den Händen," Mutti used to specify. With the hands, not with a fork or a potato masher. On a normal evening Ricky and I would sit with TV trays in the living room, but he'd never admitted the existence of a girlfriend before, let alone brought one of them home for dinner, so I took pains to make the evening elegant, with candles on the table and real cloth napkins and even a bottle of wine for us to share.

When they arrived, Ricky opened the front door and yelled "Hello!" so that I could hear him in the kitchen. It was strange, since it was his house too, and his voice had a kind of jaunty pitch to it that made me think, for an instant, that a complete stranger had walked in. When they came into the kitchen to greet me I was pressed with my bottom against the stove, taking care to stand straight and not slouch, as was my habit. I saw the look that passed over Carla's face when she saw me. It lasted only a fraction of a moment, but it was a clear transformation that involved all her subtle features. Eyes flashed their whites, eyebrows made a tiny leap, nose twitched, top lip curled ever so slightly. Then her eyes shot to my bosom. By some kind of instinct, mine went to hers also. There was barely a shadow to announce the two pointed teats curtained under her blouse.

"So nice to meet you," she said, cocking her head to the side. "Regina, is it?"

"Yes, it is. And you're Carla."

"So nice to meet you," she said again, looking to Ricky. "Should we just sit down at the table?"

I giggled out of nervousness as they escaped into the dining room. She was not what I had expected at all. When Ricky had told me she was coming to dinner, he called her a "nice lady." "She's very nice," was all he could seem to articulate when I asked for more. "A very nice person. Kind. And proper. Old-fashioned." I'd been left with no choice but to picture her as a chubby aproned grandmother offering a plate of warm cookies and a permanent grin. This woman, however, seemed the opposite—thin and small, with slick black arcs drawn onto her face in place of eyebrows.

When I brought out the meatloaf, Carla and Ricky were both seated on one side of the table, facing forward with their napkins and hands already laid on their laps. As I set the platter in front of them, she said, "Sorry," though I had no clue what for. "Work was just—murder," she continued. "Just paperwork all day long."

"It was a busy day?" I said.

"Yes. Busy. Very busy." She nodded and nodded.

Neither she nor Ricky said anything as I brought out the other dishes and sat down across from them. Ricky picked up his fork and Carla gave him a look, prompting him to set it back in its place. There was a moment of silence through which Carla and Ricky looked at me as if I'd something important to say.

"Shall we eat?" I said. I realized then that they were waiting for me to serve. I had to lurch across the table to spoon food onto their plates, and I caught Carla's eyes again on my swinging bosom more than once.

Ricky and I began to eat as Carla spoke more about her paperwork, how getting signatures was "just murder," how she would "strangle the next person who conveniently forgot about section 4.44 of the Commissioner of the Environment's report," which was, by the way, "appallingly inadequate" compared to American standards.

She'd barely touched her meal when she announced, "Well. I hate to be picky, but I can't eat this." She sighed, folded her napkin, and laid it neatly next to her plate. "It's just too heavy, you know? Rich. I mean, don't get me wrong, it's great. If you like that kind of thing."

Later, she left for the bathroom and didn't come back for twenty minutes. Ricky and I were silent the whole time, both finishing our plates and taking second and third helpings to fill the space. When Carla finally returned, her cheeks were pink and her eyes bloodshot. "Sorry," she said again, tucking herself back into the table. "I thought schnitzel was typical German fare," she declared. "I had a meal at a restaurant once—a German one, I'm sure of it. It was a side dish, like dough, little dough rolls. Like this." She used her fingers to mime a small shape.

"Spaetzle?" I asked.

"No, I don't think so. I don't think it was pronounced like that. Anyway, they were delicious. Just melted on my tongue." She stuck out the tip of her tongue for effect.

"Spaetzle comes from southern Germany," I explained. "Mutti's family came from the north."

"She means our mother," Ricky cut in.

"Oh, okay. Okay." Carla dabbed at the corners of her lips with the tip of her index finger as though she'd been eating along with us. "My mother's family is from northern China," she continued. "The food there is actually much lighter than in the south." She picked up her fork and touched its tines to the edge of the slice of meatloaf that still sat on the plate in front of her. "This is ... heavy."

They left promptly after dinner, and I was told the next day that Carla had to return to Phoenix. I saw her only one other time before the wedding. She and Ricky were walking down Centre Street, her in front and him trailing behind. I was just coming around the corner when she nearly ran into me.

"Oh, it's you," she said with that same look of shock. "What are you doing out?" I wished that I had worn something more decent as she looked me over, eyes combing my matted hair and the old housedress that had once belonged to Mutti. She was wearing a black leather skirt that flashed like a camera as she moved.

I made an excuse about needing to be quick because I had baking in the oven, and mercifully our conversation ended. I can admit that I never took a liking to her, but I'm sure she would say the same of me.

Regardless, she did offer to pay for my flight to Phoenix for the wedding, which was generous since it happened that I required two seats, at my girth. Perhaps that was the kind of thing Ricky meant by "nice." Even though I could not like Carla, I suppose it was nice to be invited to the wedding, especially because I hadn't been to one since Tante Regina's when I was a child.

After the ceremony, I went with the newlyweds and Carla's family inside the community centre, where the reception was going to be held that evening. We crowded in a little room off to the side, and although there was air conditioning, I sat fanning myself with the orange paper fan that all the wedding guests had received, while Carla's family members lined up, oldest to youngest. Carla and Ricky knelt in front of them on silk-upholstered cushions, offering each relative in turn a cup of tea from a fancy porcelain cup decorated with Chinese writing. Ricky had explained to me that it was a Chinese tradition, and though Carla wasn't really very Chinese since she was born in America, her mother had insisted. According to this tradition, the newly married couple needed to serve tea to all the family members and their spouses so that they could welcome the new spouse into the family and offer their gifts, which were small red envelopes that contained money. The envelopes they piled in a golden bowl. Carla wore a red Chinese silk dress that gave her the look of a bloodied arrow, and Ricky wore a matching smock. He looked very rigid in his costume, as though he were afraid to ruin it, and he bowed stiffly each time he offered a cup of tea.

Carla had many relatives to work their way through the queue, so it wasn't until the last couple was receiving their tea that I hoisted myself out of the chair and stood behind them for my turn. It seemed a very official kind of ritual, so I removed my hat out of respect, even though my hair was stringy from the sweat. I had no red envelope, but I figured that keeping the money secret was not so important among close family.

Carla turned away when I approached them. All the other relatives had left the room and were milling about in the foyer and chatting, waiting for the reception to begin in the gymnasium. Carla and Ricky had already stood up from their kneeling positions and begun helping Carla's sister to stack the cups on the table behind them. Carla went on with the task as though I weren't there, speaking to her sister in whispers.

"What is it?" Ricky said to me.

I understood then. It was not my turn. I had no turn. This ritual was reserved for Carla's family, not ours. And while Ricky was now an official member of that family, I was not.

Later, when all the speeches had ended and the lights had dimmed and the guests were dancing the YMCA, I returned to the tea ceremony room. It was unlocked and the lights were off, but the stacks of teacups still stood on the table, shining in the street lights that came through the window. The cups were layered neatly with saucers stuck in between so that they looked like miniature temples. I picked one up and felt the cold porcelain. It was thin, thin enough that I could see the delicate writing on the outside ghosted on the white inside when I held it up to the light. They were expensive, to be sure.

Seven years later and Ricky still has yet to say anything about what happened after I left that evening. The cups were remarkably easy to break. They exploded into thousands of pieces as soon as they made impact. Some of them I even stamped on to crush into tinier pieces, and before I knew what I was doing, there was only a scattering of porcelain shards and fine powder strewn across the tiles.

I suspect Carla must have known.

7

FALL FINALLY BEGAN to creep in, with its crisp mornings and stark light, which seemed to throw everything into sharp contrast, turning it new and strange. I'd expected it to feel freeing, a long-awaited relief from the heat, but it felt unnervingly quiet instead. It was as though the heat had made a low, constant hum that had become a comfort, and only now, in its absence, was I suddenly noticing. And it wasn't only me; the whole neighbourhood seemed skittish. Though Ricky and Jez had been living with me for nearly a month by now, the neighbours stared when Jez and I ventured out to the front yard on a Monday after- noon and began to rake leaves. The oak spread its branches over us like shadowy fingers, letting pockets of light make shapes in the grass. The old woman across the street in her purple pantsuit was mowing her lawn and stopped midway to observe us. She made a visor out of her hand to shield her gaze from the sun, apparently unconcerned that we could see her eyes focused on us. The man two doors down with thick, wire-rimmed spectacles was pretending to check his mail and stood at his mailbox for much longer than necessary to steal peeks at us. It seemed that a large woman living with her large brother and six-year-old niece was somehow unacceptable. Obscene.

Jez was small enough to fit in the pit of my arm. Perhaps that made me a danger to her, in their eyes. As if my very existence could swallow her. There were only enough fallen leaves to make a small pile between the two of us, her working feverishly to snag each and every stray piece with the tines of her miniature rake. But as soon as I set her to collecting the leaves in a trash bag, she quickly abandoned her rake and sat herself next to the pile. She began to pick up the wilted yellow leaves one by one, stripping the flesh off the vein running down their middles, careful to rip them clean. Her bird-claw fingers picked at the tiny triangles left behind until all she had was a bare stem, slightly curled at the end like a ribbon. She then held it up to the light, and when she was satisfied, let it float away.

The mildewy taste of dying leaves hung about the house.

The next morning, the phone rang. The sound pealed through the hallways as if heralding a momentous arrival, if only because I couldn't remember the last time I'd heard the phone make any sound at all. It was an ivory-yellow thing whose square buttons clicked like tapping fingernails, and the spiralled cord had gone slack in places from years of Mutti coiling it around her finger. Mutti had hung the phone on the wall in the kitchen, where all women of her generation seemed to keep their phones, perhaps so that they could cook and talk at the same time, which Mutti never did. Instead, she'd sit at the kitchen table with her heels crossed on the vinyl tablecloth, smoking cigarette after cigarette, talking to Tante Regina in German for what seemed like hours. As a child I could only pick up a word or two here and there as I listened. I was always convinced they were talking about me and would pester Mutti to translate, tugging on her dress as she swatted me away. To this day I still don't know what Mutti and Tante Regina talked about, how they could sustain those conversations for so long, with so much boisterous laughter peppered throughout. The only times I got to speak to Tante Regina directly were on special occasions—Easter, Christmas, and my birthday—when she would ask me, "You are a good girl?" and I would reply yes, after which point she would quickly run out of English words and ask for Mutti again.

Though the phone still hung in the kitchen, I had come to think of it as Mutti's and therefore as something defunct, belonging only to the past. When it rang that morning, its robotic bleat clear and loud as ever, I happened to be standing right in front of it. I was so taken aback that I stared at it for a few moments as it rang twice more, and when I finally picked it up I managed to forget what I was expected to say.

"Yes, what do you want?" I said.

Ricky was microwaving a bowl of instant oatmeal for Jez and perked his eyebrows at the sound of my curt greeting.

There was silence on the other end for a moment. Then, "I'm so sorry to bother you. I'm looking for Regina Bergmann." The voice was a woman's, and she spoke in a way that sounded rehearsed. But there was also a strange softness to it that implied a familiarity I did not share.

"This is she," I replied, an edge of skepticism on my voice.

"Oh, hello. Miss Bergmann, my name is Claudia Myers, and I'm a journalist for *Extra Magazine*. I'm doing a story about Adam Ortiz and other children across Arizona and New Mexico in similar circumstances. I've been trying to get ahold of Richard Bergmann to ask him a few questions … he's your brother, I believe?"

My mind spun, scanning the bits and pieces of what I'd just heard.

"Yes," was all I could muster in response. That Ricky was my brother was the only thing she'd uttered that made any sense to me.

"I was hoping I could speak to you about Jesmin Wang. Now, I want to stress that I'm not interested in calling into question the facts of the case or casting blame. I'm looking for all sides of the story. I'm not at all interested in villainizing anyone."

I said nothing. My eyes couldn't help but look to Ricky, clearly betraying my confusion, because Ricky mouthed *Who is it?* I cast my eyes down and found myself coiling the phone cord tightly around my pointer finger.

"Miss? Miss Bergmann?"

"Yes," I said. My voice had gone squeaky. I'd turned to the wall, but I could feel Ricky's gaze on my back.

"It might reassure you to know that Gloria Ortiz agreed to speak with me, and I've already interviewed her for the story."

"Who?" I said.

"Gloria Ortiz. Adam's mother?" Her voice was now quieter, more hesitant. It was clear that she was beginning to see I was of no use to her.

"Oh. Yes, of course," I said.

The woman made a small sighing sound, a sound of satisfaction. "You see, I want to be sure I am fairly representing everyone involved. I see victims on both sides here. Of course, I understand that your brother may not want to rehash the past. I'm sure it's very painful for him and your family, and that you all want to move on. I promise I won't be hindering you. My goal is to be objective and fair."

"All right," I said. "What are you asking of me then?"

"If you'd like I can send you some links to other articles I've written on the subject. Do you have a preferred email address?"

"No," I said.

"Oh. Okay. Not a problem. Perhaps I could just ask for a bit of your time then? It doesn't have to be right now if you're busy."

"Time for what?"

"To ask you some questions about Jesmin and your brother. Do you think you would be open to that? You would be compensated, of course. And our interview would be strictly—"

I hung up. The sound of the phone clicking on the receiver was like the clop of a shoe on pavement, just a single step. I stood for a moment, facing the wall, my hand still clamped to the handset. I uncoiled my finger from the cord, slowly.

"What was that all about?" Ricky said, blowing on the surface of a bowl of oatmeal as he stirred and stirred. Jez pranced into the room and sat herself at the table, propping her elbows up on the edge. "Just wait," Ricky said to her. "It's hot."

"I want brown sugar," she said, her head flopping into her palm.

"I don't know," I said to Ricky. "A journalist, she said. She mentioned your name."

"Oh?" Ricky said. He set the bowl down in front of Jez and went to the sink. He turned on the tap and wrung his hands beneath it. His face was stony.

"She also mentioned someone named Gloria," I said.

"Hmm?" He dried his hands on the dishtowel, and the way he looked down at them, concentrating too hard on the act, told me he knew the name.

"That's Adam's mummy," Jez said, blowing on a spoon of oatmeal and sending a few chunks flying onto the table.

"Oh," Ricky said. His face glowed red. "Gloria from Phoenix, you mean?" He shrugged and balled up the towel in his hands. "She was just our neighbour. Lived next door to us. What about her?"

"This woman—this journalist—said she spoke to Gloria."

Ricky's face had now taken on a queasy look. He looked at Jez, contemplating something. Then he began to busy himself with his own breakfast. My eyes followed him as he rooted in the fridge, clinking jars and peering into containers. He settled on an apple and bit into it immediately, as though he were afraid it might squirm away. The words balanced on the tip of my tongue. *Who is Adam?* I knew it was a question he would not want me to ask.

"Ricky," I said.

"What?" He chomped again on the apple and slurped up the juices that leaked from his mouth.

"Just tell me what's going on." I turned out my palms in the manner of the Virgin Mary, which seemed the calmest way to plead with him to speak to me.

He swallowed loudly, shaking his head. "Regina," he said in a low voice, almost a growl. "You need to stay out of it. Please. If she calls again, hang up. Don't say anything to her or anyone else. They're vultures, all of them."

"I just want to know—"

"Trust me, Regina. It's better if you don't know. Just stay out of it." His hand sliced the air and his eyes bulged from his head in a way that was so reminiscent of Mutti that I could not help but submit. He left the room and went into the living room, where he clicked on the TV and switched it to the weather report, dialling the volume way up.

Jez seemed unperturbed. "Can I have some brown sugar?" she asked.

I found some in the cupboard and dropped a spoonful in her bowl, which she quickly scooped up and swallowed in one spoonful.

"Can I have some more?" she said. I acquiesced, feeling inundated by all the confusion left hanging in the air, and gave her three more spoonfuls. *It's better if you don't know.* What did he mean? Clearly this was something that Jez knew, so why would it be kept from me? It occurred to me then that even at six years old, Jez might have a far better understanding of her situation than I had previously thought. After all, Marilyn had once told me, when speaking of how her grandson was handling her daughter's divorce, "Kids are just so perceptive. They know so much more than we think." My frustration with Ricky gave way to pity for Jez. She was only a child, burdened by something that Ricky, a full-grown man, could not even seem to cope with. And now abandoned by her mother. One word that the woman on the phone had used, *victim*, sat like an enormous rock in my stomach.

8

I HAVE NOT always been large, but I have always felt large. There's a gravitational pull to my body that makes all eyes in a room steer themselves toward me. They stare and stare, and because there are no words, I begin to turn my vision inward, imagining each part of my body as belonging to some threatening, wild animal. The haunch of a woolly mammoth, the chest of a gorilla, the giant, quivering eye of a squid.

After the phone call, I felt as though I'd grown larger. When Ricky and I found ourselves in the same room, it seemed there wasn't enough space, like we'd suffocate if one of us didn't escape quickly enough. A tremor of panic began to develop deep inside me. I began to slink in the shadows, skirting the perimeters of the rooms of the house, as though there might be quicksand hiding beneath the floorboards, ready to suck me under if I stepped too close. At one point, when Ricky was in the shower, I picked up his laptop, which he'd left lying on the kitchen table. It was heavier than it looked, and the screen flashed on as soon as I lifted the lid, making me jump and nearly drop the thing from my fumbling hands before I could set it back on the table. I held my breath and dragged my finger along the pad, making the arrow whiz across the screen. I managed to click on the *e* that I knew was the internet, but nothing happened. I clicked again, then again. A window sprang up, Google, with a bar for typing. In my head I gave myself a small round of applause for getting this far. I typed *news*. Articles about Trump rising in the polls and Typhoon Meranti. I put the cursor back in the bar at the top and typed in *Richard Bergmann*, which seemed to take an eternity, for I kept accidentally tapping two letters at once and then having to erase a bunch of letters and retype. Something about Ingrid Bergman came up, but that was all. I felt exhausted with the effort of it all, though it had only been minutes. Then I heard the water turn off and Ricky's steps across the bathroom floor. I erased all the letters I'd typed, but the screen stayed the same. When I heard the bathroom door opening, I gave up, snapping the lid shut and making sure to position the laptop on the table at the exact angle it had been left there before. I tiptoed out the door into the back garden, praying that my slapdash reconnaissance work would go undetected.

I felt wretched for having tried. Foolish, yes, for I was no whiz with technology, but mostly ashamed for thinking that anything the news might have to say about him could be more truthful than Ricky's own words. He was good, in his heart, and always had been. Far better than me. Who was I, after all, to doubt him?

For many years, having accepted that I could not change my size, it had been my goal to shrink my presence down to something that could pass by invisibly. Even before that, as a teenager, I did not attempt to make friends. Walking through the halls at school, I imagined myself a speck of dust, floating by on the gusts caused by the movements of the enormous people walking to class, brushing against each other, laughing, high-fiving, slamming lockers. I was not teased or bullied because I had no ambitions to be important or noticed. As Mutti would say, *The best swimmers often drown.*

But Ricky, for all his shyness and aloofness, wanted to be the best. Special. There was just one year when we both attended the same high school—he in grade nine and I in grade twelve. He spent most of his time in the mechanic shop with his teacher, sheltered under the hoods of cars, where conversation about anything other than tasks and technicalities was not necessary. There he thrived and became the best in the class, earning himself a certificate that he tacked up above his bed.

One day, out of nowhere, Ricky appeared in the kitchen before breakfast with his hair dyed a glossy black. Mutti nearly tossed her plate of toast in the air when she saw him.

"Who did this?" she said.

Ricky shrugged. "I did it," he said. "I did it myself."

"What for?" Mutti asked. "It's too strong for you. With that stuff in your hair." She made a little swoop with her hand to indicate the gel he'd used to smooth his hair back. "You look like Stalin," she said.

Ricky rolled his eyes.

"It's for a girl," Mutti continued. "It must be."

She was right. Ricky's face turned almost purple, and he snatched the toast off his plate and stormed out of the house.

I'd never thought of Ricky as a normal teenage boy with desires and secret wishes about girls. Until then, he was just my shy little brother. I wanted to know who had caught his eye, so I began to pay attention. The only way to learn anything about Ricky's inner life was to observe him closely. The first clue was his hair, and the second was a silver chain he bought to link the wallet he kept in his back pocket to the belt loop of his jeans. The chain hung at his side, swaying back and forth and clinking with his steps.

Then, one day after school, I saw him standing at the bus stop. Ricky and I never took the bus because we lived close enough to walk, but there he was, standing and checking his watch. I observed from a distance, and after a few minutes he stepped toward a girl who was also standing and waiting. Her name was Robin, and she was in my grade. We were in the same biology class, in fact. We were not friends and barely spoke to each other, but she was difficult not to notice. She wore black lipstick and had piercings like a connect-the-dots on her face— eyebrow, nose, upper lip, and lower lip. Her hair was bright pink that day—one of the rainbow of colours she had been experimenting with over the school year. She wore a baggy, grey T-shirt and jeans with rips travelling up the thighs like gills.

We had once been lab partners, and she had asked to be excused from the dissection of the sheep's eyeball. Rather than allowing her to leave, our teacher permitted her to be excused from the act of cutting the eyeball, but not from watching me do it. Her eyes squeezed shut as I slid the scalpel into the sphere. It felt like slicing into a water balloon, giving way to an inky black liquid. She read the instructions out loud to me, holding the paper up to her face as a barricade while I performed each task. Then she transferred her eyes straight to her notebook to record my observations as I reported them.

Later, when we wrote up the final report together, I kept staring at the red and inflamed hole in her lower lip where she had removed the spike piercing that normally filled it. I felt guilty when she covered her chin with her palm and held it there for the rest of our discussion. It wasn't that I thought the hole was unsightly; rather, I was interested in the idea of what could pass through it—air, and maybe even liquid—like a second mouth. She was a good writer. We received an A on that lab report because of her.

And now, Ricky had his hands in his pockets and was talking to her. He smiled, and I could tell she was smiling too, even though her back was turned. The bus drove up to the stop and they got on together.

Ricky got home an hour late that day. He told Mutti he had been in detention for neglecting to do his French homework.

For about a week or two after that, Ricky stood at the bus stop every day after school, coming home late by at least an hour and sometimes even two or three. Mutti stopped expecting him to be home on time.

"You'll be suspended soon if you keep going to detention," Mutti remarked, but I know now that she knew more than she let on.

I asked Ricky one night if Robin was his girlfriend, and he looked up from his textbook and blinked at me, as though just waking up.

"Who?" he said, and turned back to reading. He did it so convincingly that I was almost fooled into thinking I'd been seeing things that weren't real. And so, just to be sure, I decided to follow him.

I wandered up behind him and Robin at the bus stop and stood along with the waiting crowd. Ricky was large for fifteen, and though she was three years older, Robin seemed small beside him and less severe than usual. Ricky didn't notice me until the bus pulled up and everyone clumped together to get on. He saw me in his peripheral vision and his face turned grave, but he resisted looking at me directly. He and Robin sat on the bench at the very back of the bus, and I took a two-seater nearer the middle, close enough to make out bits of their conversation behind me.

"What about bungee jumping?" she said to him.

"Naw," Ricky said.

"You afraid of heights?" she said.

"I just don't know why anyone would," he said. "Is it meant to be fun? Hanging by your ankles?"

"It's the thrill," Robin said. "It's exciting. You just need to feel it once and then you want more."

"Until something goes wrong and you die," Ricky said.

"You can die from anything," she replied. "You can die from a broken heart, for god sakes."

"No, you can't," Ricky said. "That's a myth. No one could."

"People are so afraid of dying, you know? Like we pretend it's not real, it's not going to happen to all of us. So who gives a shit, right?"

"Yeah," Ricky said.

They went on to talk about their mutual fear of clowns, and Robin said the scariest thing she'd ever done was to pull down a clown's pants at a birthday party. Ricky laughed in a way I'd never heard him laugh, a way that seemed warm and coaxing as a campfire.

Robin got off at her stop on the corner of Sixth Street, and Ricky pulled the string for the next stop. He got off on Eighth, me following behind him. He stopped after a few steps to let me catch up.

"Where are you going?" he said.

"I don't know," I said. "Where are you going?"

"To the mall," he said. "To Tugs."

I had expected him to be embarrassed and lash out at me for following him and invading his privacy. Instead, he appeared completely at ease with my presence and my witness to his conversation with Robin. He had rehearsed this answer, this confrontation, in his mind. He had been prepared. And it was as though he had truly convinced himself that he was only there to go to the comic book store, and that Robin had simply been there, a convenience, for casual and meaningless conversation. So, we continued the small talk as we would on a normal day, talking about the tediousness of our homework and what we hoped Mutti was making for supper that evening.

We parted ways when we reached the storefront and he stepped in.

"See ya," he said as I continued down the sidewalk.

Truth be told, he had convinced me. I believed then that Robin was a mere acquaintance, and that in reality he had just become obsessed with comic books, which was evidenced by the growing collection of them that he'd piled on his nightstand.

But then, I found the letter.

It must have been in his back pocket and slipped out on the armchair in the living room. I found it wedged in the crack between the chair back and the cushion. I unfolded the paper, and the word *Robin* was written in cursive at the top. I read feverishly, as though I'd stumbled on buried treasure and was digging it out of the earth.

Robin,

I'm sorry to say that I love you because I know you are still hung up on Ian. But let me say this: he doesn't deserve you. Believe me, I've been as open with you as any person could possibly be, and I am not the least bit afraid of that. I haven't seen many girls before, but I still think that your body is perfect and your breasts are not at all small, they are like perfect apples.

Yours,

Ricky

At the bottom of the page was a little drawing of an apple with a leaf sticking out the top.

I realized then that Ricky was a stranger. I did not know him at all. Or if I did, I knew only one half of him, which was entirely separate and even enemy to the person who had written the letter. The Ricky I knew would never even utter the word *breasts*, let alone have the courage to look at a pair of them and think to compare them to apples. Perhaps it was love that transformed him, just for that little while, and I had no understanding of that since I'd never experienced any sort of romantic love, and still haven't to this day.

I folded the letter back up and returned it to its place in the cushions. By evening it was gone. I didn't say anything to Ricky because it hadn't even occurred to me. We had an unspoken pact; this was Ricky's secret life, and I had no business meddling in it.

Silence had always been our default, and it still is, though I'm told now that feelings ought to be expressed among families. Ricky, of course, had his heart broken by Robin, but Mutti and I heard not a word about it. I found out not through words, but through pictures.

One morning, not long after I'd found the letter, I saw the photographs pinned to a board along with notices about report cards and the school dance. I had come in early to visit my math teacher for help, and there were only a few other students walking the halls. Ordinarily I would have walked past the board without a pause, as I did every other morning, but the corner of my eye caught Ricky's face in one of the photos. He was sitting on a chair, naked, his legs spread. On his face was a smirk, a bit washed out in the poor lighting of the photo. His skin, too, was lit up, much whiter than in real life, and blanker, unblemished. His privates hung there, resting on the chair, like a skinned weasel.

There were other photographs on the board, each displaying Ricky in a different naked pose. In one, he was standing, legs apart, arms folded, like he always did when he was waiting around for something. He couldn't let his arms go slack and hang at his sides when he was standing idly because he would feel too exposed. I knew because I was the same. I could see in his expression that he was trying to be brave for the camera, tilting his chin back to give the impression of confidence. But in his eyes, behind that mask, there was terror, as though the camera pointing its lens at him could just as easily have been a gun.

I could have taken the photos down, but I didn't. If I took them down I would have had to put them in my pocket or my backpack. I would have had to own them and make them into the truth. Instead, I could ignore the titters in the halls, avoid the cafeteria for the rest of that week. I could forget that I'd found the letter and instead adopt Ricky's version of things, believing that he and Robin had only struck up a casual friendship that fizzled out when he began to lose interest in comic books. And someone else would take the photos down, a friend of Ricky's or perhaps a teacher, and save us—me and Ricky—the shame of having to acknowledge that we were real and human. It was easier that way. It was better.

Years later, when Ricky told me he was moving to Phoenix, the first question I asked was why.

"Why not?" he said. "We only see each other twice a month. And her contract ends soon."

"What will you do there?" I said. "For work?"

"Her father found something for me at the airport. Aircraft Marshaller."

I grimaced, picturing Ricky in the orange reflective vest and earmuffs, waving batons at airplanes.

"It's a good opportunity," he said. "It's important work."

These were certainly Carla's words. *Important work.* Things seemed to click together then, and when he told me he would be marrying Carla, I understood his decision. I could see how they fit with each other when I thought about who had come before—Robin, and before her, Mrs. Nakamura. Ricky wanted to become new. It was what he had wanted for years. The origami, the black hair, his joining the yearbook club, his one night of underage drunkenness with the boys on the football team—these were his failed attempts to transform himself.

What I knew immediately about Carla was that she was a fixer. She saw things that were slightly damaged or out of place and felt a compulsive need to correct them. I saw this at the dinner at our house, how she shifted the candles on the table so they were perfectly positioned along the centre line. She moved the potatoes on her plate to create a buffer zone between them and the meatloaf and the spinach—everything in its proper place. There was sheer joy on her face when Ricky thanked me oh-so-politely for the lovely meal, like he'd performed his trick flawlessly. Carla could not stand the look of me because that impulse inside her kicked into overdrive, but she was unable to do anything about it.

Ricky, on the other hand, was a project. Ricky was yearning to be fixed. Now, as I watched him pace across the porch with his cellphone pressed to his ear, me inside and him outside, the glass between us seemed solid as rock. I stood still, invisible to him. *Please don't*, his lips seemed to be saying, though I could not hear the words. *Please.* I wondered then at what point fixing could go too far. Fixing to the point of breaking.

9

RATHER THAN GET a job, it seemed Ricky decided to channel his energy into a frenzy of projects around the house. Over the course of three days, he built a new trellis for the clematis and the sweet peas in the backyard, patched up the holes in the gutters, repainted the front door, and even replaced the hot water tank. I could hardly complain, though I knew his real motive was to stake his claim on the house. "So much for your knees," was all I said, but he didn't bother to respond.

His latest project was a new bed frame for Jez. He insisted that Mutti's old bed was too large, and so he was making Jez a smaller one. He'd cut the piece for the headboard and was spending what seemed like endless hours in the garage, sketching hearts across it and sawing them out by hand. He was in there now, having asked me to get Jez fed and bathed and ready for bed so he could spend some time working on it. He'd even taken his dinner in there. It occurred to me that there might be another reason for all his busying: avoiding me.

I marched into the garage and let the door wham shut. Ricky's eyes stayed on his task of madly scrubbing the edge of the headboard with sandpaper.

"Right," I said, and he stopped. "This has gone on long enough. What are you doing here, Ricky? What happened with Carla?"

He sighed like a teenager. "I told you," he said. "She left. I'm starting over, Regina. From scratch. I can't do it alone." He put his fingers into one of the hearts he'd carved out and stroked it as if it were an emblem for his words.

"But that woman … the journalist—"

"Just leave it alone, for Christ's sake," he said, his voice ratcheting up. He scratched at his head. "We need your help to move on," he said, quietly now. "Jez and I. Especially Jez."

Jez. There he went as usual, trying to tug on my heartstrings. That word again, *victim*, pinched at the edges of my mind. Ricky was trying to protect her. Perhaps he'd already failed.

"Will you help us?" Ricky said. "Let us stay?"

"Yes," I said, my anger fizzling out. "Of course you can stay."

We were silent. It seemed there was nothing else to say.

"Thank you," Ricky said, and returned to his sanding. "She's ready for bed, I guess? I'll be there in five minutes."

I felt blank, like I'd been erased. It was clear we'd fallen into a pattern: I would stoke the fires and Ricky would snuff them, over and over. I wasn't going to get anywhere with Ricky. But maybe I could get somewhere with Jez.

Her hair was wet and ropy from her bath, and she was playing on the living room floor with two blocks of scrap wood, both of which came to a slivered point on one end. They were discarded bits of the lumber Ricky had cut up for the bed frame.

"*Chya, chya,*" Jez said to herself, knocking the blocks together like swords.

I bent down so I could speak quietly, right into her ear. It took me a moment to muster the courage to ask the question; I could not ignore the sinking feeling that it would open a door to something I might not want to know. Jez wriggled, tickled by my breath on her neck.

"Who is Adam?" I asked.

"He's my best friend," she said without hesitation. "Well …" she paused and sat back on her haunches. "He *was* my best friend. Not anymore."

"How come?" I asked.

"He had to go away," she said. "He said he was going on a trip. I think he said"—and here she poked her finger into her cheek—"something about the Arctic. He had to go far away."

"I see. Are you sad? Is it sad that Adam went away?" I expected this to be a simple question for her to answer, but she looked at me as though I'd asked her to solve a riddle.

"I didn't like him when his eye went all funny," she said. "I stopped being friends with him after that. Do you wanna play narwhal sword fighting?"

≈

In the morning, I marched into the living room and announced to Ricky that I would be taking Jez on a field trip to the hoodoos. He lowered the volume on the TV.

"Did you ask her about that?" he said. "Does she even want to?"

"Let's see, then," I said, and Ricky followed me back into the kitchen.

"How would you like to do something fun with your Auntie Regina today?" I said to her.

She looked between me and Ricky, apparently weighing her options, and said "I suppose," then passed her half-finished bowl of oatmeal to her father and sauntered to the front door.

I gave Ricky a gloating smile.

"Well, it's nice to see you two getting acquainted," he said.

I laughed in his face, and he gave me a scowl. He knew I was no good with Carla's brand of decorum.

In the garage, I went about strapping Jez into her booster seat. She sat with her hands folded, patiently watching my hands fiddle with the buckle. When I clicked it in and pulled it snug, she patted my head and smiled.

"Your oma used to take me to this spot," I told her as I drove. "Many years ago. She would take me to find fossils. Do you remember what a fossil is?"

"A dead thing," she said. "When you die, you might turn into a rock."

"Very good," I said. "You could turn into a rock if you were buried in just the right way."

"Are we gonna see them?" she asked.

"Fossils? I hope so. If we're lucky. Maybe we'll even find one from a dinosaur. A footprint."

"Do you know what my mummy says about dead things? She says, 'That's disgusting.'"

My heart jumped a bit at the mention of Carla, and it took me a moment to think of how to respond without judgment. "It's true that death isn't very pretty," I said.

"Yeah. There was that boy who got killed in the olden days, the one with black skin? Some mean guys beat him up and then tied a rope behind a truck and put his neck on it and then drove away."

"Where did you hear about that?" I asked. She shrugged, her eyes following the cars swooshing past the window.

"His mom was so mad she made everyone look at him dead," she went on. "At the funeral. She didn't want to cover up his dead face because she was mad that the bullies were mean to him."

"Don't worry," I said, although she did not seem at all worried. "We won't see any scary dead things. These animals died naturally, and it happened a long time ago, so everything is dried up. We'll only see an imprint of the animal, like a shadow."

"His face looked melted," she said, then raked her fingers over her own face. "*Bluueh*, like that."

"Mmm," I said, hoping that if I appeared to lose interest in the topic she would too. The girl had been cursed with an oblivious father and a melodramatic mother. Ricky was always watching documentaries on the History channel, and he'd clearly underestimated how much attention Jez actually paid to them. And Carla's way of being horrified by any minor impropriety was really only going to encourage the exhibitionist in Jez. I was beginning to think I'd have made a rather competent parent, if given the chance.

Mercifully, once we got beyond the city limits, Jez grew quiet. The river running alongside us was low in the wake of the hot summer, rocks poking out and winking wet in the sun, and the hills seemed to loom even larger now that we'd left the buildings behind. I felt a tinge of civic pride that Jez seemed to be in awe of it all, her eyes scanning the landscape, darting back and forth.

I'd packed a couple of apples and juice boxes in Jez's backpack, which I slung over my shoulder when we arrived. The straps were so small that the pack perched on my shoulder like a parrot. Jez ambled out of the car and rubbed her fists in her eyes as though emerging from a cave.

"Where are the fossils?" she said. She stamped her foot into the dirt and peered around. We'd arrived in a parking lot filled with vehicles, people with wheelchairs and baby carriages unloading their various colour-coded gear. Across the road, a wire fence marked the designated walking trail, and I could see that a steel staircase had been built around the hoodoos that lay ahead. I realized how long it had really been since I'd last come to this spot. From what I remembered there had only been a sun-bleached sign, and in the dirt the vague shufflings of feet that had walked there before.

Now my confidence in my mothering abilities was rightly squashed. I'd made a grave mistake; Jez had taken my mention of fossils as a promise I was now sure I could not fulfill. When Ricky and I were children, it had seemed as though fossils were as abundant as any other attractive rock. I distinctly remember fossil hunting one afternoon by the river and tossing the pieces that were not as complete or the ones that had an ugly shape into the water, even skipping them like ordinary river stones. I'd somehow forgotten that in recent years they'd become much more scarce, and that even the faintest carbon film of a mangled fish corpse would get whoops and hollers from the tourists, thinking themselves intrepid and fat with luck.

"The fossils may be tricky to find," I said to Jez. "But we'll try, by gum." I cringed at my own false enthusiasm. "Keep your eyes open for funny-shaped rocks. Or rocks with pictures on them."

Bestowing a task on her seemed to energize her, and she plowed forward past a family of five, cutting between two little blond girls who were about to join hands. The parents turned in unison, throwing dirty looks my way. The icy-eyed baby strapped to the back of the man had a little canopy over his head, which made him look like a miniature emperor.

We climbed the staircase that travelled up to the hoodoos and around their backs, where the path spread out into the badlands. The crumbly bentonite underfoot had been caked by the heat, so our shoes rasped with each step. For a person with such short legs, Jez was especially quick. She had her eyes trained on the ground, darting from one rock-strewn seam to the next, and she might as well have had a magnifying glass for the way she resembled an inspector looking for clues. I was huffing like a rhinoceros within minutes, the space between us growing larger.

"Fossil-bossil-bo-schmossil, banana-fana fo-fossil, me my mo-mossil, faw-sil." Jez sang the words over and over in monotone, like a Druidic chant. "This one?" she said, plucking a small rock from the ground. I was thankful for the chance to catch up to her as she stood examining the rock.

"Let me see," I said as I approached her. I took a moment to slow my heart, turning the rock over in my hands. It was smooth and sandy-coloured all over. "It's not shaped like a bone, is it. Do you see any pictures on it?" I asked.

"Right there," she said, pointing at nothing in particular.

"No," I said. "It's not a fossil." She threw it back at the ground and it nearly hit a boy in the ankle when it bounced. He hopped up on one foot and glared at her as he passed.

"This one?" She grabbed another rock, right next to the one she'd just dropped.

"No," I said, ushering her behind a patch of sagebrush so that others could pass us on the narrow trench that had been carved by so many walkers before us. "That's not one either. See, there are no pictures on it. Blank." I dropped it between my feet. "It might take us a long time to find one," I said. "They're very rare and very precious."

Jez wiped her hands on her shorts. "We better find one," she said.

Of course we didn't, on such well-worn trails. Just when I thought we'd found a route less travelled, I'd spot a shard of green glass from a beer bottle or a discarded can wedged in the silt. We looped back around the hoodoos, and while other children made their oohs and aahs and begged their parents to climb on them, Jez refused to pull her eyes from the ground. I managed to yank her to a stop at one of the information signs.

"Here," I said, pointing at the pictures on the sign. "Those are fossils. See? It says this one's called a trilobite."

She ran her fingers over the picture.

"See?" I said. "We found them!"

The way she rolled her eyes at me made her look about ten years older than she was. "I want a real one," she said.

"I can show you one at home," I said. "As soon as we get home. I'll show you one I found here years ago."

"No, thank you," she said, and continued on her way. She seemed to realize that we'd gone in a loop only when we arrived back at the start of the trail. She looked up then, and turned around in a circle.

"Well, that's it," I said. "It used to be different here, you see. When I was a girl you could walk much farther out, past the fence there and right into the coulee. I suppose they've decided it's better for the wild-life and such to keep humans out of there."

"Ohhh!" Jez cried, jumping straight up in the air. "I want to go there!" Her voice was now squeaky and her eyes had grown to globes. She clasped her hands together and squeezed them between her legs.

"No, no," I said. "It's not allowed. We stay where the fence tells us."

"But!" she squeaked. "You got to do it before! You got to do it and now why can't I do it?" She blinked once, and a great splash of tears poured out and splattered in the dirt. I'd never seen tears develop so instantaneously. And the way her scream emerged from her open mouth was like a siren, sudden and piercing enough to make the dozens of people in the park turn their heads at once and stare.

I'm fairly accustomed to receiving damning stares from strangers, but these were of a different nature. I'd come to terms long ago with being a curiosity, but I had never before considered the idea that in the minds of these unknown people, I was the mother of this child.

My first impulse was to clap my hand over her mouth and throw her over my arm like a coat, but then something unexpected happened. My limbs began to harden and I became filled with rage. Not at Jez, but at them. The young blond with the garish red curl of her upper lip, the old man with his coal-hard eyes, all the mothers and fathers who touted their well-behaved children around like solid-gold trophies, so eager to bludgeon anyone they deemed less righteous than themselves. Their presumptions, their stupidity, the way they all thought and felt with the same brain. I was a bad mother. Jez was a bad child. That one—Jez, a bad child—was even more enraging, and I was all the more enraged by how impossibly helpless I was in the face of it. It was a feeling that I hadn't experienced for many years, a feeling of needing desperately to clench all parts of my body at once. And so that's what I did. I stood in front of screaming Jez, clenching my face and my neck and my fists and my buttocks, positively vibrating with rage. The staring faces disappeared, or if they didn't, my mind made it so. Instead of seeing their faces, I was seeing a knifepoint sliding into a soft belly. How perfect and crisp the sound would be, like scissors cutting paper. Then into a back, right between the shoulder blades, a red bloom growing across the cotton shirt. Then the top of a head, right through the skull. I could not open my eyes, not for anything. I was afraid of what I might do.

It was only when Jez tugged on my hand that I realized she'd stopped screaming. My eyes flicked open. An arc of emptiness surrounded us, the other visitors doing their best to evade us by skirting the perimeter fence on the far side. She pulled on my hand again and I crouched to her level, my knees going slack.

Jez leaned into my ear. "You want to do something bad, don't you?" she whispered.

Her face had flattened, with no trace of the anguish of moments before. "Come on," she said, beckoning with her hand. Just steps away was a small sign affixed to the fence that said KEEP OUT: *Protected Area*. Jez threw one leg over the wire of the fence, then the other. I followed without a word.

No one tried to stop us as we ventured off, shuffling up into the hills, our feet skidding on the bentonite. The heat pounded, and the hem of my dress dripped sweat into the dust, but I followed Jez's steps automatically, as though pushed along by my own chugging heart. We scrambled down a rocky trench and into a coulee. We did not speak. Both of us scanned the ground as we walked, picking up rocks intermittently and tossing them back to the ground. A sharp ache began to creep down my neck and across my shoulders, but it turned out that searching for fossils was quite calming, even meditative, now that we'd left the crowds behind. Jez, having gotten her way, was cheerful and well behaved, breaking into a skip every once in a while and tossing handfuls of little rocks in the air to dance in them as they fell.

We walked for what seemed like an hour, the sprays of dry grass scratching at our legs, the dust turning our socks the colour of milky tea at the ankles. I knew we would not find a fossil. The trip had been a failure. But it hadn't mattered, in the end. At some point, out of nowhere, Jez stopped and said, "I know what a fossil is."

"Oh?" I said.

"It's this," she said, and pressed her hand into a patch of silt nestled between rocks. Her little fingers made an imprint that could have been confused for a bird's.

"Yes," I said. "That's it. That's a fossil." I bent down and made my own handprint next to hers, thumbs touching. "Someday, hundreds of years from now, someone will find our fossil and wonder what kind of strange creature we were."

On the drive home, Jez fell asleep in the car. When I picked her up out of her booster seat, she groaned and wrapped her little spindly arms tightly around my neck. I felt a flood of warmth for her; the day hadn't been without its trials, but I was convinced that we had bridged a gap.

She'd lost control of herself, but then so had I. It was a kind of union, a call-and-response that had joined us in some invisible way. I recognized now what had always been true: that Jez and I belonged to each other, bound by blood. If I were asked to call it by a name, I would call that feeling love.

PRESS

*The layers put tremendous pressure on the bones,
compacting them as they begin to decay.*

10

I AM NO EXPERT, of course, but it strikes me that love is actually quite a lot like rage. The thing about love is that it can sit inside you like a hibernating animal, so quiet and still you don't even know it's there. Then all of a sudden it wakes and bursts out into the blinding light before you even realize it belongs to you. It's the same with rage. I suppose I can really only speak for myself, but I see rage as a kind of rite of passage just the same as love—full of pain, but also growth.

The last time I'd felt the kind of rage I'd felt at the hoodoos was eighteen years ago. I still can't be sure, however, if what happened that day was really my fault. I hadn't considered the consequences, in the moment. How could I have known that her femur would be shattered, that she'd never walk without a limp again, that her face would have to be jigsawed back together? That part hadn't been me. All I had done was open a door.

It was after Ricky and Robin had stopped seeing each other, after the photos, after Mutti had been called into the principal's office to discuss Ricky's misfortune, after he'd moved to a different school on the other side of town. I was sitting in the back seat of the car, parked alongside the street and waiting for Mutti, who was running into the dry cleaner's. I remember the weather on that morning: it was early winter, and the land was coated with a layer of shimmering frost, the atmosphere all around icy and dreamlike. The World's Largest Dinosaur, towering over the buildings at the end of the street, was an affront to the frozen badlands that stretched out on the horizon behind, the hills like delicate skiffs of snow about to be dissolved by the slightest breath. The fake against the real, I remember thinking.

In the rear-view mirror, I saw her coming. Robin. Lime-green hair flapping in the wind, black lips like a beetle pinned to her face. She was on her skateboard, coming up fast on the side of the road, and I was watching her leg pumping forward and back, forward and back, thrusting her toward me, faster and faster. She was blind to me sitting there. For some reason that made me angrier than what she had done with the photos. That she could live this way, speeding down the street, flaunting her freedom, wanting so badly to be seen as tough, daring, even invincible. I felt my muscles begin to clench, my limbs hardening. My body going rigid, shuddering with rage, and the wild impulse to act—to let the energy explode out of me—but pushing against it, the fear.

I opened my door. Just as she was about to whiz past our car, I pulled the latch and swung it out wide. The sound of her body slamming into the door was a kind of splitting, like a pumpkin dropped from a great height.

I don't remember much of the rest. Mutti ran out into the street, turned her body over, and then lifted her into the fold of her arm. There was blood, flesh hanging loose from her face, and Mutti was pressing the flesh back in, holding it, her hands painted red. I remember watching it all, the paramedics swarming and ushering Mutti away, and me still sitting in the car with the door open, my legs stuck out and my feet on the pavement. The realization that the person being lifted onto a gurney and loaded into an ambulance was not Robin creeping upon me slowly like a rising tide.

The woman's name was Michelle Landry. She was a tattoo artist on her way to work that morning. She was twenty-two. She'd only looked like Robin from afar, but when I saw a picture of her in the paper, she looked nothing like Robin at all.

The only thing Ricky ever said to me about it was, "How could you be so stupid?" He thought it had been a careless mistake. They all did. I had to give a police report, and I told them I'd opened my door because I was cold and wanted to turn the heat on, so I'd been trying to move from the back seat to the front. There was no reason for anyone to doubt me.

Except Mutti. We had sat on the curb together as the ambulance sped off and a fire truck pulled up in its place. Mutti propped her elbows on her knees and let her bloodied hands hang.

"I thought she was Robin," I said to her.

The way Mutti looked at me, I knew I should never have said it. I should have kept it buried deep inside, in the darkest parts of myself, where no one would ever find it. It was a look of despair so penetrating that it seemed to take hold of my heart, squeezing so hard I had to gasp for air, and then I was choking, my chest collapsing in on itself.

"She's in shock," I heard someone say, and then an oxygen mask was strapped to my face, my breath making clouds of steam inside, my head tilted back to look at the grey sky, flat as a sheet of paper.

That evening, Mutti came into my room after I'd gone to bed and shook me awake, though I was not really asleep. I gave her a look of dazed bewilderment, as if I didn't know why she was here.

"No one can know, Regina," she said. Her eyes bored right into me, sharp and bright even in the dark, waiting for a response.

"I know," I whispered.

"Listen to me," she went on. "No one can know. Do you understand? If they find out, they will take you away. They'll treat you like a crazy person. You'll go to Ponoka."

Ponoka. Where Mrs. Nakamura had gone. I'd seen her just before her husband took her away. She had found her way into our garage in the night. In the morning I'd heard the scratching and shuffling and thought it was a raccoon. Armed with a broom, I went into the garage and found a pair of white feet sticking out of an empty cardboard box that had been turned on its side. Mrs. Nakamura was crouched inside, wearing a baby-blue nightgown and no shoes. She looked so small, small as a child. I kept saying her name, but she seemed not to hear or see me. Her eyes were open but gazed into nothing.

Mutti called her husband to retrieve her. He knelt down in front of her, his hard face unchanging, and spoke a few words to her, so quietly that I could not hear. Then he pulled on her leg and her whole body went slack, sliding out of the box like a dead fish. He hoisted her over his shoulder and carried her like that, through the alley and back to their house.

We didn't see her again for two years. As children, two years seemed like eons. When she finally returned, she had become a different person—no longer a person, really. Gaunt and grey, like she'd been emptied out inside. She would stand in her front yard sometimes and look at her neglected garden, but she no longer tended it. She no longer waved to me and Ricky. Ricky asked Mutti if we could go see her and Mutti said no, she wasn't able to see anyone anymore. They'd given her electroshock therapy, Mutti told us. She'd never be the same.

Michelle Landry, on the other hand, was only damaged on the outside. Somehow, the world thought that was far more horrifying. When I saw the story about the accident in the paper, along with the picture of her from before, fresh-faced and grinning in the sun, I understood Mutti's words. There was Michelle Landry's life story—that she'd grown up in small-town Hanna, was a gifted and imaginative artist, that she planned to travel the world and pursue a career in illustration— written with a tone of lament, as if all her promising dreams were now dashed. Even after she recovered, her scarred face was so monstrous that she became a cautionary tale. I learned later that she became a safety advocate, travelling to schools across the province to speak to children about road-sharing protocols and the importance of wearing a helmet.

The story in the newspaper made no mention of me at all. I knew it was because I was a minor, but I couldn't help but feel like a kind of ghost, there but not there, in control and yet completely out of control. It was a relief. To be a ghost was to be free.

"No one can know," Mutti had said, over and over.

≈

Carla appeared like a moth in the night, rapping her hand once, twice, three times against the glass pane of the front door. When I opened it, she stood under the porch light looking powder white all over. She wore a long white sash around her shoulders that was so papery it looked as though it might blow away in the breeze. Her face was drawn, her eyes showing the whites.

She didn't speak, and neither did I. Jez had gone to sleep hours earlier, and Ricky was parked in his usual spot in front of the television. Now, I felt him at my back, making a slow approach to the door.

"What do you want?" he said. I stood like a gate between them.

"May I speak with you?" she replied. She stood stiffly, and in the harshness of the porch light she appeared to be made of plaster, her skin finely textured as though sanded down.

Wordlessly, Ricky sidled past me and pulled the door wide open, sweeping me behind it. Carla strode in like a queen. The heels of her white boots stabbed little holes into the carpet as she followed Ricky into the living room.

I went out onto the porch, feeling cast out like a bad dog. Through the sheer curtains in the window I could see Carla's spiky silhouette sitting in my chair.

They were getting back together, I knew. I played out my imagined version of their conversation as I waited outside. Ricky would say he'd been a mess since she left, he didn't know what to do with himself, without her. Carla would say she forgave him for everything, she wanted to get through this together, let's start over. They would come out onto the porch, shining with hope, and announce their reconciliation as though it were a second engagement. They would make a plan to leave tomorrow and put their house in Phoenix up for sale, move to a new neighbourhood or maybe even a new city where they could forget whatever tragedy had happened. Jez would have her mother again and would not bother to give me a second glance when she climbed into the back seat of the Buick, and the Buick would round the corner, windows flashing in the sun so that I couldn't tell whether or not anyone was waving. Everything would settle like a cake just out of the oven, sinking slowly back to normal.

Carla came out, alone, only a few minutes later. She stood in front of me, waiting for me to look up at her. It was all I could do not to spit on her face.

"Don't worry," she said. "Everything's fine."

"Is it," I said, my voice a hiss.

Carla's gaze fell from mine. "You don't know what it's been like," she said quietly.

"I know my brother," I said.

"He's not the same," she said. "None of us are." Her face was slack, her tone softer than I expected. Not defensive. Her words sounded genuine—something I'd never thought Carla capable of being. The tiny thought sprang into my mind that perhaps there was truth to what she was saying. But then her features turned hard once again, her words measured. "I'm going to fix this," she said, pressing her hands together like a prayer. "My family won't be your burden anymore."

"*Your* family?" I said, standing to meet her eyes. She had to take a step back to make space between us. I bolted into the house as though it were a race. I saw a flash of fear cross her face as I slammed the door shut.

Ricky was in the kitchen cracking open a beer. He sat down at the table, and I began filling the kettle and putting it on as though that were my reason for being there. I could hear the faint slam of a car door and an engine starting outside.

"She's staying at a hotel," Ricky said.

"Oh. Which one?" I said, though I did not care.

"The Marriott. She won't stay anywhere else. Hypoallergenic pillows."

I nodded as though I understood. "So she's come to beg you back?" I said. I'd meant for it to sound like a joke, but it didn't.

"Well," Ricky began, "sort of. Not beg, but. There's a few things I have to think about."

"What things?" I said. "Are you thinking of saying no?" I tried not to sound too hopeful.

"No ... no. It's just, she has some conditions."

"Conditions," I repeated. I could not help but roll my eyes, and Ricky scrubbed at his hair, pretending not to see it. I got a sudden surge of bravery then, seeing how weak he had become. How weak he had always been, perhaps. A blast of heat rose up in my chest and I blurted, "This is not right, Ricky. I may not know much about relationships, but it seems to me that a person should love her husband no matter what. You shouldn't have to meet her demands like a circus animal. That's just what I think."

Ricky held his head in his hands. "You don't know what you're saying," he said. "You don't know any of it."

"I know you," I said. "I know you'll bend over backward for a woman and that you don't know when to stop."

"Jesus Christ, Regina. You're like a child. You oversimplify everything."

"It all seems simple to me. She wants you to be the villain. She wants you to accept all the blame. Simple."

"See, you're just wrong. You have no clue. It's not even about me at all."

"Who then?" I demanded. "Is it Gloria? Did you have an affair?"

"Jesus! No! It's not me, for Christ's sake. It's Jez."

"What?" I sat across from him, the fire inside me fizzling out. I tried to find his eyes, but he was trying his best to bury them in his lap. "What about Jez?" I said.

Ricky sighed, hanging his head on the exhale. "She wants Jez to go see someone. For treatment."

"What kind of treatment?"

"Psychiatric."

It took a moment for the word to register, and once it did I pictured Jez curled up inside a box, only her feet sticking out, small and white as a rabbit's. "But," I said. "But she's only six years old."

"I know," Ricky said. "It's not as crazy as it sounds. Carla read an article in the *New York Times*. She said it made things clear—I don't know. It was something about child psychopaths, and now she's got it in her head that if we can just get Jez some treatment—"

"Stop," I said, covering my ears. Jez's limp body slung over Ricky's shoulder, head lolling. "Forgive me, but this all sounds—well, it sounds

117

insane, to be perfectly honest. I'm afraid you married an insane person, Ricky, and it's not fair to Jez."

"Calm down," Ricky said. He scratched his head all over as though it were covered with ants. "We don't know anything yet. It's not that Jez is a psychopath or anything. It's not that simple. I don't know."

"It's absurd, Ricky. It's absurd and you know it."

"It's not. It's more serious than you think."

"Serious, yes. You're talking about your own child." Jez with electrodes suctioned to her forehead, blank eyes staring into nothing, and Carla and Ricky on the other side of a glass window, watching.

"I need to do whatever it takes, Regina." Ricky sighed again, and this time looked me straight in the eye. "There are things you don't know," he said slowly. "I didn't want to have to tell you."

"Well," I said, sinking into the chair across from him, "now you have to."

〰

When I crept into Jez's room at three a.m., her eyes flicked open as soon as I whispered her name. It was clear she had been pretending to sleep, for she sat up without a blink. I had a suitcase in one hand and laid it on the floor in front of the dresser.

"He told you, didn't he," she whispered.

"Yes," I said. "Time to go."

11

THERE WAS A BOY, six years old, like Jez. His name was Adam. He lived with his parents in the Phoenix suburbs, in the gated community of Blossom Hills. I could picture the manicured lawns, palm trees placed at perfect intervals, sidewalks dotted with white-haired seniors taking their daily air, shuffling about with canes and walkers. It was uneventful. Safe.

And this, I'm sure, is why Ricky and Carla bought the house next door. They had moved Jez to a new school. Carla had switched to a smaller firm and could now drive Jez each day to the school, which was too small and exclusive to offer a bus service. Ricky's commute to the airport doubled in distance, but of course, Ricky being Ricky, he did not complain. Things were going to be better, they told themselves.

Naturally, in the absence of any other children their age in the neighbourhood, Jez and Adam struck up a fast friendship and began spending much of their summer days at each other's houses, but mostly Adam's, because his mother did not work.

So there was Adam, blond and fair, small for his age, a ball of energy and a handful for the parents but still their boy, their only child.

And then there was Adam's father's shed in the backyard. The father was a sport hunter—a serious one, before he'd settled down with his wife—and in the shed were his trophies, hung all together on the back wall. Two deer with five-point antlers, and several exotic specimens he'd brought back from his excursion in Africa, including an antelope and a warthog with tusks like yellow crescent moons. His wife would not allow the heads in the house because, as she said, the living room was for the living, not the dead.

The shed became something of a playhouse for Adam and Jez, seeing as the father had developed shingles and grown too frail to keep up with hunting. He rarely ventured out into the shed now, and it was too charming with its cedar shake roof and painted shutters for the children to resist claiming it as their own. The father's things stayed in there, despite the urgings of his wife to make more room for Adam and Jez and their toys. But the children did not mind; they invented their own games, as children do. They had a game, in fact, with the animal heads. They would tie strings to them. They got into the mother's yarn. Once, they tied red strings all over the antlers of one of the deer. Dozens of tight little knots, and lengths of it stretched between the antlers, criss-crossed and woven and looped under its neck to create a giant tangled web that shrouded the deer's face. The father had to snip them off, one by one. After that, the children were not allowed to touch any of the father's things. But he was at work most of the time, and the mother was too soft to disallow them from using the shed altogether. Kids needed to be kids, she reasoned. They needed their space to be kids.

The mother would check on them every so often to see what they were up to. Once, she caught them exploring their bodies. When she walked in, they had their shirts and pants and underwear off and were spread naked on the floor. Side by side, but not touching. No hint of shame crossed their faces when they saw the mother walk in. It was only a game to them. Harmless.

But then came the day of the incident.

It was a hot summer afternoon, around lunchtime. The mother, Gloria, saw Jez emerge from the shed and enter the house. This was not unusual; sometimes one of the children would get fed up with the game and take a break from the other, venturing to the kitchen to ask for a snack or a drink of chocolate milk. Jez sat down at the table and folded her hands in her lap. She was very quiet, again not all that unusual for Jez, and nodded when Gloria asked her if she'd like a bowl of soup.

The soup was tomato, and Jez spooned it carefully into her mouth, making sure not to spill a drop and dabbing her lips with her napkin every so often. Gloria was preparing steaks for dinner, seasoning them and rubbing them down. They sat on the plate in a pool of blood, sparkling with grains of melting salt, waiting for the evening, when the father would return home to barbecue them for his favourite meal. Gloria expected Adam to wander in on his own time, but once Jez had spooned her last mouthful and said, "Thank you very much for lunch, Mrs. Ortiz," she simply sat on the chair with her hands pressed between her knees rather than running along like usual. Gloria asked her what was the matter, but Jez did not answer. She sat still, as though hypnotized, staring at the empty bowl.

Gloria knew then. A sudden feeling like falling rushed through her body. She knew something was wrong.

Gloria ran, but it felt as though her feet couldn't move fast enough, like she was on a treadmill, the distance between her and the shed expanding, expanding, with every step. Time slowed. Her feet finally reached the bricks that she and her husband had piled to create a step up to the door, and the sound of her foot stomping against it seemed to echo. Her hand on the knob, turning, turning forever. The door opening, a single hairline of space, a fracture, as though the thing inside were alive and hatching, using all its feeble strength to crack the shell from the inside, bit by bit. Adam's shoe coming into view, the white sole pointing at her, smeared with grass stains. Then the legs, the bare belly, the T-shirt ridden up and bunched around his chest, the arms spread out. The light from the open door shone on his skin. Everything was Adam, just as she knew him, just as she'd seen him that morning. Except the face.

Adam's mouth was slightly open, lips soft, as though he were about to speak. The bullet had hit him in the eye. On the wall behind him, red. Not just a spray, but great gobs of it hanging, clinging like giant amoebas to the animal heads—their fur, their antlers. The animals' eyes stared out through the muck, and frozen inside was the moment, the single instant of mortal fear, the blink-fast acceptance of their fate.

Adam's face was not a face anymore, without the eye. It had become meat—some inert thing, shapeless and leaking.

Ricky had not, of course, described the scene to me in such detail. He'd told me the story as though recounting a myth, as if it were something far removed from him, almost fantastical. We'd sat in the stewy heat of the kitchen, steam billowing from the kettle that was boiling dry on the stove, both of us sweating but choosing to suffer through it, like we deserved it. He told me that Gloria hadn't heard the gun go off because her ears were bad without her hearing aid. That she didn't think anything was wrong because Jez seemed fine and ate a whole bowl of soup. That she found Adam lying there on the floor of the shed. That he'd been shot.

Some of the other details I heard later, in scraps here and there, some from Ricky and some from Jez, some from the interview with Gloria in the magazine. The rest I invented on my own because … why? Perhaps because I am a sick person. Because I did not cry, not a single tear, even when Ricky began to sob, his whole face wet and crunched and grotesque. Perhaps I had some need to imagine the bloody spectacle in order to make sense of it in my head. It happened without my control, and once it did, it became the truth, just like any one of my own memories. It was as though I'd been seeing the world upside down, and only now had I been flipped back onto my feet.

After he'd finished, I asked Ricky for only one more detail: how the children had gotten hold of the shotgun.

"We still don't know how they got in there," Ricky said. "It was locked, in a locked case. They said they were sure it was locked."

I pictured Jez's tiny fingers handling a paper clip, feeding its end into the keyhole.

"Carla can't let it go," Ricky said, wiping his snotty nose with the back of his hand. "It's just one of those terrible things. A tragic accident. It wasn't anybody's fault."

But it was, I wanted to say. It was everyone's fault. It was the father's fault for keeping a loaded gun in the shed. It was Gloria's fault for neglecting to protect the children. It was Ricky and Carla's fault for putting blind faith in veritable strangers. It was Jez's fault. She was a child, but she knew. Carla knew it too. And perhaps it was because of some mystical bond that allowed me to see through Jez, or perhaps because Ricky had created his own ending in order to survive, but the story forked there, at the very end—Ricky's version versus mine. Mine was not neatly boxed away as pure tragedy or accident. In my version, there was something else, some invisible, sinister thing crawling its way out of the seams. I heard Mutti's voice in my head. *No one can know.*

They found a large bruise on Jez's shoulder. It was from the butt of the gun, which had kicked back when she fired, slamming into her small body and knocking her to the ground, like a bird hitting a window.

12

WE WENT NORTH.

Jez insisted on sitting in the front seat, spreading a map over her legs, which were so small for the seat that they stuck out straight. With a bright pink marker, she scribbled along the highways splaying from Drumheller, where I'd placed a great X to mark the very spot from which our trip had begun. Then she recognized the white shape of Greenland at the top of the map and asked if we were going to the Arctic.

"Yes, we are headed toward the top of the map," I said. This way I did not have to lie.

"Will it be cold there?" she said, and I nodded.

"Good thing we remembered our winter coats," I said. Hers was tucked under her bottom and was a shocking thing as white and furry as a polar bear. Jez had put on a face like a movie star as she draped it around her shoulders and strutted down the front steps, lips pursed and chin held high. "Let's go, dahling," she had said, which she must have learned from a television show, or perhaps from Carla.

It was quite eerie to be out driving at such an hour; the night seemed to have claimed the world. The streets were perfectly still, not a leaf blowing, and it occurred to me that the only thing moving was us. In the absence of any human beings, every waste bin and fire hydrant seemed to be alive with watchful gazes. The flash of a little dog skittering across the street, quick as a bird, was enough to make me jump in my seat. I drove more slowly than usual, perhaps waiting for some kind of reason to dawn on me and force me to turn the wheel round before we got too far from home. We passed the water tower and it seemed to gaze upon us, following us with an invisible eye. Once it had passed out of sight, however, I felt impelled to speed up. My mind was oddly vacant, and Jez seemed quite happy drawing a route up to the Arctic on the map. The overhead light cast an angled beam over her, turning her face a ghoulish orange.

We passed through the badlands and into the patchwork prairies. Fields of grain stretched out endlessly, and the sky pressed down on them as it lightened to a dusky blue. Tiny grain elevators jutted from the horizon like teeth on a key. The radio hissed static.

We were quiet and still, our minds as stretched as the landscape. At one point we came upon a collection of wind turbines stoic as statues, their giant propellers slicing the sky. Jez traced their slow turning with a finger on the glass of her window.

As the winking lights of Gasoline Alley came into view, I counted in my head the years since I had been this far from home. Eleven. I'd come to Red Deer to buy a space heater at Walmart. This was before we'd gotten our own in Drumheller, when Walmart was still magical to those of us who'd lived our lives in a small town. You'd have thought we were on the brink of apocalypse the day it opened, hordes of people streaming from the doors with overflowing carts. On my way inside I saw one woman emerging with a whole cart brimming with cans of frozen orange juice. It was my very first time visiting such a store, and sure enough I got lost in the household goods section for well over an hour. A few people passed me, but all of them had a shifty, foreign look about them even though I was only an hour away from home. So distraught was I by the time I had found my space heater and paid that I had to have an elderly employee carry the box out to my car, and he saw the McDonald's wrappers strewn across the passenger seat. I caught a glimpse of his nose crinkling and then gave him a dollar tip. He shrugged as he slipped the coin into the pocket of his blue Walmart vest.

The memory of it made my heart drum louder in my chest, and I clutched my hand to it as if to keep it from bursting out.

It might all prove to be too much for me, I realized. Poor Waldo was roaming free in the back seat. His hutch was far too large to fit in the car, so what could I do? I'd emptied a bag of wood chips and spread them as best I could across the seats, but most of them were already on the floor, having been kicked about by Waldo's mad hopping back and forth. As far as I could remember, he had never been inside a car.

I had no plan. Once I reached the QE2, I knew I would go north, but I did not know why. Perhaps north seemed the best direction in which to get lost.

Jez, on the other hand, seemed not at all concerned. She had now let the map fall to the floor and sat on her knees on the seat, watching the sparse scenery go by without a care, as if we were on a regular Sunday drive. After I'd gone into her room to wake her, we'd worked together in silence by the glow of her night light, filling the suitcase with her socks and undershirts and slacks and dresses. She'd collected Earl and a few other stuffed animals from her bed and thrown them into the suitcase as well, tiptoeing as she moved across the creaking floor.

It crossed my mind then that secrets were likely a natural part of her environment; I wondered if it was something of a routine for her to be whisked away in the middle of the night. It struck me as something Ricky likely would have done to avoid facing Carla.

As if to affirm my thoughts, I found something I did not expect at the bottom of the last dresser drawer, nested in a crumpled T-shirt. It was my egg. My dinosaur egg, its two cracked halves glittering. Upon seeing them, Jez snatched them up and dropped them into the suitcase like pennies, and I hadn't time in that moment to ask her how she'd found them. We had to be long gone before Ricky suspected anything.

Now, as I peered at her slant-wise, I felt content to imagine what had happened rather than ask. She'd snuck inside my room when I was at work. She'd gone through my things, drawer by drawer, cupboard by cupboard, taking out each trinket in turn to examine it and then putting it back just so. She'd seen my panties, each pair huge as a tent, and scoffed at the ratty ones that should have been thrown out long ago. She'd seen the photo of Mutti in a red bikini that I kept in my bedside table. And she'd found the dollhouse in the corner of my closet and inspected every room, her eyes quickly catching the glint of the geode's insides. How to resist such a pretty thing?

I'd found it when I was a child, not much older than Jez, on one of my fossil hunts with Mutti. We used to make regular trips to a particular spot at the edge of a coulee, not far from Horseshoe Canyon, but far enough off the trail that tourists didn't dare venture near it, at least not in those days. Seeing as the spot was filled with water in springtime, we had only a small window of time in the year when conditions were ripe—the land dry, and the weather mild and not yet scorching. I would take off my shoes to let the sandy dirt catch between my toes and skip between the sharp rocks and thistles that poked up slyly from the sparse grasses. Mutti picked the new growth from the stunted bushes of sagebrush and rolled it between her palms. Then she pulled me near and ran her hands through my hair to transfer the musky scent. Whenever I smell it now, I travel back to that time when each day had a clear purpose—when it was enough to unearth a rock that hadn't seen the sun for hundreds or perhaps thousands of years, as though raising it from the dead.

Mutti would allow me to keep just three rocks each trip, subject to her approval. They had to be rare, was the thing; Mutti was not about to let me hoard every bit of commonplace quartz or limestone that my untrained mind deemed worthy. So she'd examine each specimen before allowing me to place it in our basket, first turning it over in her hands, which was often enough to make a firm judgment, and then, if need be, holding her magnifier up to its surface to assess its structure in more detail. There were times I'd thought I found something precious—a piece of amber, or once even an emerald. I remember how the green face of it winking from a nest of dull rocks seemed to signal a kind of destiny. I tore at the rocks to recover it and held it to the light, triumphant. The prospect of presenting my treasure to Mutti was perhaps even more exhilarating than finding it; I knew that Mutti would gasp, praise my keen eye, and offer to take me for ice cream to celebrate our luck. But it turns out I never managed to develop a keen eye. The amber I found was only a particularly orange chunk of iron ore, and the emerald was a piece from a shattered beer bottle, the edges worn smooth over years of abuse from the elements. Mutti needed only to take a glance at these before she dropped them to the ground for some more ignorant treasure hunter to find.

Once I found a stone, spotted and oblong in shape. It was chalk-white in colour and in the powdery feel of its surface, and about the size of a hen's egg. Indeed, I was convinced it was an egg, but one belonging to a small dinosaur. With my X-ray imagination I could see the reptilian body curled up inside. It had been warm in there, and safe, and after the mother was unceremoniously eaten it knew nothing but the blank walls of its shell. It would not have known that the cold air, seeping through the shell and into its veins ever so slowly, was sinister enough to kill.

I did not tell Mutti about my finding. I knew somewhere inside myself that it was an illusion, but it was one I preferred to keep. I hid the egg in an open seam in the waistband of my slacks, seeing as I had no pockets on my clothes that day, and it kept falling out over the course of that day so that I had to scramble after it and tuck it away before Mutti noticed. When I got it home safely, I found a hiding place for it in my dollhouse—a place that Mutti would never have cause to look—and it stayed there for years, occupying the miniature four-poster bed in the master bedroom.

Sometime later, I decided it was time to test my theory. I brought the egg outside and set it on the pavement, then proceeded to smash it over and over with a slab of shale from the garden. To my surprise, it was not easy to break the egg open; the shale cracked and sloughed away much sooner than the egg showed any signs of distress. But I had set my mind to seeing its insides and, as Mutti always said, I am as stubborn as a billy goat. So I gave up with the shale and began throwing the rock at the pavement with all my might. Still no success. It was clear that I needed to pierce the thing in order to start a crack, and so I retrieved one of Mutti's gardening trowels and a hammer from the shed and set the sharp end of the trowel against the centre of the stone. Imagining myself a paleontologist chinking away at the unyielding earth, I hammered on the end of the trowel. It took some artful positioning to make the trowel stay against the stone without jigging off with each blow, but I managed to set it against a notch that held it still, and eventually, finally, I made a small fracture that spread its way around the egg and severed it into two jagged halves. The halves rolled away from each other and wobbled, baring their insides.

They were filled with crystals. Thousands of tiny white crystals that sparkled like sugar. Fused to the heart of one half was an orange nugget, which I was immediately convinced was the remnant of a yolk. That was enough evidence to persuade me that this had truly been an egg, and that the half-formed dinosaur embryo had transformed by some miraculous geological process into crystals.

This was the real thing, I knew. This was something that had never been seen before. I would become famous. Mutti would jump out of her stockings when she saw what I had found. She would beam, she would cry. We would take it to the museum and receive a sack of money in exchange, so long as they agreed to display the egg with a plaque noting me as the blessed discoverer.

"What do you have there?" said Mutti as I approached her that evening. She was just coming home from work, hanging her coat and shucking off her boots. I was cupping the egg in my hands like a trapped creature so that I could orchestrate a dramatic revelation. I stood in front of her as children do, legs apart and belly stuck out, and opened my clamshelled hands to present my treasure.

I suspect she was expecting some insignificant thing, like a pussy willow or a dead moth, so she only half looked at first. But once her eye had caught the sparkle, she peered in for a closer look.

"Hil-fe, Regina," she said, grabbing my wrist. "Where did this come from?"

"It's an egg," I said. "A dinosaur one. I found it and cracked it open. See, there's the yolk."

Mutti heaved a sigh and shook her head, then began pulling the ends of her mittens and peeling them off. "Silly," she said. "That's not an egg, Regina. It's a geode. And you've gone and ruined it."

She explained then that geodes were most valuable when sliced with a special machine that could cut rocks like butter. The imperfect edges that I had created around my geode made it virtually worthless.

"What do I do with you?" she went on, taking the two halves from my hands and shaking them before me like evidence. "It might've been worth something, you know. I think about four hundred dollars, maybe more. But there you've gone smashing it to bits. Must you go around smashing everything, Regina?"

This story makes Mutti sound cruel, though she really wasn't. She did not know how I had stretched the egg's significance far beyond its beauty or rarity or value and had begun to see it as part of myself. It was true that in trying to make it my own, in loving the egg, I had ruined it. I held the ball of devastation deep in my throat and blinked and blinked to keep back the tears. If it is possible for an object to break your heart, that egg broke mine.

I kept the two halves hidden away in the dollhouse, where they stayed for almost thirty years; it seemed wrong to move the egg from its snug spot in the bed. Perhaps because within the walls of the dollhouse, the egg was still allowed to be an egg. And while it would have been the decent thing to drag out the dollhouse, dust if off, and pass it on to my niece, I did not do so precisely because it had at some point become like a gravesite to me, a place frozen in time that I felt should not be disturbed.

Now, as the egg halves rode in Jez's suitcase in the trunk, I could not help but think of them as stowaways hitching a ride on a journey on which they were not welcome. Knowing they were there felt like a bad omen.

"Are we gonna spy?" Jez said, and I jumped a little at the break in the silence.

"Spy?" I said. "On whom?"

"Like I spy, my little eye." It seemed she'd given up on being subdued and was now wriggling in her seat like a lizard.

"Oh," I said. "Your papa taught you that game?"

She nodded, rubbing her little hands together.

"All right, then," I conceded. "Here we go. I spy with my little eye …" I peered about the car, making a show of moving my eyes this way and that. "Something that is yellow."

"Lights!" Jez said, bolting in her seat as though a wasp had stung her bottom.

"Yes! How did you know?"

"Oh boy," she said, now flopping back into her seat. "That was a dumb one."

"It was dumb of you to suggest such a dumb game," I shot back.

Laughter spurted from her lips, sending flecks of spit flying.

"Now how does that feel?" I said.

"Dumb dummy dumb game!" Her laughter was like air escaping from a balloon.

"Fine," I said. "Never mind, then. Just finish this silly mood of yours."

"It's my turn," she said, thrusting a crazy grin at me. "I spy, my little eye … my little eye, my little eye …"

I ignored her, eyes on the road. She was behaving like a child, which I was not so much accustomed to. Twinges of regret began to creep into my belly.

"Something that is grey!" she cried.

"I give up," I said.

"No fair," she said. "You didn't even guess."

"The road. The dashboard. That handle."

"Nope, nope, nope."

"Auntie Reg is tired."

"Wrong."

"Look," I said, pointing ahead. "The sun is rising."

"It's pink," she said. "Something that is pink!"

"Lovely, isn't it?"

"Are we gonna get out soon?" she said, shoving her arms under the seat belt.

She was restless, to be sure, and I admitted to myself that taking a break was probably best for us both. I pulled over onto the shoulder.

"Would you like to stretch your legs?" I said.

Jez hopped out of the car, and I followed quickly, grabbing Waldo's leash. I harnessed him up and set him in the gravel. Jez picked a few foxtails from the ditch and dangled them in front of his nose while I filled a little dish with some water.

"What's that?" she said, now looking down the road in the direction we'd come from.

"That?" I said. "Well, that's a man. On a bicycle."

"Is he going to hit us?"

"No, no," I said. "He'll go around us. He's trying to get somewhere, just like us. But it will take him much longer, I think."

The man was burdened with a huge sack that made him look like a hunchback, and the wheels of his bicycle were turning so slowly that it was a wonder he could stay upright. The brim of his red baseball cap was bent up, and a pair of small dark eyes looked out from beneath.

"Hi, guy!" Jez yelled as he approached.

"Shh," I said, batting down Jez's waving arm.

The man began to slow down, and there went my heart again, thumping away. My instinct was to pick up Waldo and press him tight to my bosom, but when I bent to grab him I found he had wandered underneath the car.

"Waldo," I hissed, tugging his leash.

"H'lo there, missy," the man called out as he brought himself to a stop in front of us. "Missy one and missy two, I guess," he added. He was breathing quite heavily, and now that he was directly in front of us I could see the sweaty stripe of his hat at the brim and strings of oily black hair like seaweed coiling out from underneath. With a great snort he sucked his nose drippings back into his throat and swallowed.

"What's in your bag?" Jez asked.

The man smiled at her and heaved the bag to the ground. It was a duffle bag that he'd simply slung over his back, and it landed in the dirt with a clumsy flop. Perhaps it was unfair of me, but I could only picture dead body parts inside. Mutti had always said that the fools who rode their bicycles on the highway were the scourge of civilized society. "Verpiss dich!" she would yell out the window.

"In here?" the man said to Jez, pointing a knobby finger down at the bag. "I bet you'll never guess what I have in here." He looked at me and winked.

"We need to be off," I said, tugging and tugging at Waldo's leash. His little claws scratched maniacally at the dirt, digging in. It's a well-known fact that bunnies have a sixth sense for danger, which, being Waldo's mother, I could easily pick up on. But Jez saw fit to take up the man's challenge and toddled up to the bag, prodding it with the toe of her shoe.

"Something soft," she said. "Is it teddy bears?"

"Nice try," the man said, now dismounting his bicycle. "Missy two, you wanna take a shot?"

"We're in a rush," I said. I reeled Waldo in like a fish on a line, cringing at the thought of the harness squeezing his throat. I practically threw him into the back seat, leash still attached, but by the time I turned my attention back to Jez she was already kneeling next to the bag as the man unzipped it. Her hand reached inside and I lunged, grabbing her shoulder.

Jez looked up at me blankly and showed me her fist. In it was a clump of hair, and when she saw the terror in my eyes she opened her palm and let it drift to the ground.

"Whoa, whoa," the man said, "watch it." He began plucking the fallen hairs out of the gravel. "Took me forever to collect all this. Grade A human hair, you know. People will pay up the wazoo for this shit."

I saw now that the bag was full of dark, thick hair, piles and piles of it in varying lengths, and the way the man jostled the bag about by the handles to show off his bounty made it move together in clumps, like some inchoate animal about to emerge.

We left Waldo's water dish behind, and as I veered back onto the highway I could see it in the rear-view mirror, the sheer whiteness of it blinking through clouds of road dust. Just beyond it, the man was waving, and Jez waved back.

13

THE STRIP MALLS and motels of Edmonton went by in a blur. My heart was galloping with the chaos of it all—the early morning light blaring, vehicles packed on all sides, from compacts to semi trucks, construction workers directing traffic out of lanes where the smells of fresh tar mingled with clouds of exhaust. It seemed that driving the speed limit was some kind of unforgivable offence in the city. I kept my hands gripped tightly on the wheel, face forward, each time a monstrous truck veered around us, the driver's steely eyes trying to bore a hole through my window as he passed. So that I would not lose focus, I set Jez to counting all the red and white signs of the Tim Hortonses along the highway. Six. The traffic did not seem at all distressing to her, though. Her only acknowledgment of it was to cluck her tongue when one driver nearly cut us off as a way of making his point. "Watch it, buddy," she said under her breath.

Truth be told, Edmonton was a harrowing place in my memory because of the time I'd visited with Ricky and his father when I was young. Unlike me, Ricky had known his father for a time, although a short one. He worked as a guard at the penitentiary and was a born-again Christian evangelist. In fact, it was his faith that prompted him to seek out Ricky and begin what he called "a relationship" with him, which mostly involved taking Ricky out to Arby's and the mall every odd weekend and buying him some extravagance—once a Hot Wheels racetrack, another time a ghetto blaster, then a Nintendo. Ricky always gloated over the gifts, and I pretended not to be jealous. "Regina doesn't want such silly boy things anyway," Mutti would say in my defence, which was true, but we all knew it wasn't really the gifts I was secretly coveting.

The first time Clint came to our house, I was struck dumb by the way he moved and talked like Ricky, his face morphing in and out of Ricky's expressions, and how he had Ricky's same nervous laugh that he kept trapped in his throat. I saw him as a kind of mischievous shape-shifter, cloning pieces of Ricky one by one and using them whenever he saw fit, though of course it was the other way around; Ricky was a copy of him, with the cheeks and jawline of Mutti mixed in.

It was obvious to me that Ricky liked Clint for the gifts and attention he would provide on those rare Saturdays, but that Clint himself was something merely to be endured, like the doctor's checkup before the lollipop reward. It was Clint's preaching, especially, that prickled Ricky. Clint would say things like, "Every good gift and every perfect gift is from above," and "Forecast for tomorrow: God reigns, and the Son shines!" and Ricky and I would look at each other like he'd just pulled his pants down right there in the living room. He would go on about the "sinners" he oversaw at the penitentiary, how some of them were repentant but others would not let Jesus into their hearts. He tried to get Ricky to join his church, of course, and I suspect Ricky did attend a couple of times, though he would never speak of it.

Once, Clint offered to take us both on a weekend trip to West Edmonton Mall. We stayed at the Fantasyland Hotel in the Polynesian Room, which had a hot tub in the shape of a volcano with fake palm trees around it, and a waterbed made to look like the prow of a ship. It would be an understatement to say the whole thing was cheesy, but Ricky made not a single mocking quip the entire weekend. Clint bought us a huge bag of candy, which we spread out on the bed and gorged on while watching pay-per-view Disney movies. At the mall, we got novelty T-shirts and ball caps, and Clint and Ricky rode the roller coaster while I watched from below, their twin faces slathered with glee as they plummeted down big drops, swooped around curves, looped upside down. Ricky's face when he came off the roller coaster, windswept and pink with thrill, might have been the happiest I've ever seen him.

Later, we all went to the water park. I was eleven and had just begun to develop breasts like small tents on my chest, and I was wearing a bathing suit with a frilly skirt round the waist that Mutti insisted would accentuate my curves, though I was not at all eager to accentuate them. When I was not in the water, I kept my arms either crossed over my chest or pinned to my hips at all times, except when the creeping hem of my bathing suit forced me to slide a finger beneath the wet fabric to extract it from my bottom. The waterslides were unthinkable to me. I saw how Ricky and the other children flew off the bumps and slipped around the turns, their legs flailing about like paper caught in the wind. So I stood in the pool, hopping into each measured wave and letting it drift me back, little by little, toward the shallow end, until I was sitting on my bum, rocking back and forth, my hair dipping in and out of the water. Then, when I got all the way to the edge of the pool, I'd go back and do it again.

"Having fun?" Clint said to me as I rocked in the shallows. He was standing in the water, looking down on me.

"Yes," I said, sitting up.

"I'm glad," he said. "You deserve to feel special once in a while." He looked off to the far end of the pool as though he were looking out over a vast landscape. There was Ricky, coming toward us. "I know it's difficult for you," Clint said.

I nodded, though I had no inkling of what he was talking about. Ricky splashed up to us and stood by his father.

"But it doesn't need to be," Clint continued, as though Ricky weren't there. "Jesus reminds us of the dangers of gluttony."

"I'm going for another run on the slide," Ricky said. "Anyone want to come?" By anyone he meant Clint, of course. Clint only looked at him, his hands on his hips, and blinked. Clint's wet hair dripped on his shoulders, and from where I was sitting below with the sun coming in through the glass ceiling, I could see a collection of hairs sprouting from each shoulder, like tiny corkscrews. Ricky had his back turned to me so I couldn't see his face. After a moment, he leapt into the water and swam off, back to the slides on his own.

Clint carried on. "Do you know that word, gluttony?"

I nodded again.

"Proverbs 23, verses 20 and 21. 'Be not among drunkards or among gluttonous eaters of meat, for the drunkard and the glutton will come to poverty, and slumber will clothe them with rags.'" He recited the verse in a different voice, putting a little vibration on each of the words as though he were half-singing them.

I said nothing. I was getting cold with my chest out of the water. I brought my knees up and curled into a ball, holding my body tight so I would not shiver. What he was saying hardly meant anything to me, but the word *glutton* put pictures in my mind of people with the faces of pigs, stuffing themselves with doughnuts and cake and hamburgers. Clint had let us choose whatever candy we wanted at the store and paid without a word. He'd sat on the armchair in the hotel room and crossed his legs, watching with his lips pursed, as we laid our bounty over the bright-pink duvet.

"Do you see?" he said. "Powerful, isn't it. That was a powerful verse for me. I'm a recovering alcoholic, you know. Two years sober."

I wanted to leave. I thought about saying I was going to the hot tub, but then I would have to stand up and out of the water, my wet bathing suit dripping and sagging and sticking to my skin, suctioned to every lump and crease of my body.

"It's not too late," he said. "You and Ricky. You don't have to follow your mother's sinful path."

"Okay," I said, hoping this would be enough to make him stop. I was already imagining how I would tell Mutti, how she would be outraged, would threaten to wring his self-righteous neck and might even forbid him to see Ricky again. But in the end, I never told Mutti. I waited out the rest of the weekend, wishing for home, while Ricky and I declined every chocolate bar and every bag of caramel popcorn that Clint offered, knowing by the look on his face that it was some kind of test.

Clint offered to take me along again the next time he visited, but I said no. Mutti was smug about it, but Ricky seemed bothered and would not speak to me for a day or so afterward. I know now that it was not disappointment, but shame. He knew that he'd been found out; he could no longer pretend that visits with his father were full of carefree fun and father-son bonding. Clint's visits became less and less frequent over the months, until he stopped coming altogether. Then he moved away, to someplace in Ontario, to live with a woman he'd decided to marry.

He did return once, however, for Ricky's high school graduation. Even after I'd surprised Ricky with a green silk tie for the occasion, he had insisted that he wasn't going to the graduation ceremony, that it was a big deal made out of nothing, that it was a superficial waste of time. But when Clint showed up, Ricky changed his mind. He felt obliged, I suppose. Clint stayed at our house for two days in Mutti's old room, stinking up the whole upper floor with the smell of Drakkar Noir. He took Ricky to buy a new suit to go with the tie I'd given him, and since neither Ricky nor I had ever tied a tie before, Clint showed him how. They both blushed at having to stand so close to each other, at Clint having to look Ricky straight in the face and touch him at the nape to get the tie around. From where I stood, they were exactly the same height. Even though we hadn't seen Clint in years, Ricky seemed to belong in that moment more to Clint than to me, and I got a sinking feeling in my gut so intense that it was everything I could do not to wrench the two of them apart and plant myself in the middle.

I had to sit next to Clint at the ceremony, of course, our thighs brushing against each other and his cologne hanging like a cloud around us, so oppressive that my head felt as though it might detach itself and float away. But then, when it was Ricky's turn to walk across the stage, I was glad he'd come. Ricky looked out into the audience as he shook the principal's hand and accepted his diploma, and his eyes caught us. Clint did not hesitate to wave, to put two hooked fingers into his mouth and blast a sharp whistle, then grin and clap with pride.

The clapping seemed thunderous, particularly because no one else was doing it but Clint. It emboldened me to join in, and then it was the two of us, clapping and cheering madly in the sea of bored onlookers. And Ricky, rather than being embarrassed, like I expected, grinned back. It was Clint's smile on his face, not Mutti's.

Jez, on the other hand, had somehow gotten a smile just like Mutti's. I had too.

≈

Once we'd left Edmonton far behind and were sailing again through the open prairies, I felt my stomach churn, and it let out a deep, roiling growl.

"I'm hungry," Jez said, as if to give a caption to my stomach.

We stopped for brunch at Mike's Pizza & Restaurant in Athabasca. I ordered scrambled eggs, six rashers of bacon, and two slices of toast.

"So you want the Traditional," said the waitress, pointing her pen at the menu board behind her. She was trim, with a soft pouch that stuck out around her middle, and though her eyes were small and heavy lidded, I could see her gaze flick to my midsection as well, no doubt estimating how many of her could fit inside me. The smell of fresh bread lingered about, and the tables were edged in chrome, which all made the place feel like the old commercials for things like Shredded Wheat and fabric softener. Wholesome. Except that the waitress was now sliding her gum against her teeth as I tried to convince Jez that eggs were not made of baby chicks and would not put her cholesterol through the roof. We finally settled on ordering her a Kids' Pepperoni Pizza. She must need the protein, I reasoned with myself.

The waitress shrugged without bothering to scribble anything on her notepad and went away.

Jez set to work making little piles of salt and pepper while we waited for our meals, shaking out a bit of each at a time and then using the edge of her finger to sweep the grains into neat, separate mounds.

I folded my hands on the table as though conducting an interview. "So," I said, but she remained fixated on her task. "I think it's a good idea to make an agreement." Her eyes showed no signs of recognition, and my first thought was to poke my finger into one of her piles. But then I remembered that Ricky too was a fiddler when he was young. Mutti took us out to restaurants only when she wanted to give us a lecture, knowing that we were too meek to throw tantrums in public. Ricky would slump into the table as though burdened by the weight of Mutti's words, and would tear his napkin into tiny pieces and collect them in an empty creamer cup. It drove Mutti wild that he would refuse to look at her. To her, it was a sign of defiance, but I knew it was really that Ricky wanted to be adored, always, and the idea that Mutti was in some way disappointed in him was too much to bear.

I unfolded my hands at the thought of this. "Sometimes," I continued, "there will be bad men. Bad people, I should say. Your Auntie Reg is a lot older than you, which means she has seen a lot of bad people in her life and knows how to spot them."

"How?" said Jez. She rested her chin on the table to examine her piles at eye level, her finger adjusting them to some invisible standard.

"Well," I said, "it's difficult to explain. It's like an impression." I paused here to find the words that a child might understand. "Like a funny smell. The bad people have a funny smell about them that only this special nose of mine can smell." I twitched my nose at her like a bunny, even though she wasn't looking. The sudden reminder of poor Waldo hopping about in the back seat and longing for a sprig of grass or a dandelion to chew on was enough to make me heave myself from my seat for a moment to look out the window and spy the car. The distance was too great to see anything in the back seat.

"Does my papa have a funny smell?" Jez said.

I settled back in my seat and pondered her question. I knew that any questions she asked about Ricky had to be handled carefully.

"Yes," I said, "he does. But he didn't used to."

"I can smell it too," she said.

"But the point," I went on, anticipating another silly game, "is that we need a secret signal between us. So that if we come across a bad person and one of us can smell it, we can signal to the other person to say, 'Let's get out of here.'"

"What kind of a secret?" Now her attention was on me. She brushed the salt and pepper off the table with one big sweep of her hand, and the grains made a tiny showering noise against the tile floor. I sat back, pleased with myself.

"A gesture," I said. "Some kind of action. Something only you and I will recognize. It has to be subtle."

"Like this?" She stuck her pinky finger in her mouth and clamped her teeth down on it one, two, three times, as though she were chewing a chicken wing. Then she slid her finger through her lips to wipe off the saliva.

"This?" I echoed her movements exactly. She grinned and did it again, with even more fervour.

"Good," I said. "That's it. But remember—subtle. That means we want to keep it a secret. So we can't let other people know it's a signal."

She nodded her head.

"All right," I said. "So when I do this"—I gnawed my finger—"it means?"

"Bad person," Jez said, grinning away. It seemed as though all the light in the room was reflecting off her shiny teeth.

"And what do we do?" I asked.

"Get out of here!" she squealed, ducking under the table. A man sitting at the breakfast bar swivelled in his stool to look over at us. I put on a polite smile.

"Come now," I said, knocking my fist against the table. "Our food is coming, I think. Any second now." Thankfully it was not a lie, as the waitress came sashaying between the tables toward us, balancing her tray in the air. Jez popped up and settled back into her seat, swiftly unfolding her napkin and laying it across her lap.

"The Traditional," said the waitress, setting a plate of faintly grey eggs, leathery bacon, and butter-soaked toast in front of me, "and a pizza for the little princess."

Jez licked her lips at the sight, and indeed the pizza looked far more appealing to me, with its golden crust and glistening pepperoni slices, than the meal I'd ordered.

"Auntie Reg," Jez said, peeling off a slice of pepperoni, "what do we do if he finds us?"

"Who?" I said.

She did the signal again, this time chomping on the pepperoni at the same time as her finger. "Papa," she whispered.

"No, no," I said. "The signal isn't for your papa. Your papa isn't the bad man." I realized I was confusing her. "The man on the bicycle. He's the kind to watch out for."

"He smelled like shampoo," she said.

"Well, that's because you need an extra-sensitive nose, like mine." I twitched it at her again. She touched a finger to her own nose, leaving a greasy spot.

"My nose can smell whatever's beneath the shampoo or perfume or any other smell," I added.

"What's my smell?" she asked.

"Hmm," I said. "A sweet one, but also spicy. Cinnamon buns."

"Yep," she said, nodding, as though she knew it all along.

"So if we see your papa …" I began. I thought the answer might become clear as I spoke the words, but I found I had no idea how to finish. I imagined us stopped at a gas station, me pumping gas into the car and seeing Ricky's face rise up from the vehicle across, pointing a look of murderous rage directly at me. He would not understand, I knew. To him, I was probably a kidnapper. What could we do in that instance but admit defeat?

"We hide," Jez said. I thought at first that hiding would be childish, but her expression was serious enough to make me realize that it was our only choice. Yes, we would have to hide. No more driving through big cities or stopping along the highway. We would need to move about like true fugitives on the run.

Strangely, the thought of this gave me some comfort. I'd been worrying about having a plan, some kind of clear destination that would bring all the answers to whatever it was I was doing with Jez. But I knew then that the plan was simply to evade Ricky and Carla. As long as they couldn't find her, she would be safe.

Jez finished nibbling her pizza down to the crusts, which I collected in a napkin as a snack for Waldo. It had been so long since I'd eaten in a restaurant that I couldn't remember how much was customary to leave for a tip. I stacked three loonies and a quarter on top of the bill and scooted Jez out the door before I could risk glimpsing the waitress's look of disapproval.

It was apparent when we returned to the car that Waldo was not taking well to his new enclosure. The smell that hit my nostrils when I opened the door to the back seat was much more rancid than I expected, and I realized that we hadn't noticed it before because we had grown accustomed to it as a result of stewing in it for hours. I had left the windows cracked open, but Waldo was panting like a dog, his little pink tongue darting in and out. I cradled him in my arms and promptly felt the squish of fresh stool against my skin. He'd mussed up all the wood shavings and pushed them to one side on the back seat, and the spots he'd scraped bare were moist with patches of urine, his brown beads smeared into the upholstery here and there. I held him up to my face and whispered into his fur to calm him, but his back feet kicked at my arm.

"Waldo needs a break for a while," I said to Jez, who yawned in response. She was standing on the other side of the car at the passenger door, flipping the locked handle over and over again.

"We'll find a campground somewhere nearby," I said, redistributing the wood shavings and placing Waldo back on top. "There's got to be one around here. Have you ever been camping?"

"Nuh-uh," Jez said. Now she was pulling her weight against the door handle, swaying lazily on one foot and letting her head loll back.

"You'll like it, I think," I said. "It's the best way to relax. And we might see some frogs, or chipmunks. And maybe deer."

"Okay," she said, tugging on the door handle once again. "Let's go."

I unlocked the door and she climbed in, quickly strapping herself in and placing her hands on the dashboard as though readying for a carnival ride.

"Is camping the one with the tent?" she asked.

"Yes," I said, "sometimes you sleep in a tent. Or sometimes you can drive a house on wheels way out into the country and live in the wilderness for a while. Or there's a thing called a tent trailer that you haul from the back of your car." I was making myself sound like an expert, though I'd only been camping once in my life, with a girl named Chelsea and her family, who lived across the street from us. Mutti always said camping was barbaric, and it was true that when I came home after four days in the woods, I had burrs tangled in my hair and scratches all over my legs from running through the brush, and I'd accidentally peed on my shorts when Chelsea tried to teach me how to squat on a log to go to the bathroom. I told Mutti that Chelsea had given me a leaf to wipe my privates and she immediately ordered me straight into the hottest bath I'd ever felt, scrubbing me all over until my skin was pink as ham. Chelsea never asked me to go camping with her again, which was a great relief to Mutti. A campground was not a place that Ricky would think to look for us.

There was indeed a campground down a small township road off the highway, right on the edge of Baptiste Lake. The day was becoming quite warm, but it was a Tuesday and the place was nearly deserted. A few RVs poked their noses from campsites as we rolled through. A black-haired boy on a bike rode up alongside us, apparently deciding that we would make a good racing opponent. Jez's gaze followed him as he pedalled madly past us and zoomed around the next bend.

I pulled into an empty campsite with a giant oak stretched above it, just like the one in our front yard. All but a few of the topmost leaves had already fallen, now crunching against the car tires. The sharp pinch of homesickness rose up in my gut for a moment before I forced it back down.

"There," I said shutting off the engine. Jez peered around.

"Where's the tent?" she said.

"Oh," I said. "We don't have one. You need to bring your own, you see."

Jez made a pouty face.

"But it's still camping, even without a tent. The point is to be out in the wilderness, surrounded by trees and wildlife and nature." I unbuckled my seat belt and climbed out of the car to set an example for her. "See?" I said, taking a seat at the picnic table and raising my hands up to the sky. She only sighed and turned her head away.

"Fine," I said. "Just take your time. Come out when you're ready. Waldo and I are going to explore."

I looped Waldo's leash to a leg of the picnic table and anchored him there on his harness. He hopped tentatively on the gravel, his nose sniffing away, no doubt detecting all the strange animals that were skittering about the woods. In hopes that a treat might ease his worries, I tossed a pizza crust in front of him.

Jez was still sitting in the car, arms crossed. I began to wonder if breathing in the stale ammoniac smell might actually do her some harm, so I thought it best to try to coax her out. I knocked on the window and waved. She unrolled it partway and curled her fingers over the edge.

"Can I help you?" she said.

"Welcome to McDonald's," I announced. "What would you like to order?"

She grinned, catching on immediately. "Umm ..." she said, chewing a finger, "chicken nuggets?"

"One order of chicken nuggets, comin' up!" I said, punching buttons into my invisible computer. "Would you like fries with that?"

"Yes, please."

"That'll be five dollars and eighty-eight cents," I said, sticking my open palm through the window. Jez reached in her pocket and slapped imaginary bills into my hand.

"Thank you, ma'am. Here's your food." I mimed passing a bag through the window. "Enjoy!"

She rolled up the window and took hold of her steering wheel. I waved goodbye.

"What now?" she said, her voice muffled behind the window. I shook my head, pretending not to hear her.

What? I mouthed.

"What now?" she yelled, cupping her hands around her mouth.

I shook my head again and mouthed, *I can't hear you.*

She rolled her eyes and opened the door. Success.

"What are we doing now?" she said.

"We're letting Waldo take a walk," I said. "He is a wild animal after all. He needs to be outside every once in a while."

She pushed the door open and swung her legs out, stretching. "I'm a wild animal too," she said.

"Is that so?" I said. "Then you must need a walk as well."

She stood and shut the car door behind her. The sound of a vehicle rumbled toward us, and I saw coming round the bend a white truck with a rake sticking up from the box at the back. Behind the wheel was a white handlebar moustache that seemed alight against the shaded face of an elderly man. I watched as he came closer, even giving him a friendly wave and smile. I expected him to roll past without a glance, but his truck slowed and turned into our campsite, stopping right behind our car.

The old man took his time climbing out, collecting a clipboard from his passenger seat as he did so.

"Howdy," he said as he approached me. He wore a tan-coloured shirt and matching shorts that were unsettlingly close in colour to his skin, making the white moustache so bright it seemed ready to leap off his face.

"How many nights?" he asked, raising a pen to his clipboard.

"Oh no, we're not staying," I said. "We'll be leaving within the hour."

He wrinkled his brow. "Can't take a campsite if you're not staying," he said. "Day use area's on the other side." He waved his clipboard in the direction we'd come from.

"Right," I said. "Of course. Sorry." I'd begun to sweat. How stupid I had been to come here when I knew nothing at all about camping. The old man's eyes were travelling all over the car now, undoubtedly surveying the mess of rabbit feces in the back, my silence now making him all the more suspicious as he looked over my matted hair, my faded brown dress that had taken on the look of a potato sack in its old age, my dusty feet peeking out of my Crocs.

"I'll move right away," I tried to say, but the words tumbled out over my tongue.

"Take your time," the man said, having somehow understood my mumblings. He ambled back to his truck, and I tried to look purposeful by opening the trunk and shuffling the suitcases about. Once the noise of his truck had faded away, I slammed the trunk shut.

"Jez," I called out, "time to go."

She was sitting at the picnic table, dangling her legs and kicking at the leaves.

"What did the guy want?" she said.

"He said we need to move somewhere else." I had just uttered the words when my heart seemed to drop out of my chest.

"Waldo?" I said. I had tied him up there, right there, at the corner of the picnic table. Was it there, or had my nervousness gotten me turned around? I spun in a circle, scanning the whole site. Nothing. But now I saw that there was the pizza crust, a few feet ahead and seemingly untouched. I saw no trace of his footprints, no sign of any animal at all having tramped through the blanket of foliage. Weeds and grasses and bushes skirted the campsite, undisturbed and austere in their silence.

Dropping to my knees, I groped in the leaves. There was his leash, buried among them. At the other end, the clasp, perfectly intact, but unattached to anything.

14

WHEN I BEGAN to realize that Waldo was gone, really gone, the sweat pooled in the crack at the base of my neck in a matter of seconds. It did not help, of course, that I was tramping through the brush like a stampeding rhinoceros. *He can't have gone far*, I kept telling myself, apparently out loud, because Jez's voice piped up behind me.

"He went that way," she said, and I turned to see her pointing toward a tree a few yards away.

"You saw him?" I barked, grabbing her shoulders. "Why didn't you go after him?"

"He was taking a walk," she said.

Of course it was her. The clasp had not, of course, unhooked on its own. Jez had done it, and now her small fingers were entwined at her chest as if to proclaim their innocence.

"Jez," I said to her, taking a deep breath so as to slow my speech, "did you take Waldo off his leash?"

She nodded, her face smooth and vacant. She raised a finger to her scalp to scratch it idly, and the action gave her the look of a wooden marionette.

I caught a glimpse, then, of something I hadn't seen before. It was something about the way her eyes lost focus, as if deliberately, and I thought I could see the softest shadow of a smile on the corners of her lips.

But we were losing time.

"We need to find him," I said, and a quaver leapt out of my voice. "It's too dangerous for him out there by himself. You show me which direction he went."

She looked me in the eye, biding her time, as if calculating her response. "He went …" she began, "that way!" She shot her finger to the sky with a joyous little leap. The finger lingered there, waiting for my eyes to follow, while Jez's teeth peeked at me through her grin.

The feeling of dread, the weight of a pile of cinder blocks, settled even more deeply in my gut.

"Now Jez," I said, my voice low and growling. I knelt in front of her and looked directly into her flat brown eyes. She blinked twice, and even her blinks seemed forced, as though part of a performance.

"I'm serious," I went on. "Tell me where he went."

"He went …" she began, and then whipped around to break my gaze. "That way!" she said, pointing back at the car. "Or maybe this way!" Now she pointed at her own belly button, poking the flesh there. "Or this way!" she said, spraying spittle through a fit of giggles as she turned and stuck out her bum, her curved finger pointing at it from below like a claw.

What I felt then was something beyond rage. I felt some sort of trigger go off in my brain, a kind of animal instinct to look inward, as though my eyeballs were sinking back in their sockets and shrinking down inside, travelling to the bubbling core of my unconscious brain. The world outside my body melted away, and there was that stiffness again, the hardening of the shoulders that I'd felt that day at the hoodoos. It gripped me, from my shoulders through my arms and down all the way into my toes and back up through my neck. She had done it on purpose. Perhaps she'd done it to hurt me, but really it would do more harm to Waldo. He was only a helpless creature who had no idea what was being done to him when his leash was unclasped. I would not be able to protect him. And even if he did survive, it might be without me.

It was too much to bear. My skull began to vibrate under the pressure. And then it all came shooting out like a bullet from a gun. I felt the pressure lifting, from the centre and back up through my eyeballs. The whole thing must have lasted only a second or two, because when I came back to earth, my vision jackhammering, there was Jez, still standing in front of me with her bum cocked toward her finger.

I struck her. Swift and hard, across the head. The fine hair that had grown tangled and stringy over the course of the day leapt in the air like a writhing rodent, and it was the hair that I watched fall to the ground. The hair was a cover, a shield over the moment as she lay face down in the dirt and leaves for what seemed like minutes. I could not see her face, and so I could believe for that short time that she was not real, not a person, not a child.

"Bad," I said quietly. I found it was all I could say, but I did not know if I was speaking to her or myself. An odd feeling of calm settled over me, warm as a bath.

But I was losing time, I knew. I pictured Waldo in my mind's eye, hopping farther and farther into the brush, and the vision was enough to send a surge of adrenalin through my legs. And so I left Jez there, lying in the dirt, and began calling Waldo's name. With every step I envisioned the scene of his grisly death, bloody limbs trapped in a snare, or torn apart by coyotes, cougars, bears, or squashed on the side of the road, his gangrenous intestines spilling out of his belly. I made my way through the brush, straddling small trees and fallen stumps and branches that poked up my dress. The ground was the brown of Waldo's furry coat, shrouded by a labyrinth of weeds and saplings. At one point I saw a flash of fur and lunged at it, but it turned out to be a squirrel, who quickly shot up a tree trunk. I began to follow a trail of dandelions, tramping through thistles with no care of the spines collecting on the flesh of my ankles. I collected a few dandelions in my fist and began waving them about, calling his name as though I could lure him like a dog. But before long I gave up on any method; nothing here made sense, not to me or to Waldo. The sound of my feet crunching on dead leaves began to crackle in my ears like a broken television, and before long the look of the ground followed suit, blurring to an endless screen of static.

I don't know how long I searched. I meandered through the brush, zigzagging between tress, scouring surrounding campsites, until I came upon the bank of the lake. There was no wind, and the water was still. The way the sun glinted across it seemed maddeningly careless, but by now I had no energy left to be bothered. In the distance, a man and two boys were floating in a canoe, the man paddling capably in the back while the older boy scooped his paddle in the water like a spoon, splashing the child seated in the middle. His cry echoed across the water, and from where I was standing, I could just make out the grimace on his little white face.

I crouched down and let my bottom fall into the pebbled beach.

I cannot say why, but I thought then about a memory I had long ago forgotten. We were children, Ricky and I, quite young. I must have been five or six, which would have made Ricky no more than three. I had his little foot in one hand and the toenail clippers in the other. I'm certain this was not something Mutti would have allowed, seeing as my hands weren't nearly coordinated enough at that age to use the clippers safely. And yet when I placed myself back in that memory, I was quite certain of my capability, and I remember thinking that I could be a mother, and this would be the feeling—taking something sharp to a child's tender little toes, knowing that the tiniest mistake could pierce him, fearing the immense guilt that would come with a single bead of blood. I had been careful, oh so careful, up until the thought arose, and then I was struck by an overwhelming urge to do the opposite. It was an urge not to protect him, but to harm him. And so I edged the clippers down under his pinky toenail, right to the very edge of the quick. I held my breath and clamped down.

The blood bloomed from his nail immediately, a red crescent moon, and Ricky's scream followed close behind. Mutti came running, of course, and pushed me out of the way to console him, snatching the clippers from my hand as she did so. I'm sure I received a good scolding, although that part I don't remember. While Mutti tended to Ricky's wound I sat in my bedroom under my blanket, not out of shame but out of awe at my own power. It was as though I had discovered I was magical, the tips of my fingers sparkling, seething with electricity that only I could see.

I'd lost Waldo. I would not see him again, I knew. My love for him was fierce. And yet, even though I hated Jez for what she had done, I thought I might love her more than I'd ever loved anyone.

What would she think of me now? The thought that she would probably ask to go home, back to her papa, back to things that were familiar and safe, made the panic rise up once again. I'd no idea how long I'd been gone from the campsite where I left her lying on the ground. I pictured her lying there still, a dead animal with a glossy eye peeking between the hair that shrouded her face.

Then came the crunch of leaves behind me, and though for a moment I allowed myself to imagine that Waldo had miraculously returned, it was Jez who came to rest by my side.

And she'd brought someone with her.

15

"WHAT ARE YOU DOING HERE?" I sprang up, scrambling from my haunches to my feet, spraying dry leaves and twigs around me. "Did you follow us?"

"Whoa, whoa there, relax, Missy," the man said. "Name's Sal. Remember me? From back on the highway." His duffle bag was nowhere to be seen.

Jez remained seated on the bank, sucking her thumb.

"I found this poor little missy all by her lonesome over there," Sal continued. "Do you know what happened?"

"Go away!" I shrieked, kicking dirt at him. Some flecks flew into his face and he coughed and spat at the ground.

"What the hell, lady?" he yelled back. "What the hell's going on here? What happened to that kid?" He pointed at Jez.

She stood then and turned her face to mine. The skin was swollen and red on one side. A bruise, purple as an eggplant, had begun to emerge just below her temple. Her eyes were dry and blank.

"Leave us alone," I said to Sal. My voice was strange to me, deep and hollow.

Sal shook his head. "Somethin' ain't right here," he said. "Now I'm trying to help you, see. I think I better call the authorities. We'll get you some help."

Jez let out a little whimper, and a few tears began to drip from her eyes. She was playing along, playing the part she knew she was meant to play.

"I'm warning you," I said to Sal, my gaze fixing on his. He was holding his hands up now, waving them in surrender.

"Look. I dunno what's going on here. I think you got the wrong idea."

I took a step toward him and he stumbled back a bit. I realized then that my fists were clenched.

"I'm just gonna go, okay?" he said, backing away.

I lifted my pinky finger to my lips and tucked it into my mouth, biting once, twice, three times, my teeth bared.

"I'm leaving, okay?" Sal said, shuffling back. "I'm leaving."

Jez and I exchanged glances. We both knew that Sal would not leave without telling. I might have imagined it, but I'm quite convinced that I saw Jez's eyes dart to the large rock in the brush near my feet. An igneous rock it was, sticking out of the dirt like it didn't belong, round as a loaf of bread. We were in the woods, and there was no one else around. The canoe in the lake had disappeared. The gravel road was just out of sight, the mostly vacant campsites at the fringes quiet.

I picked up the rock.

≈

Mutti said it was a woman's pheromones that attracted men. Men were like bloodhounds, always following their noses, and the scent of a fertile woman could drive them mad with desire. It had little to do with looks, she said. Women's noses, on the other hand, were far too sophisticated, and could pick up the nuances of a man and immediately pinpoint his failings, which were always numerous. The problem was that most women were not conscious of these powers, so the key was to learn to interpret the intuitive twinges and make decisions accordingly.

Mutti spoke about her own men as though they were souvenirs—no use at all but good for a fond memory. When I was young I asked her for stories about my father. She would respond with a sigh and one of her many glib tales.

"He was an astronaut, Regina. He flew to Mars. He'll be back in sixty years," she said. Or: "He baked the most wonderful cakes. But he died in a freak baking accident. Something to do with expired yeast." Or sometimes, "Well, he was a dog, you see. An actual dog. I got tired of all the shedding."

I don't recall most of the men—that is, those that Mutti allowed me and Ricky to meet. But I have a vague image of them—all of them grouped into one composite body—as having a reptilian face, wide mouthed and beady eyed.

There is one man who stands out among the rest. Leon had fiery red hair, curly as a doll's, and skin so fair it was nearly blue. He wore a white crystal on a leather string around his neck, and when he caught me eyeing it once he took it off his neck and placed it in my hand.

"It's a magic crystal," he told me. "Healing properties, that kind of thing." The crystal had an oily shine to it, as though it were coated in gasoline, but it was smooth and cold to the touch. "You ever heard of opalite?" he said.

I shook my head.

"It's for psychic abilities, you know. Woooo." He laughed and fluttered his fingers. It was meant to be a joke, but I believed that he could in fact read my thoughts, which was only confirmed when I caught him fondling Mutti's bottom in the frozen foods aisle at Food for Less. Mutti had sent me to get the lemon we forgot, and when I came around the corner to meet them there was his hand, stuffed down the waistband of Mutti's skirt and rolling about beneath the fabric like a pig in mud. At first it seemed he thought no one was looking—the aisle was deserted, just the two of them and the fish sticks, a box of which Mutti was holding, poised to place it in her shopping cart. She put her hand on his shoulder and whispered something in his ear.

I watched them from the end of the aisle, peeking around the corner. I'm embarrassed to admit it now. But the scene was thrilling to me at twelve years old, perhaps because I was just beginning to envision the possibility of my grown-up self having her own romantic liaisons. There was a little tingle in my groin, as though someone had sprinkled a bit of fairy dust there, and in the next instant I was seeing Leon's hand on my own buttocks, kneading them like balls of dough.

At that very moment, Leon's head turned and his eyes found mine. But he did not quit his fondling. He simply watched me, the slightest hint of a smile on his lips. I was convinced then that it was true. He was reading my mind and seeing the dirty thoughts that passed through it.

Mutti, however, was not aware of my presence until I marched out from my hiding spot and announced that I had the lemon. She pulled away from Leon and smoothed her skirt back down.

"What else to go with these?" she asked Leon, holding up the fish sticks. Her cheeks were pink. "Rice?"

It was a strange age, twelve, which is perhaps why I am able to remember it so clearly. Around this same time I'd been having a recurring nightmare. In the world of the dream, I was losing my teeth. They were not simply falling out the way a baby tooth does, releasing itself neatly to create a clean space for the adult tooth to grow in. Rather, my teeth were cracking, breaking at the root to leave jagged shards protruding from my gums. The pieces crumbled out of my mouth, a rock slide in miniature scale. And I was panicked, frantic in front of the mirror, watching it happen, desperate to collect all the fragments of tooth and fit them back into place as though mending a china vase. But there was no glue, no way to fuse the pieces together again.

There was never any blood at all in this dream, which made it somehow more terrifying. My mouth an alien part of me, like a secret prosthesis.

I had a children's picture book that I kept hidden away in my nightstand as a weapon against the dream. The story was about a bunny who gets lost in the woods at night and encounters a host of terrifying creatures on her search for home. In the morning, however, her papa takes her back along her route to show her that the hulking bear she saw was really just a rotted old log, the howling banshee was an owl in a tree, and so on. The moral of the story, as you might guess, is that the world is always more frightening in the dark, but in the bright sunshine of the day you can see things for what they truly are.

Even at twelve years old, I could return to this storybook and fool myself into forgetting the horror of the dream, and I wouldn't have to leave my room to find Mutti's bed cold and empty, the sheets still tucked and stretched tight as a trampoline. I was old enough to know that when Mutti stayed out all night she was with a man, but young enough to be wilfully ignorant about what they would be doing together for an entire evening. But on occasions when Mutti was home, I preferred to go to her, descending the stairs to see her curled up on her armchair with a teacup in her hand. She would set the tea down, open her arms, and let me become a baby once again, wrapping and rocking me and smoothing my hair.

One particular night began as usual: the dream came, and the panic, and I woke with a start. I opened my eyes and saw out my window a bright star in the clear midnight sky. There was a moment of perfect release in which I emerged, sweaty with relief, creeping out from the bounds of the dream and back into reality, with all my teeth firmly in place. But here, in the real world, something was different.

What I heard was white noise, like a blank channel on a television, which was what I pictured—the flickering snow of the screen—as I lay there, calming my beating heart and slowly coming into my body. I turned onto my side and the sound stopped, then started again. It was not a television, I realized. It was water. Running water. Mutti was in the kitchen, making herself some tea, I presumed. The clock on my bedside table clicked to 3:42 as I climbed out of bed and made my way downstairs.

It should have been so ordinary; it was not unusual for Mutti to be awake and making tea in the middle of the night. But something about the rhythm of the tap turning on and off planted a seed of worry in my gut, and without thinking, I tiptoed down the stairs, making sure to avoid the creaky spots that I'd memorized over the years.

Mutti's coat, left in a heap on the floor, met me at the foot of the stairs. A few steps beyond it lay her rumpled cardigan. I stood there for a moment surveying the trail of clothing that led from the front door to the kitchen. The water kept pouring—on, off, on, off. From the kitchen came a soft blue glow. I crept toward it slowly, feeling heat flare up once again against the damp of my nightshirt.

Mutti was standing at the sink, barely lit by the stray light from the stove, which was always left on as a kind of night light for midnight wanderings. I could make out only the outlines of her body, shifting side to side like a skipping record. Her head was bent and therefore seemed to be missing. I flicked on the overhead light.

I saw the sponge of her bare bottom flash as she turned, then her unbound breasts, which hung and jiggled like the chin of a turkey. Her gaze, like a predator's, pinned itself to mine. In her hands was a bit of fabric, waterlogged and milky white between her clutching fingers.

"Oh," she said, her shoulders falling as she turned back to the sink. "It's you."

It seemed an odd thing to say to me, her daughter, and I wondered if she hadn't recognized me on account of her glasses being set on the counter beside her instead of perched on her nose. I didn't say anything, but she went on with her task, which I could see now was scrubbing the fabric. Wetting, scrubbing, wetting, scrubbing. She did not seem bothered by the fact of her nakedness. Mutti was the kind of woman who was fond of closing doors and wrapping herself in a long robe that covered even her ankles when she passed from bathroom to bedroom after her bath, and yet here there was no shame at all in her look, her posture.

I sat down at the table, unsure about what I was doing there. I remember saying something silly like, "Am I awake?" because I felt as though I must still be floating in a kind of dream world, but Mutti did not answer. Instead, she said, "I'll tell you something, Regina." She went on working the fabric. "There's something in a man that can turn him bad," she said. Her voice was strange and deep.

I knew better than to ask questions.

"It's something you cannot control. Neither can he."

I waited for her to give an explanation, but none came. Instead, she threw down the fabric with a wet smack.

"Throw it out," she said. "What am I doing, just throw it out." Then she showed me the thing. I do not know why. She held up the fabric by its ends, letting it drip on the linoleum, and I saw that it was a pair of her underpants. The white ones with little strips of lace around the leg holes. I had an identical pair, same size and colour. The only difference now was the copper-coloured stain that bloomed from the centre, a goblin emerging from a cave. It was far more frightening than my dream, precisely because it was entirely unknown and beyond my understanding—I had never imagined such a sight. And now that I had seen it, the other parts of the room became clearer as well. I saw then that the shirt on the floor was torn, and imprinted on Mutti's thighs were vague shapes, indistinct islands of shadow floating on her skin like a topographical map.

I do not know what became of Leon in the end. After that night Mutti continued to see him for many years, all the way up to the day she left, but she rarely spoke of him or brought him to our house, which kept him at enough of a distance that he could never conceivably become a father figure to us. But for some reason Mutti felt compelled that night to finally tell me about my real father—a story that sounded banal enough to likely be the truth. Mutti said he was a professor of geology at the Freie Universität Berlin, and that he had been obsessed with honey. He'd keep stacks of little jars of it in his office, different flavours and types—clover and buckwheat, alfalfa and huckleberry, creamed and golden. I liked this about him. I asked Mutti why she did not stay with him in Germany, and she laughed. "I would have finished my studies if not for him," she said. And I understood then that he was really no better than Leon. None of them were, according to Mutti. And Ricky, sleeping in the room above us, not yet a man but doomed to become one.

16

"LITTLE BUNNY FOO FOO," I sang as we sped down the highway. My voice was trembling. "Do you know that one?" I asked Jez. "Hoppin' through the forest." The road stretched ahead, straight and clean as a knife.

Jez said nothing. She only stared ahead, her palms flat on the seat at her sides. The bruise on her face seemed to throb like a heartbeat.

"Scoopin' up the field mice," I continued, feeling out the melody. "And boppin' them on the head."

I'd left him. Waldo was gone. I'd abandoned him there, somewhere in the wild. He might live, but it would be a life of constant fear.

"Will he be okay?" Jez said quietly.

"Yes, of course," I said. It occurred to me that she might not have meant Waldo. Either way, I could not answer truthfully. The whole world seemed unknowable now.

"I can't remember the rest," I said. "Something about a good fairy who tells Bunny Foo Foo to stop boppin' the heads of the poor little field mice."

"She turns him into a goon," Jez said.

"Ha, oh yes. You're right." I patted her knee, and she did not flinch.

The trees stood uniform as matchsticks alongside the highway, making a dense shroud as we rushed past.

"Jez," I said, and she turned her bloated, purple face toward me. "I lost control. I'm terribly—" and here I began to blubber, a tangle of regret coming up in my throat. I let out a sob, and then sucked it back in. "I'm so sorry."

"Sorry for what?" she said quietly, twisting Earl's horn in her fingers.

"I didn't mean to hurt you. Or frighten you," I said. "Sometimes I can't seem to stop myself, something takes over and—no. There's no excuse for it."

"You didn't," she said.

"Didn't what?"

"Didn't frighten me."

"But—your face. Is it—painful?"

"Not much," she said, poking her cheek with her finger. "It'll go away."

My guilt seethed, a physical agony, like my insides were being squeezed slowly and steadily. Some part of me wanted her to be upset— to scream and cry and beg to return to her parents. If she were upset, I would have a penalty, however small, to suffer. But instead, I took the way out and buried it like always. Even though the reminder of my cruelty was right there on her face, it was easier to go on like it hadn't happened. *It'll go away.* Truth be told, it was what I needed to do to live with myself.

I pulled in at a gas station with an old, graffitied pay phone mounted on the outside wall. I left the car running with Jez sitting inside while I thumbed coins into the battered slot. Ricky picked up immediately, before the first ring had finished.

"Hello?" he said, his voice pinched.

"Ricky," I said. "Don't worry. Everything is okay." It was a bald-faced lie, as much to him as to myself.

"What in god's name, Regina? Where are you?"

"We're just taking some time," I said. "We're giving you and Carla some time to think."

"Where the hell are you?"

"Away," I said. "I can't say. I just wanted you to know that Jez is fine. We're having a fine time." I sounded like the worst liar there had ever been.

"You've got no idea what you're doing, Regina. This is not going to go well for you. You don't want this."

"Are you going to call the police?" I goaded.

He hesitated. "You know I won't do that," he said. "You're lucky that Carla is in such a state that she's not pushing for it either. But I will come after you."

"You don't know where we are," I said.

"I can find out," he said. "I can dial star-sixty-nine and find out where you're calling from. It'll tell me exactly where you are."

I said nothing. I could not tell if he was bluffing. Was such a thing really possible?

"Just stay right there. I'll be there soon. Listen to me, Regina. You aren't prepared to handle this. Just wait for me to come and we can forget all of it."

I hung up the phone. The car's engine hummed. Jez's big brown eyes stared at me through the reflection of the gas station logo in the windshield.

We needed to get off the QE2. We got back on the road, and I told Jez to watch out for signs for the 2A. When we took the exit, the already sparse traffic fell away, and I felt a slight loosening in my chest.

Jez sighed, apparently disappointed that this road looked exactly the same as them all. "When will we get there?" she asked.

"It's very far away," I said. "But we can stop for a break soon." I began a silent countdown in my head. Two more hours. If we could just get two hours away from the place where I'd called Ricky, two and a half from the campground at Baptiste Lake, we'd be able to find a place to safely stop for the day.

"You don't even know where we're going, do you?" Jez said.

My first impulse was to reject her. *Of course I know where we're going.* But I decided instead that it would not make a difference, that I might as well be truthful to someone.

"No," I admitted.

Oddly, this seemed to satisfy her. She rested her head against the window and watched the road whiz by. "There wasn't too much blood," she said. "You won't turn into a goon."

"I hope that's true," I said. I kept driving forward, my eyes pinned to the road.

After some time, I thought she'd fallen asleep. But then she sat up straight in her seat. "Look," she said, pointing out her window.

I looked. Smoke. Plumes of smoke were rising from somewhere behind the trees like the fingers of a blackened hand.

"Must be a fire," I said. "A forest fire." As if on cue, the smell of burning wood hit my nostrils. I sucked it in.

"Mmm," Jez said, doing the same. I drove on, watching the sheaf of smoke move nearer and nearer. It appeared we were driving toward it.

"Is it a big fire?" Jez said.

"I'm not sure," I said, though inside I was certain it was. How had I not noticed the smoke earlier, I wondered. My head was not right; my brain felt as loose and gelatinous as a collapsed custard. "Perhaps. It's quite a lot of smoke." My jaw clenched tighter, sending a pang of electricity up the back of my neck. On the other side of the highway, a grassy field splayed out into the distance, an old farmhouse perched on the horizon line like a paper cut-out. Another car passed in the opposite direction, the shadowed head in the driver's seat flicking between the road and the smoke.

"Hopefully someone has called the fire department," I said quietly. I had no idea what one was meant to do in this circumstance. Surely the authorities were already aware. There hadn't been a drop of rain for months and the summer heat had been unrelenting, so the forest was undoubtedly parched enough to make a fire inevitable. I turned on the radio and twirled the dial, searching for an information station. There was nothing but the effervescent fragments of a twangy country song.

"Can *we* call the fire department?" Jez asked. She was pulling on the ends of her hair, her hands clenched in tight little fists.

"No," I said.

"Why?"

"Because someone else will. Probably already has."

"How do you know?" she said, looking behind us at the deserted road. "What about all the creatures? The chipmunks and beavers and lions?"

"There aren't any lions here," I said, and then realized I was wrong. Cougars were lions. There might be cougars. On some silly impulse I scanned the trees for a slinking feline body until my reason kicked in. I wondered briefly how Jez had become so well versed in the wildlife of these parts.

"Can we stop?" she asked, rolling down her window. Her hair flew up around her like frantic bats. The hot air filled the car, and I coughed a bit with the strength of the smoky smell. The wind must have picked up or changed direction, because the smoke was now visible in the air, clouds of it puffing through the window.

"Jez, it's not safe," I barked, just as we rounded a corner and came right up against the edge of the fire, creeping to the ditch that lined the road. I slammed on the brakes and pulled up on the shoulder.

"My god," I said, clutching the wheel. The flames alongside us were not yet high—only knee height—but the fire that burned in the forest beyond was raging. The heat pressed in on us from the passenger side.

"Whoa," said Jez, her head poking out the open window. She coughed but did not move to cover her mouth.

I regained my composure and pressed the button to roll Jez's window back up before veering back onto the road. I coughed, my eyes watering. The smoke seared my throat.

"What are we doing?" Jez said, smearing her arm across her own watery eyes. "Aren't we stopping?"

"We can't stop," I said. "The firefighters will come."

"I'm not afraid," she said, crossing her arms.

"I know," I said. "Of course you aren't." I pressed harder on the gas pedal. The speedometer surged to 130.

Jez let out a sudden gasp, and I pounded the brakes again in my nerve-racked state. The car snaked. The wheel wobbled, left right left, before righting again. I caught my breath and slowed the car steadily.

"Hokay, phooooo," I said, forcing air out and in, out and in, to settle the quake of my hands.

"It's a doggie!" Jez said.

At the brink of the forest, something was emerging from the trees. It was grey-furred and slender, and if it wasn't for its rust-coloured haunches it would have blended seamlessly with the smoke in the air. Its pointed ears perked at the sight of us.

It was a coyote. And then another, and another. Three coyotes, running from the flaming forest. We swooped past and I slowed even more, watching them in the rear-view mirror. They looked with their sly, pointed faces diligently up and down the highway before crossing, their feet gambolling over the black asphalt.

"Stop," Jez said, and for some reason I did. Before I even grasped what was happening she jumped out of the car and ran out into the road, following the coyotes' path. It looked as though she wanted to chase them, but they were already slinking into the trees on the other side of the highway.

"Jesmin," I said, stumbling out of the car after her. The air was thick and hot. "Please don't."

I can still feel the twist of my heart when I think about how Jez began to cry. She stood in the road, choking and coughing on smoke and tears, and I knew that she was imagining the animals in the forest, trapped, the flames licking their legs and crawling up, up their bodies. She was imagining them burning, slowly, their flesh falling away into sizzling meat. I was too. And of course, even though the campground was far in our wake, I could not help but imagine Waldo in the flames, his body a marred heap of glowing ash, his eyes burned to holes. Somehow, it was better that way.

Back in the car, as the road took us away from the fire and the smoke began to dissipate, Jez said, "I wish it was me."

"Who?" I said. "Do you mean in the fire?"

"I wish it was me who got shot." She pressed her fingers into her swollen eye socket. "Me instead of Adam."

We drove for miles and miles, until the fire was beyond our sight and the gas light on the dashboard flashed on. I breathed a sigh of relief that a clear next step had presented itself. We stopped at a small roadside station where the rusted pumps were ancient and so necessitated a visit into the convenience shop to find an attendant. I poked my head in, ringing the little bell on the door, but the place was empty. The aisles were tightly packed with all manner of plastic trinkets, salty snacks, and candies. I paced through them and plucked a bag of Cheezies and a carton of Junior Mints from the racks.

"Hello?" I called out. No answer. Jez was sitting in the car alone outside. The seconds ticked by like hours. I moved toward the washrooms to listen for rustlings inside. I heard a flush, then the whishing of a tap. The box of mints jostled in my hand as though something alive were inside.

A man wearing overalls finally emerged from the washroom and jumped at the sight of me standing at the entrance to the hallway.

"Jesus!" he cried out, clutching his chest. One of the straps of his overalls was much longer than the other, making the front bib sag on one side. "Sorry, you gave me a start." He looked me up and down, wiping his damp hands down the front of his legs. His slow gaze settled on the snacks in my hands. "I'll get you all sorted out here. You need some fuel as well?"

I nodded, but just as I was turning to follow him something caught my eye. Among a rack of pamphlets and brochures was an advertisement. The huge black letters against a bright yellow background read MAKE YOUR ESCAPE. I yanked the pamphlet out of the rack.

"You aren't headed toward Athabasca, are ya?" the man asked as he rang up the snacks. "Heard there's a big wildfire right up on the road." He was not old—maybe forty—but the way he pressed the buttons with a searching finger, squinting at the screen, made him seem withered and helpless.

"Really," I said, avoiding his eyes. He paused, waiting for more, but I pressed my lips together and held out my hand for the receipt.

It wasn't until I was back in the car, waiting for the man to fill the tank, that I read what the pamphlet was for.

VIA Rail Adventure Routes: Jasper to Prince Rupert

*The Jasper–Prince Rupert train travels 1,160 km between
the Rocky Mountains and the northwest Pacific Coast.
With its dramatic and diverse landscapes, the route takes in
some of the most stunning scenery in Canada.*

Come escape with us!

It was a sign, surely. It was too fortuitous to overlook. We could make it to Jasper by tomorrow afternoon. We could leave the car behind, rid ourselves of Waldo's vestiges scattered across the back seat and the sweat and dirt and tears and smoke that had seeped into the upholstery, the mingling stink of it all that was impossible to ignore. We could let ourselves be taken away, let the train determine our escape.

I rolled down my window as the man finished up. "Thank you," I said to him, reaching out a hand and pressing it to his bare, hairy forearm. I scarcely knew what I was doing, and apparently neither did he, for he blushed and took a step backward. I'm not one for gestures of affection, but I felt an overwhelming gratitude, as though he were some kind of saviour.

As my window slipped back into its casing, sealing us into the fuzzed silence of the car, I turned to Jez. Her eyes were still red, from crying or the smoke or likely both, and the bruise on her face had deepened to the colour of a blueberry. Her legs were drawn up on the seat, her chin resting on her knees, and it occurred to me then that she looked like a blueberry, a half-formed blueberry that had shrivelled in the sun.

"How would you like to meet your oma?" I said to her. I turned the key in the ignition.

The overalled man waved goodbye to us as we pulled out of the station, his smiling face bright and benign as snow.

ALTER

Minerals replace the decaying bones. What is left is no longer bone, but rock—a replica of the original.

17

Dear Regina and Richard,

I will not try to apologize because I know it's too late for that. I don't expect forgiveness. I only ask you to consider this. What is the worst thing I could have done? Now think about how I chose not to do it.

I will tell you something about what the last twelve years have been like, not as an excuse but perhaps a kind of explanation.

For many years, I woke up each morning thinking I would be hearing the knocking at my door, and that would be it. The fact that this never came tells me that Leon was even more ashamed of what happened than I. But I have had much time to think over the passing of years, and what I realize now is that I had to leave, even if I had no repercussions to fear. I left because I was afraid of

*myself—what I could do. And what I could not do. So I ran
away. But of course one cannot escape oneself. Still, I am
better for having left, and I am certain you, my children,
are as well.*

*Anything I have left at the house is yours. You can give
my carbon film fossils to the Tyrrell Museum. I told them
to expect the donation and they offered to name me as
a benefactor, but I gave your names instead.*

All my love,

Mutti

I have always thought myself an honest person, but I also believe that some things are better buried inside. Hiding the truth from someone is different from telling a deliberate untruth. It would not have been constructive for me to reveal to Ricky all the truths about the letter Mutti had sent three years ago. After all, as it turned out he was not eager to hear any of it. So I chose not to tell him that the letter had arrived in an envelope that had Mutti's return address written in her sprawling cursive hand in the corner. While Jez used the bathroom at a Subway in Swan Hill, I dug the letter out of the front pocket of my suitcase. I looked at the address on the envelope. The words *Prince Rupert*, BC seemed to lift off the paper. I left the letter folded inside the envelope and slid it into the glove compartment.

It now made perfect sense to me that Mutti would have found a train when she left Drumheller. She once told me that in Wuppertal, the magical city, the train is a kind of parallel universe. She described how thousands of people move, every day, on a different plane, a layer above the river and the roads and the sidewalks that roll out across the land below. I can picture her, Mutti, standing on the street and looking straight up at the train as it speeds away. She would feel a strange sensation, I think, of being upside down—suspended herself, caught between the sky and the moving train below, waiting for something solid to land on.

I remember also Mutti's stories about the terminal station of the Schwebebahn, where the rail mechanism has its own enclosed room. Though Mutti had no photographs of the place, she described it to me as an attic, walls made of wooden planks, which meets the wheels at the end of their journey. She told me that as a teenager she used to sneak past the signs and barriers, climb inside the attic through the panel for maintenance workers, and watch the wheels moving across the floor, like miniature trains themselves, coming to a rest for some indeterminate time before surging without warning back in the other direction. The way she described it made it sound comforting—an enclosed, secret space that seemed to belong only to her.

Mutti hadn't told me those fifteen years ago that she planned on leaving. But I knew. I knew it as soon as I saw the bruises, which she tried to hide all day with a white silk scarf that she'd looped in a tight spiral all the way up her neck. With her red-faced head perched on top, she looked like a dollop of whipped cream topped with a cherry. When I walked into her room just as she unwrapped the scarf, revealing black shapes like shadow puppets on the skin of her neck, she said, "It's not what you think." I did not know what I thought, but I turned around and tiptoed back down the stairs, where I found Ricky eating leftover chicken in the living room. I stood behind the couch across from the armchair where he sat, unsure about what to do with myself. He was watching a new episode of a boorish reality TV show that he'd decided he liked all the more because I so disdained it, and on the screen the contestants were being shown something that looked to be a horrible dead worm the sickly colour of pantyhose. Ricky was gnawing the knob of a chicken bone as he watched the host of the show dangle the flaccid worm, the camera cutting to close-ups of coagulated chunks dripping from its end.

"It's a pig rectum," Ricky announced, not taking his eyes from the screen.

"A pig rectum," I repeated. "But … why?"

Ricky shrugged. "I suppose for many people it's the worst thing you could imagine eating. So that's the point. It's all about how far you're willing to go." A heavily tanned woman in tight athletic pants with pink stripes at the hips was now tearing the meat into chunks, the tube stretching and flopping like a rubber band, and shovelling the chunks into her mouth, retching as she chewed.

"Ugh," Ricky said, tossing the bone to his plate and pressing the greasy side of his finger to his lips, but it was clear from the sparkle in his eyes that he was enjoying it. I stood by, watching with him but finding myself unable to sit down. The woman threw up once, then sucked a deep breath of air through her nose, smearing her chunk-coated hands across her cheeks to get the stray hairs out of her face, and resumed shovelling. Her jaw worked at a ferocious speed, her chin jerking mechanically up and down. The host of the show and another man, who appeared to be her husband, watched at the sidelines, delivering gasps and claps and cries of shock to which the woman seemed oblivious. The husband periodically cheered, "Babe! C'mon! Yeah, babe! You got this!" A clock at the bottom of the screen counted down, pulsing with each second. The woman gave no reaction to the cheers; she appeared to be somewhere else entirely, disembodied from the task she was performing.

When she finished swallowing the last quivering blob, the woman opened her mouth, stuck out her tongue—whitened down the middle like the tail of a skunk—and raised her hands in victory. Though her husband grinned as he ran to hug her, she did not. She had the triumphant look of a warrior on her stony, wide-eyed face.

"She did it," Ricky said, wiping his fingers on his pant legs. I could not watch any more after that, even though I longed for a distraction from the image of Mutti's bruises, which kept screening itself over my eyes, refusing to dissolve no matter how much I tried to blink it away. Then I began to picture Leon's hands on her neck, squeezing slowly, that same impish smile on his face as that day in the grocery store. Mutti with that same stony-faced expression as the woman on TV, still and unblinking as a doll.

The last time I saw Leon was the very next day. I was in Mutti's closet, having just discovered that half of her clothes were gone and the rest had been left in shambles, tossed and heaped in piles on the floor. Leon burst into the house, calling Mutti's name. I ran to the top of the stairs and he was already halfway up.

His face was ghastly. I let out a bit of a yelp when I saw it. One eye was swollen shut, purple and wet as a ball of chewed-up bubble gum, and the skin all around was patchy and red. The hair on half his head had been shaved off, a ragged line down the centre where stubbly head met orange hair. His eyebrows were gone.

"Where is she?" he screamed.

I was so shocked at the sight of him that I could not speak. He looked like a bug-eaten potato, his pitted face and mouth gaping black in the floodlit corridor.

"Do you see this?" he hollered, pointing a finger at his eye. "I fucking woke up like this!" He tore up the stairs and stomped from room to room. I stood out of his way, my back up against the linen closet, my limbs stiffened as a mannequin, vainly wishing I could become inanimate if only I could hold my position for long enough.

"Your mother is fucking crazy," he muttered as he searched all the corners and closets. He stopped in front of me once he realized she was nowhere to be found. I tried not to breathe. "She's a sick bitch, you know that? Don't believe anything she tells you. She asks for it, for fuck's sake. She asks me to hurt her, begs me, and I don't even like it but I just fucking do it anyway." His voice was shaking, breaking like a little boy's. "And you know the craziest thing? She thought I had my eye on *you*. Like some kinda twisted fuck. I mean, who's the twisted fuck here?" He turned and fumbled his way down the stairs, his shoes leaving skiffs of mud on the carpet. He left the front door open behind him.

Just outside the house, watching Leon stalk across the lawn, stood Ricky. As I descended the stairs I saw him there, framed in the open doorway. He was eighteen years old, but there was that round baby face, a look of sheer terror carved across it.

Ricky and I never talked about that day. As we did with anything that would force us to acknowledge we were human beings with frail hearts, we buried it deep, pushing it down through the layers until it seemed so far away it no longer existed. And even when the police came to visit our house, asking where Mutti had gone, and Ricky heard my account of everything Leon had said about Mutti, he never brought it up again.

There was just one time, however, after Ricky began dating Carla, that he accused me during one of our domestic spats of having "abandonment issues." It was obvious to me that this was a phrase Carla had been feeding to him, and that he was beginning to buy into it.

"What does that mean?" I asked him, laughing in a way he surely knew was phony.

"It's not funny," he said. "It means that you're afraid all the time. Afraid of opening up. Afraid of taking risks."

"What risks would you have me take?"

He wouldn't answer at first, just shook his head. Then, "What about Mutti? You could have gone after her."

"And done what?" I said. "Dragged her back here to rot in a life she didn't want?"

His face was stunned. "Unbelievable," he said. "How could you be so pathetically naive?"

They were only words, and I have a particular talent for seeing words as ephemeral things, fleeting and powerless. Sticks and stones, as they say. *The rocks don't care.*

≈

As the orange sun sank low in the sky, I pulled the car into a roadside motel. It had felt like the longest day I'd ever lived. I thought of one of Mutti's sayings: *Anfangen ist leicht; beharren eine Kunst. To begin is easy; to persist is an art.* Neither Jez nor I had slept since sometime around two o'clock that morning. Even so, we slept fitfully in the queen bed we shared, wearing only our underwear on account of the heat and stuffiness of the room. Jez's tiny body kept rolling into the trench made by my weight pressing into the pillowy mattress, and each time she shimmied back over, the skiff of her callused feet against my bare leg would jar me to alertness. And of course I was plagued by thoughts of Waldo, drifting into half dreams and then out again, with an ache like a fist cinched around my heart. Waldo hopping through the campground, sniffing my fading tracks, Waldo falling off a rocky bank and splashing into the lake, Waldo being torn to shreds by a bear, Waldo in the dark woods, trembling.

We gave up trying to sleep around six a.m., slinking out of bed and dressing in the dark in the same clothes we'd worn the day before because I'd been too exhausted to unload our suitcases. Jez put on her furry coat and it looked limp and dirty, as though it had ventured into a swampy lake sometime in the night. She looked like Ricky in that moment, the way she held herself with shoulders slumping under the weight of so much disappointment.

18

BY NOON THE NEXT DAY we'd made it to the foot of the Rockies. The mountains seemed to grow upon us, shearing higher and higher, edging out the sky as we neared. There is something about watching a wall of solid rock moving steadily toward you, the dimensions of its surface shifting with each slight change in view, that makes it seem alive, like some mythical beast drawing you into a fantasyland. At one point I even thought I glimpsed a giant face etched into the rock, its eyes black gashes narrowing on us as we passed.

Neither I nor Jez had ever seen such mountains up close—pointed, snow-capped peaks like the ones out of storybooks. Jez's head was tipped back, her forehead resting on the window, eyes pointed up at the jagged line where peaks met sky. I thought I caught her eyes move for a split second to her own face in the side mirror. The swelling had gone down, but the skin all around her right cheek was still purply blue, like a grape stain. Was she thinking about Sal, I wondered. Or Adam? Her expression betrayed nothing.

We'd been driving for five hours. To throw off Ricky, I'd opted to circle back south and then head west on the 11—a less-travelled route than the Trans-Canada. The clock on the dashboard flashed to 12:27, and I thought about how I was scheduled to work at noon. Darrell would be calling. I'd never been late, never in fifteen years.

We were climbing steadily, up, up the mountain road, curving around cliff faces and blasted-out passages through the rock. We came around a bend, and a cluster of mountain goats were licking salt off the road, to Jez's delight. I advanced the car slowly, and they parted lazily to let us through.

Jez's demeanour seemed to be lightening the higher into the mountains we climbed. She bounced around in her seat, looking here and there, pointing at each little glassy pond and every sign for a hiking trail or a campground and asking to stop. We'd received a brochure from the attendant at the Jasper National Park entrance, and because the picture on the front was of a giant grizzly crossing the highway, she was convinced that bears were roaming all over the woods. Her excitement was rather infectious; I began to feel lighter myself, or perhaps it was the relief of the cold mountain air that smelled of ice and pine.

A sign for the Columbia Icefield popped up along the road just as it was coming into view. There it was, a blot of white like a fallen cloud on the grey mountains. It was indeed a field made of ice—a huge sheet of it spread across a valley between two enormous mountains. I believe I gasped at the sight. I'd never have thought that ice could inspire such a feeling of awe. But it was not really the ice itself, more so the enormity of it and the way it seemed to be one huge animal, frozen in action, like a still frame from a movie. You could see from its shape, the way it seemed to be pouring over itself, that it was creeping forward ever so slowly.

Jez saw it too, and stared as we drove toward it, her eyes shining. "We made it," she said. "It's the Arctic."

I hadn't the heart to crush her fantasy. "Amazing, isn't it?" I said. At the base of the glacier were clusters of people, tiny as insects, walking on the ice.

"That's where they found the mummy," Jez said.

"What? Whose mummy?"

"The mummy, the body of the explorer. He died and they buried him in the ice, and the ice kept him from coming apart."

"Ah," I said. "A mummy. Interesting."

"There!" She pointed to a turnoff into a parking lot. The sign read *Athabasca Glacier Trailhead*. "That's where we can stop. See?"

Against my better judgment, I took the turnoff. It was foolish to be stopping at a tourist attraction, I knew. There were dozens of other cars taking the turn. But it seemed impossible not to let Jez see the glacier up close for herself when she was practically glued to the window with fascination.

We followed the road up, our view of the glacier sliding away behind the mountains, and ended up in a gravel parking lot. When I opened the door a blast of icy air swept over me, like opening a refrigerator. I shivered, my skin still damp with sweat. All around were scattered boulders and piles of loose grey rock, backed by the endless mountainscape in the distance.

"Come on, Auntie," Jez said. She was already out of the car, her feet crunching on the gravel. A path began at the edge of the parking lot, and a few other groups of people were ambling out of their cars and walking toward it.

My dress was so wrinkled around the waist it looked like crumpled paper, but I smoothed it as best I could, caught my breath, and followed Jez to the path. Everyone around us seemed to be dressed in brightly coloured athletic gear. Some even carried hiking poles. They stared at me, huffing along on the path. It was nothing I was unaccustomed to, but their eyes felt like accusations. I remembered then that Jez's bruise was still there.

"We can't stay long," I told her. I was trudging behind her, her legs moving too quickly for mine to match. A crude fence made of rope strung up on metal poles marked the path. Jez stopped at a blue sign up ahead and beckoned for me to catch up. I had to bend over and put my hands on my knees once I reached her. I breathed deeply, filling my lungs with the cool air. Although I was out of breath the cooling sensation was a relief, like my insides were being washed clean.

"What is that?" Jez asked, motioning toward the sign.

"It says," I said between breaths, "the glacier. Was here. In 1982."

She thought about this for a moment. "That was a long time ago, right?"

"Well, sort of," I said. "The glacier is slowly melting, you see. So it used to be much bigger. It used to come all the way down to here. I was even smaller than you when it was this big." I held my hand down to demonstrate how small my stature would have been as a toddler.

She tilted her head. "You got a lot bigger, and the ice got a lot smaller," she said.

"Yes. Precisely."

She continued up the path. "I'll show you where they found the mummy," she said.

It seemed too late to explain to her now that this was nowhere near the Arctic. I suspected that even if I did try to tell her, she would refuse to believe me. She'd brought Earl along with her, tucked up into her coat sleeve, and she whispered to him from time to time as she walked.

By the time we reached the base of the glacier my face was dripping, my knees aching. I sat on a small boulder next to a cairn of rocks someone had built. Groups of people milled about, taking pictures of themselves in front of the flood of permafrost spreading out behind them. Jez and I looked out upon it, saying nothing. The snow was a dirty grey from here, tinged with patches of soft blue. Cracks like giant claw marks splayed out toward us.

"There," Jez said, pointing way out into the distance. I couldn't see anything but snow, all the way into the horizon. "That's where it was," she continued. "They found a grave and they had to dig deep deep down to get the body."

Another child standing nearby looked at Jez, then at me. The look on his face was like he'd been caught doing something naughty.

"Shh," I said to Jez. "I don't think any bodies were dug up here." I shielded my eyes from the sun and looked anyway in an effort to see what her mind had invented. The little boy's father looked at us too, then pulled his son nearer.

"But they did," she said. "They wanted to know why he died."

"I see." I pulled Jez in, her bruised cheek against my thigh. "And did they find out?"

"Yes. It was something inside him. Something that no one could see. It wasn't his fault, he didn't know."

I heard a story on the news when I was a girl. Some scientists had found the remains of a lost ship of explorers who had been looking for the Northwest Passage. They'd found a corpse preserved in the ice and exhumed it. There was even a picture of its face. The skin was still there, but it was brown and dry as leather, pulled tight over the bones. The eyeballs were still there too, the wet crescents of the whites floating beneath the half-closed eyelids. The lips had peeled back like split fruit, baring clenched, yellow teeth.

Mutti had caught me and Ricky watching the news story and had quickly shut off the TV. "Disgusting," she said. "The poor man. Trapped there in his body for over a hundred years and they can't even leave him underground?" I remembered that I felt ashamed for having seen it, and the image stuck itself in my mind for days afterward, surprising me each time it popped up, seemingly out of nowhere. The milky, wet eyes. The bared teeth.

"Yes, I think you're right," I said to Jez. I wondered how she'd heard the story. Had Ricky remembered it too? "They got it from the food, didn't they? Their food was in lead cans. They didn't know that it was poisonous. It made them go crazy."

"Some of them ate each other," she said quietly.

"Nonsense," I said, immediately doubting myself. I hadn't heard that part of the story, but it could very well have been true.

"They had to," she said. "They even ate the bones. They cracked open the bones and scooped out the insides."

"I suppose they were desperate," I said. "People sometimes do bad things when they're desperate. But it's not really bad, is it, when there's no other choice."

"Yeah," she said. "They weren't bad. They were just trying to make it go away." She knelt down next to me, letting her shins press against the snowpack, and sat on her heels. "We're home," she whispered into her sleeve, and pulled Earl out, laying him on the snow.

"Time to go," I said, standing. "As I said, we need to get moving. We have a train to catch."

Jez shook her head. "I want to stay here."

"No," I said. "We have to go."

She scrambled away on her hands and knees and grabbed a sharp rock. I pulled on her arm, but she resisted. A few people glanced over. An old woman wearing a plastic bonnet over her white hair stared unabashedly, pointing her puckered frown straight at me, which was intimidating enough to make me let go of Jez's arm. Jez shoved the rock into her pocket and sat on her bum, then pulled up her knees and balled herself up like an armadillo.

I'd seen mothers play a certain trick on their children at Fossil Land, and it seemed an opportune moment to try it. I knew we could not make a scene.

"Fine," I said. "I'll go without you, then. Bye." I began walking away, back down the path, willing myself not to look behind me. I listened for cries of protest or the shuffling of little feet behind me, but heard none. How long to keep up the charade, I wondered. I thought perhaps if I went far enough that she began to lose sight of me, it would become real enough to trigger her reason. I followed the path around a bend and down a hill, surely now out of sight. My steps began to slow. Still nothing coming behind me.

I made it back to the 1982 sign, at which point I allowed myself to turn around. I walked back up the path, passing only strangers moving in both directions. Jez had not followed. She was nowhere along the path, and now I began to scan off the path, all across the rocky plain. It was flat and barren all the way up to the base of the mountain. Nowhere to hide. My heart began to gallop.

I huffed back up to the edge of the glacier, to the boulder we'd been resting on, hopeful that Jez was crouched impossibly small behind it, playing a harmless game. She was not there. She was not anywhere.

Now my mind began a little movie of what had happened as I scrambled back down the path, searching like a blind mole. Ricky had found us. He'd followed us here, and now the police had us surrounded. Jez had been whisked away, wrapped up like a fire victim in a blanket, and the police were now moving in on me, Ricky and Carla standing by in triumph.

When I got back into the parking lot, there were no sirens, no police, no Ricky. But there was a woman standing at the back of our car. She was hardly threatening in her bright-pink jacket and white earmuffs, but she seemed to be examining the car—looking in the windows, then standing in front of the licence plate and taking out her phone.

I nearly cried out in terror. I did not know this woman, but it couldn't be disputed. We were being pursued. I didn't know what else to do but run—run away from her and pray I wouldn't be seen until I could find a place to hide. But then there was Jez. I couldn't leave her. Perhaps she'd already been found. I was running, in such a panic that I moved without direction, without thought, without sight, my feet scrabbling across the gravel.

But then, mercifully, I spotted her. Jez, way up ahead in the distance. I planted my feet, arriving back in reality. She was there, but she was not alone. She was with a grown person, her hand holding theirs. The person pointed at me, and they began to jog together toward me, the grown person pulling Jez along. I was frozen in place, bracing for what I did not know. As they came nearer, I saw that it was a man with blond curls. He was young, with pale skin and kind, wide eyes. His features, plus the way he jogged with a kind of breezy poise, the sun shining behind him, put me in mind of a cherub.

"Is this your little girl?" he called out. "Whew," he said as they skidded to a stop in front of me.

"Oh. Yes," I said, blinking like a newborn fawn. I couldn't think of what else to do but pretend that I'd forgotten her, but then I realized that sounded far worse than the truth.

"She told us you'd left," the cherub said with a forced smile. He clearly wasn't sure whether or not to believe this. His accent was foreign—European. Norwegian, perhaps.

"I was just ..." I ventured, "trying something."

He gave me a queer look. "My wife was looking for you in the parking lot. We thought you went back to your car, perhaps."

"No, no," I said. Relief rinsed out all the knots from my insides. "I've been here, looking for her. I looked everywhere."

"She was out on the glacier, past the fence," he said.

"Was she?" I said, taking Jez's hand from his. "Sorry. I mean, thank you."

"Is she all right?" he said, kneeling down and looking into Jez's face. Jez stared back blankly.

"She had a fall," I said.

His eyes swivelled up at me, then back to Jez.

"I fell off a mountain," Jez said, a little too brightly.

"Oh dear," said the man. "That is … terrible. Well, we found your mother now."

"Thank you again," I said, squeezing Jez in close to me. She played along, wrapping her arms around my hips.

"You're welcome," the cherub said. He put his hands in his pockets, clearly reluctant to leave. We stared at each other. Behind his eyes I could see the workings of his brain, trying to decide what to think of all this. "Be careful," he eventually said. He gave me a strained smile, then jogged down the path toward the parking lot.

Jez put her pinky finger into her mouth and bit once, twice, three times.

I nodded.

Back in the car, I realized that Earl was gone. Everything kept going missing, it seemed, one after another. I asked Jez if she'd dropped Earl somewhere, but she shook her head.

"I had to leave him," she said. "The Arctic is his real home. It's not so hot. He told me it was too hot where we were. It was making him sad. He was sad all the time."

"I'm sorry," I said, pulling the car out of the parking lot and back onto the road. "I'm sorry he had to be sad for so long."

"But he's happy now," Jez said, and smiled at me. She settled back into her seat and sank down, her head nestling into the furry lining of her hood. "I buried him in the ice."

I understood. Ice was not like rocks or earth. It was clean. You could bury something and know that it would stay that way, hidden, without ever really disappearing.

"I'm happy too," I said.

And I was, I knew. I was happy when we parked the car at the train station the next morning and pulled out our suitcases, knowing we'd never see it again. I was happy looking out at the craggy belt of mountains that swathed us on all sides, the creosote smell of the train tracks drifting through the air. And even when the snippy attendant at the ticket booth implied, after sliding her eyes all around the curves of my body, that I should purchase three seats rather than two, I did not care and paid the extra fare without hesitation. It was foolish of me, I know, but at the time it truly felt like we were free—we were going to make it all go away.

19

THE TRAIN WAS not full when we embarked, which was a small mercy. There were a handful of empty seats in our car—six or seven fewer people to stare at me as I squeezed through the aisles, looking for our seats. Thankfully, most of the other passengers were part of a tour group, so by the time we set off they were pinned to the windows, indifferent to me and Jez, oohing and aahing and holding up their cameras to take pictures each time a snow-crested peak came into view between the gaps in the pine forest. Still, I felt enormous among all the normal-sized people plunked into their neat rows like eggs in a carton. I was fortunate then for the ticket attendant's indiscretion, as having two seats to myself meant I wouldn't have to suffer the flesh of some stranger, with his rancid breath and insufferable small talk, pressed up against me.

Years ago, Mutti had told me and Ricky a story about an elephant named Tuffi who once rode the Schwebebahn in Wuppertal—a story Mutti insisted was true, but seemed far too whimsical to be real. The elephant had been the star of a travelling circus, she said, and the circus director had done it as a publicity stunt. Apparently, it was something of a tradition with this circus troupe; each time they found themselves performing in a city with a train, the director would take Tuffi on a ride and invite the city folk to come along for the spectacle. Ordinarily the stunt would go off without a hitch; Tuffi, an extraordinarily docile elephant, would be led onto the train, would stand obediently inside the car while the spectators squeezed in around her, snapping photos and vying for their chance to touch her, pet her, offer peanuts from the palms of their hands to her lithe, grasping trunk. But the Schwebebahn was different. The circus director hadn't accounted for the fact that this train veered and swayed on its suspended rail, and that the elephant had no sense of reason to understand that this feeling of perpetual falling, of hovering, untethered, was not cause to panic. I could not blame her.

Tuffi lost control; she stampeded through the car, breaking things, even tearing a seat off its base. The people, trapped in the car with her as it flew through the air above the river Wupper that snaked below, were terrified, clamouring to get out of her path. Tuffi eventually found a window. She broke it and sailed through, splashing into the river. Remarkably, she survived.

I was certain that the story was only a children's tale until Mutti showed me a picture that her boss had found for her on his computer. There was the Schwebebahn, in black and white, with an elephant falling out the side. Her body, however, was not spread out as you would expect of a free-falling elephant; rather, it was posed in a casual walking stride, angled down toward the water.

"Fake," Ricky said the moment I showed him. I protested at first, but once I examined the photo carefully enough, I noticed that the ears hung loose at the sides of her head rather than billowing out and realized that yes, Ricky was right: the elephant was a cut-out superimposed on the photo, like something out of a Monty Python cartoon.

Mutti shrugged. "The story is real," she said. "That's what matters." To this day I still don't know if she was telling the truth. But I've thought often of the elephant anyway, and how she was small for an elephant, only four years old, and yet must have felt so large and out of place and always on display, a curiosity, even when she just wanted to be an elephant—a fact unto herself. How smashing the window, shattering the image of her own panicked face, then smacking the cold surface of the river would have been welcome, a kind of violent relief.

I pulled the shade down on my own reflection in the window beside me, already brimmed to disenchantment with the mountain vistas. The shade dampened the sunlight that flickered through the trees in rhythm with the trundling of the train on the tracks. Our three seats were spread across the aisle, so I had the two on one side and Jez the one on the other, next to another passenger—a woman, with long, black hair streaked with white, which looked as though it hadn't been cut in many years, as it fell over her shoulders and down her front, the ends nearly brushing her lap. I could tell she was kind; she did not do a double take when she saw me, did not give me shifty eyes when she saw Jez's bruised face. She took out her book and read quietly, the corners of her lips turned up slightly in a smile that seemed fixed on her face. At one point on the ride, when an open plain came into view at her window and a herd of elk dotted across it, she pointed it out to Jez and let her climb onto her lap for a closer look. Later, the train attendant announced that Mount Robson, the highest mountain in the Rockies, would be coming up on the right. The train slowed, passengers pressing up to the windows. The woman laid her book down and Jez stood, moving right up against the window, jamming herself into the woman's knees. They looked together, and from where I sat, they appeared to be so at ease with each other—the woman holding Jez's shoulder to brace her as Jez stood on her tiptoes—that anyone would have believed them to be together. A grandmother and grandchild, with matching dark hair. I craned to see the mountain from my side, though there wasn't all that much to see. The steep, angled face, ridged with thin lines of snow, mimicked the woman's white-streaked hair so perfectly that for a moment the mountain appeared as an extension of her head. The peak was covered in a woolly hat of fog. I imagined a tiny person—a speck, perhaps too small to see even on a clear day—standing in the fog at the tippy top of the peak with a hat on their head, an even tinier person perched atop of it. And so on and so on. Slowly, the mountain shrank away behind us.

As the day went on Jez moved back and forth across the aisle, sometimes squeezing in beside me and sometimes beside the woman. I'd gotten her a colouring book from a grocery store just before we set off, and she kept herself busy with it, though instead of colouring the pictures of rainbows and ponies she drew her own pictures on the blank back pages. I was impressed by her skill with the crayons; she was a far better artist than I, and I regretted that all this time I hadn't known. She drew Earl in every colour and in a dozen variations: swimming, jumping in the air, spearing a slice of pizza. The woman asked her about each of the pictures, and Jez had a little narrative prepared for every one.

"Earl couldn't find any fish because of global warming," she explained. "So I had to give him a piece of my pizza. Then he got a tummy ache because narwhals aren't supposed to eat pizza."

"Well, of course not," said the woman. "Poor Earl."

"And this one," Jez went on, flipping the page. "Here's the grave of the mummy."

"Je—Jennifer," I said to Jez, reaching my hand across the aisle. "Let's give this nice woman a bit of peace." I felt protective of her—not Jez, but the woman. She seemed to be so enchanted by Jez, and I didn't want her innocent perception of us as an ordinary mother and daughter to be spoiled. But Jez continued as if she hadn't heard.

"This is the ice where we buried him. He's dead now but someday we'll find him and dig up his body."

The woman laughed a little, and Jez looked at her with admonishment.

"Oh dear, I'm sorry," she said. "It can be hard to lose somebody."

Jez closed up the book and collected her crayons. "I didn't lose him," she said.

Dusk eventually fell, the windows greying over. We stopped for what seemed like an hour or more alongside a blackening river, waiting for a caravan of freight cargo to pass. Car after car after car chugged by. Jez and I had set to counting them at first but gave up after a hundred. The tourists had all quieted; most were reclined in their seats, and a couple of old people snored softly. The woman next to Jez offered to teach her how to play tic-tac-toe. I closed my eyes, and we began to move again as if by my command. In the dark, the rumble of the train became the distant sound of giant boulders slowly tumbling, down, down the mountain.

I felt something touch my arm, and when I opened my eyes the black-haired woman was leaning over to me.

"I hope you don't mind," she whispered. Jez had put her head down on the woman's lap and appeared to be asleep.

"Not at all," I said, though it was strange to me to see Jez warming to a stranger so unreservedly. She was not typically the cuddly type. It occurred to me that she had never once laid her head on my lap. Her eyelids flicked open then, flashing her wide eyeballs straight at me, then quickly shut again.

"I just love little people," the woman said. "They're so honest." That perpetual smile. I began to wonder if there wasn't something a bit off about her.

We reached Prince George shortly thereafter, where we were to disembark for the night before continuing our journey early the next morning. The other passengers took their time stretching their legs, unloading their suitcases, while I stood wedged in the aisle, a suitcase on either side of me and Jez tugging on the waistband of my dress, both of us yearning for the open door beyond the jam of bodies. I thought again of Tuffi. The smash of the window, the splash of the water.

Though it was dark outside, we walked from the station up the road, relishing the movement of our legs. It was raining lightly. Jez stuck out her tongue to catch the drips as we walked. The suitcases rolled and jostled behind me, skipping on cracks and bumps in the sidewalk. The city had a cold, metallic smell. We'd crossed into another province, and I felt the change. Though there were tall glass buildings and busy, sleepless streets, there was a roughness to the city, as though it still belonged to the earth, as if it had been built underground and had only just risen to the surface.

We ordered pepperoni pizza and ate it in our motel room with the TV blaring, sitting at the ends of our twin beds. I pulled out the map and traced the route we had taken thus far. I measured the line in hundred-kilometre half thumb-lengths. It seemed we'd already travelled more than a thousand kilometres. A lump rose up in my throat at the thought of how far we were from home, how much farther I was now than I'd ever been in my life. I scanned the spiderwebs of various routes we could have taken from Baptiste Lake, the towns and cities smattered all along them. There was no way Ricky or anyone else would know which way we went. I imagined Ricky driving the highways aimlessly, unshaven and wild eyed with panic, following the most natural route up the 2 and then taking the 35, all the way up to High Level, into the snowy North. For a moment I wondered if Carla would be with him, and she popped into the passenger seat briefly, her painted lips pressed in a tight line like a fresh cut, but then I thought better of it and erased her from the image.

We started off again the next morning at 7:30 a.m., leaving the waking city behind. We hadn't slept much; my eyes felt like they'd sunk to the back of my head. But the tourists, rejuvenated, squawked over the various points of interest that were indicated on the map we'd been given of our route. An elderly couple with their two grandsons, who'd joined just that morning for a short scenic ride, kept asking the attendant about every bridge and town, and the grandmother, whose voice was so loud and nasally that it seemed to whine straight into my ear each time she spoke, must have said "Seven Sisters" nearly a hundred times as she scanned for the famous range of toothlike peaks. The grandsons bounced about like monkeys, both wearing striped old-timey engineer's caps.

Jez was subdued by comparison, for which I was relieved. She'd stayed up late into the night watching an endless stream of reruns of old TV shows—All in the Family, Three's Company, Family Ties—before finally dozing off. Now, she could barely stay awake, her head dipping down, chin to chest, and then bobbing back up. The black-haired woman was still sitting next to her, and she leaned over and tapped me on the shoulder.

"Mind if I sit with you for a bit?" she said, motioning to Jez. "I thought I'd give her a chance to stretch out."

My heart began to pump rapidly at the thought of her squeezing in beside me. What if she didn't fit? I eyed the space next to me.

"As long as you don't mind getting a bit cozy with me," she said. I did not think I could say no; after all, she was trying to be kind.

"Of course," I said, shimmying over as best I could. The woman stood up, easing Jez down onto her side and covering her with her coat. As the woman stood and retrieved her bag from under the seat, I could see that she was actually quite thin, her hips narrow. Clearly she'd never had to consider the possibility of not fitting into a seat. As she lowered herself in beside me, I sucked everything in, and she slid into the space between my thigh and the armrest as perfectly as a VHS tape into its slot. When I let out my breath I could feel my flesh forming itself around her bony limbs. "Sorry," I said, cringing. "Is that all right?"

"Oh yes, I'm fine," she said. "Thank you." She introduced herself as Trudy, and I told her I was Lois. I bent my arm in as best I could to shake her hand, but could only reach her fingertips.

I expected her to take out her book, but she didn't. She folded her hands in her lap, smiling away. I realized then that it might be considered odd or even impolite not to make small talk in this situation of forced intimacy, sandwiched together as we were, so tightly it seemed as if our bodies might fuse if stuck there too long. I could smell her unwashed hair. The white streaks glimmered in the sunlight coming through the windows.

"I'm glad the sun is out," I said.

She looked out the window at the trees rushing past. "Lovely day for a train ride," she replied.

"You like trains?" was all I could think to say.

"I do," she said. "I've been on every train in the country, in fact."

"You must travel a lot."

"I like to roam. Back in the day I used to hitchhike."

"You've very brave."

"Not really. I was young, foolish maybe. But back then it wasn't so dangerous. At least it didn't seem so."

"How young were you?" I was faring pretty well with the idle chit-chat, I thought.

"I started when I was seventeen. Hitchhiked from my little back-woods hometown in Ontario all the way to Vancouver."

"Only seventeen? Didn't your parents put up a fuss?"

"Not really. I suppose they knew they couldn't really stop me. I thought I was my own person."

I thought of myself at seventeen, refusing Mutti's hand-me-down dresses. "A big woman cannot afford to be meek," she'd said to me.

"I was shy at seventeen," I said to Trudy. "I never would've had the courage to travel on my own." It suddenly occurred to me that I had been seventeen at the time of the accident with Michelle Landry.

"Well, I might have been more naive than brave. I'd never consider it now. If my granddaughter wanted to do it? No way. Especially not around here."

"It's dangerous around here, is it?" I looked around the train, as if only now I'd acquired an ability to spot the suspicious characters.

"Have you heard of the Highway of Tears?" she said. "That's it, right there." She pointed out the window at the highway beyond the trees, running parallel to the tracks. A semi truck gunned down it, surpassing our speed.

"No," I said. "I haven't heard of it."

"Really," she said. "Well, it's called that because many people have been murdered along that highway. Hitchhikers. Mostly women. A lot of … um … Native women."

I swallowed, my throat dry and tight. "I see."

"So that highway has a reputation. There's still a bunch of people who went missing around this area and were never found. Bones everywhere, they say."

Bones everywhere. I thought about how they said that about Drumheller too, and almost said as much before I realized that would have been insensitive. Dinosaur bones were not the same as human bones. I felt a rush of self-loathing for having to remind myself.

"Aren't the police investigating it though? Won't they find the culprits?" What a stupid, childish thing to say, I knew. But really I was trying to voice something of my own humanity, my own vain hope in goodness. Perhaps voicing it would make it certain.

"Well, I don't think so. These people, the ones who went missing ... well, it's no coincidence that so many of them were ... vulnerable, I guess. Prostitutes, teenage runaways. Drifters."

I nodded. I didn't want to look at her. She seemed genuinely sorrowful as she spoke. I could not help then but think of Sal, riding that beat-up old bike on the breakneck QE2, his duffle bag slung over his shoulder. No one driving by would ever think to slow down for him as they passed.

"They were the kind of people who were already sort of forgotten. It sounds horrible. I feel terrible saying it."

"No," I said. "Don't feel terrible." I'd been afraid of Sal. He'd been a stranger, a man I did not know, too peculiar to be trusted. Wouldn't anyone have been afraid? Perhaps not. What reason did I really have? I'd been unhinged, lifted out of my world and into a strange new one. I was afraid of everyone, everything.

"It's just the sad truth, you know?" the woman continued. "Bad people— they go after the ones they think no one will really miss."

"Yes," I said. "That is sad. Do you think ..."

She turned to me, her face lit white in the sun, the smile still there but somehow turned pensive.

"Do you think," I continued, "they do it on purpose, the bad people? They look for the ones who won't be missed?"

She blinked. "Of course," she said. "That's how they know they'll get away with it." She looked over at Jez then, at her little body unfurled across the seats, deep in a wanton slumber. "What a sweetie," she said. "A little angel."

I thought about the bones. Bones everywhere. In the ditch, between the trees, in a grassy, windswept field, the makeshift gravesites so shallow you might see the knob of a femur, the edge of a skull poking up from the dirt, moon white. They would stay there, turning ancient over the years, with no one to claim them. No one to account for what had happened. No one to blame. *The rocks don't care.*

But they called it the Highway of Tears because there was grief somewhere. Somewhere, someone was still crying for having lost them.

Trudy had been wrong about that; they weren't really forgotten. She was sleeping next to me, her cheek turned into the headrest, and I saw her suddenly for her callousness. It was easier to believe that the killers were deliberate, calculated, that they'd only gone for the ones who didn't matter. That way, you could convince yourself it could never have been you.

I woke her when I dislodged myself from the seat, momentarily lifting her out of hers along with me. But I felt sick; I needed to go to the bathroom. My stomach churned. I felt as though I'd eaten bad meat, a sour taste rising up from my throat. And with it came the image of Sal's forehead, a gash in the shape of an eye right in the middle, leaking blood. Then Michelle Landry. Her face, falling open like an unzipped coat. And then Leon's, so swollen and bulging that it no longer looked like flesh at all.

I got myself inside the bathroom stall and threw up in the toilet, a little bit at first and then again and again, a great emptying of half-digested fast food, bracing myself against the cold metal seat as I pitched this way and that with the swerving of the train. I sat on the floor, which bounced and quivered beneath me. Even though I'd emptied my guts down to the very bottom, I still felt stuffed full, like I'd been filled with sand. I stuck my finger down my throat and retched some more, but nothing came out. I slapped my head. Then again on the other side. Both hands at once, smacking with open palms. My scalp stung. I pulled my hair, hard enough to rip out a few strands. I let them float into the toilet and pushed the button to flush it all away. The sound of it, a great sucking jet, like a desperate gasp.

I leaned my back against the wall. I felt tired, and impossibly heavy. Even my eyelids felt too heavy to keep open. But my mind reeled with questions. What would we say to Mutti when we got to Prince Rupert? How to explain what had brought us there? Adam, Sal, Ricky chasing at our heels? For some reason I hadn't thought that far ahead. What made me think that she would be our salvation, only because of the simple fact that she was my mother?

Me at seventeen again—an age when any normal girl should be independent, self-sufficient, her own person. I'd gone to a movie with

Jonathan Bula, a stocky, mole-faced boy who had been in my class all through elementary and then again in twelfth grade English. I'd once overheard him telling Scott Matwychuk in class that Claire Danes as Juliet gave him a boner. Having never seen one in the flesh, I pictured it just like that—a bone, with knuckles on one end, sticking out of his unzipped jeans.

I did not like him in the slightest, but I admit I was titillated by the notion that a boy might have an interest in me beyond being scandalized by my size, so I'd agreed to the date and even dolled myself up with Mutti's makeup. I had no makeup of my own. And when Jonathan tried to kiss me in the car with lips that looked unnaturally smooth and wet, like sealskin, I had no idea what I was doing, what to say, how to act. I hadn't thought that far ahead. I cowered, shrank back to the window as far as I could, and thrust out my hand. My palm caught his cheek with enough force to make a clap.

The remaining ten hours of the train ride dragged by like a thousand while I did my best to avoid Trudy. Thinking back on our conversation, I could now hear the edge of delight in her voice as she'd told me the story, as if she owned it, as if she revelled in the power to shock me with the horror of it. *Bones everywhere, they say.* My head throbbed, prickling in the spots where the hair was missing. I spent much of the time pretending to sleep, and once Jez awoke I took her for long visits to the dome car, where we could look up at the sky through the glass ceiling and let the landscape swirl by. "We're going to the moon," Jez said, pressing imaginary buttons on the tray table in front of her. "Are you excited, Auntie?"

But Jez's surge of energy wore off by the time darkness sealed us into the train, obscuring everything outside. She'd exhausted her interest in her toys and had taken my dinosaur egg halves out of her suitcase, rolling them up and down the aisles and crawling under the legs of annoyed passengers to chase after them. Under the fluorescent lights overhead, Trudy's face had turned sharp, the ink-dark irises of her eyes making her look snakelike, and even her smile now seemed suspect, crafty rather than serene.

The windows showed only our own reflections. There was no way to tell where we were, whether we were travelling through mountains or valleys or across lakes, until the lights of the port appeared and we entered a world of brightly lit machines, huge cranes and jerking scissor lifts, and stacks of shipping containers tall as skyscrapers—red, blue, yellow, green, blue, yellow, black, green.

Jonathan Bula hadn't been angry, like I'd expected. He'd asked me not to tell my mother that we didn't make out. "She promised me a hundred bucks," he told me.

I hadn't known, of course, that she had arranged the whole thing. I was mortified enough to confront Mutti afterward, to yell and cry, to say that I would never forgive her, that she was a terrible mother, a despicable human being.

She stared at me through my tirade, silent, her face a wall. When I was finished, the sting of my words caught in the air like an echo, she put her head in her hands. "What did I do to deserve this?" she muttered. "One child a clam, the other a fucking leech." Then she looked into my eyes. "You suck me dry, Regina. What else am I to do?"

We pulled into the station in Prince Rupert just after midnight. We had nowhere else to go.

20

THE SIGN OVER the door said SHEILA'S AT COW BAY.

"What's this?" I said to the cab driver.

"It's your B & B," he said. "The address you gave me."

"No," I said. "This can't be right." I pulled the crumpled envelope out of my pocket. *107 Cow Bay Road.*

"See for yourself," he said, pointing at the numbers nailed to the siding. 107. The house was quaint, with a red tin roof and red window frames and round windows all over like the ones on old sailing ships.

We stood at the door, our suitcases at our feet. There was a brass knocker on the front shaped like an anchor with a rope coiling around it.

"Is this where Oma lives?" Jez said.

"I don't know," I said. "Let's see, shall we." I gave the knocker three sharp clacks. We waited. I knocked again, harder. I thought of the day Ricky and Jez had come to my door, with no one there to greet them, and had waited under the oak, nothing to do but wait, without knowing for how long. How small Jez had seemed when I first saw her, how much younger, though it was not even two months ago.

I could hear movement inside, the creak of old floors, foot-steps pounding slowly down stairs. It took a long time for someone to answer, which I suppose is to be expected when you show up at someone's house unannounced, well past midnight. But the wait was excruciating. I felt as though the bottom of my stomach had fallen out, and it was still falling, falling, down an endless void like the rabbit hole in *Alice in Wonderland*.

Finally, the click of the door latch. The door swooped open to the face of a man. A very large and burly man with a thick, grey beard and a mop of salt-and-pepper hair. Truth be told, I felt relieved that it wasn't Mutti.

"Yes?" he said, peering at us. "Can I help you?"

"I'm sorry," I said, backing away and pulling Jez by the shoulders. "I have the wrong house."

But then I saw her. She was only a shadow, her silhouette carved out of the darkness by a dim light shining from another room. I knew it was her by the way she moved—her small steps, brisk and dutiful. She froze when she saw us.

"Mein Gott," she whispered. "It's Regina." And she emerged from the darkness, her face coming up beside the man's like a creature surfacing from a black sea.

Her hair had gone white, short, and thin. She had a liver spot on her left cheekbone. Her eyelids had begun to droop at the corners, making her eyes seem softer, spaniel-like, and her mouth had become an arc, downturned and wrinkled all along the edges. She looked like Mutti wearing a costume.

"Regina?" the man repeated. "*Your* Regina?" He let the door swing all the way open.

Mutti nodded.

"Well, no kidding?" He clapped, his huge hands clasping each other. He looked me over, then Jez standing next to me. "This yours?" he said, grinning. He bent down and sat on his haunches. "Hiya, little lady," he said. "My name's Silas. Sy, Grampa Sy, whatever!"

Jez curtsied. "Please to make your acquaintance," she said.

"My lord," Silas said, putting a hand to his chest. "Little lady indeed."

"Her name is Jez," I said. "My niece. Ricky's daughter." I tried to catch Mutti's eye but she seemed to be in a trance, looking at me but not at me. Through me. She was wearing a fuzzy housecoat printed with pink flowers. Mutti had always hated pink.

"Pretty good knock on the noggin' you got there," Silas said to Jez. He looked up at me. "She need some ice?"

"No," I said. "It's fine. We're sorry to intrude … so late at night …" I said.

"Heck no!" Silas said. "You kiddin'? We were just watching some TV, no big deal. Well, I was. Your mom was KO'd on the couch, as usual. Ha ha. Come on in!" He held open the door and ushered us through.

"We have guests," Mutti whispered, holding a finger to her lips. We shuffled in the dark foyer with our shoes and coats. Silas lifted our suitcases as though they were made of air and placed them in front of an old wood stove. We followed them up a narrow staircase that creaked shrilly with every step. At the top was a lofted area with a kitchen. We passed through and into another room lit with lamps and the blue glow of a TV, in front of which was a saggy brown couch, a rumpled pink blanket tossed across it. Behind was a bed, neatly made with a flowered bedspread.

"We can hang here," Silas said. "We've got a full house tonight, but we won't disturb anyone from here." He closed the door.

Jez and I stood in the middle of the room. It did not seem appropriate to sit. We were in what looked to be their bedroom, after all. And now Mutti had plucked up the blanket and was folding it quickly, halving it again and again until it was a bulky package in her hands. She scurried off to a closet by the bed and stuffed it inside.

"Have a seat," Silas said, and we did, though I sat with my bottom right on the edge of the lumpy cushion. The TV was playing *Wheel of Fortune*. "I tell ya," Silas went on, turning down the volume with the remote, "I've asked Sheila to invite you to come so many times. Gee, it's great to meet you."

It took me a moment to realize that when he said Sheila he meant Mutti. She was still at the closet, her back turned, rummaging around, taking out folded piles and rearranging them.

"This is nice," I said, looking around the room. A framed picture of a baby sitting in a wheelbarrow filled with pumpkins hung on the opposite wall. A pumpkin cap with a long curled stem, sat atop the baby's bald head. His look seemed one of shock, his mouth a little O.

"Yeah, thanks," Silas said, surveying the room also. "We've been running this place for oh … going on seven years now? Isn't that right, Sheila?"

"Eight," Mutti replied. She closed the closet door.

"Jeez," he said. "Where's the time go, eh? Where're you two staying?"

"Um …" I said. "I'm … not sure."

"Oh boy, you don't have a place lined up? Might be tough this time of year. Tell you what, I'll call Murphy up the road here, see if he's got space."

"Thank you," I said. "That would be a great help."

"Let you three get all caught up," he said as he left the room, closing the door gently behind him.

There was silence. The TV flashed and murmured. On the screen, Pat Sajak gestured to the board, and the remaining letters of the puzzle flipped into view. AIN'T MISBEHAVIN'. Mutti took a chair from beside the bed and moved it nearer, across from us. She sat.

"Where's Richard?" she said. She kept her eyes on me, away from Jez, as if looking at her might turn her to stone. She hadn't looked at Jez once, not even a glance.

"Not here," I said. "Just us." I put my arm around Jez. It felt like gloating, like rubbing something in Mutti's face, though I didn't know what. Still, Mutti refused to acknowledge her.

"You look well," she said. I knew I did not. I hadn't showered since Jasper; my skin was gummy all over with dried sweat, coated in the corn-chip smell of the train upholstery, my hair matted on one side. "Your cheeks," she continued, brushing her fingertips near her own cheeks. "Rosy."

I had nothing to say. Jez had begun playing with the buttons sewn into the couch cushions. One was hanging loose by its string, and she twirled it around her finger.

Mutti sighed. "How long will you be here?" she asked.

"I don't know," I said.

"Well. Ach du lieber, Regina, I don't know what you expect. I had no warning you were coming."

"I'm sorry," I found myself saying. Truth be told, what I'd hoped for was something so foolish I could not say it out loud—a little Hollywood scene I had boxed away in my mind. One in which Mutti would break down into joyous tears upon seeing us, gaze upon her granddaughter with amazement, embrace us both. We would all know without saying it that this was where we belonged—the three of us, together. Stars twinkling overhead. The end.

Silas returned, again giving his bear hands a single celebratory clap. "Good news," he said. "Murphy's got a room. It's just a couple of blocks up the road."

"Good," said Mutti. "It's late." She stood and cinched her housecoat tighter about her waist.

It was two a.m. by the time Jez and I settled into our double bed at the neighbouring B & B. The room was freezing; both of us wore layers and used our coats as extra blankets. We lay with our sides smushed together for warmth.

"They don't know who you are," Jez whispered in the dark.

"They don't?" I said.

"They were calling you Re-*ghee*-na." She pronounced it with a hard *g*, the German way, as Mutti said it. When I was young Mutti had made a point of correcting people when they called me Re-*jee*-na, and especially if they tried to pronounce it like the city in Saskatchewan. "It's Re-*ghee*-na," she'd say. "It means 'queen.'" But rather than explain this to Jez, I said nothing and patted her leg under the blankets. After all, it was true that they did not know me. Even to Mutti, I was practically a stranger.

≈

I dreamed of Waldo. I had used to let him play on my bed, making caves and tunnels out of the feather duvet for him to explore. Sometimes I'd lie beneath the duvet with him, my body becoming a labyrinth. His soft fur would brush against my bare skin, turning it to gooseflesh. I had my hand nestled in his fur as I surfaced from sleep, and it took me several moments to realize that I was not at home, not anywhere I recognized, and the fur was not Waldo's but the furry lining of the hood of Jez's coat.

In the light of the morning, Prince Rupert was a fairy-tale fishing village—rusty boats bobbing at bay, tangled fishing nets lying about the docks, mossy, wet concrete walls against a matching grey sky. Everything was damp to the touch. I'd taken a shower but my hair would not dry, the cold chill of it on my neck sending shivers down my spine. Jez and I stood on the dock, looking out at the vast Pacific. It was blacker than I had expected it to be, colder looking.

We walked the two blocks back to Mutti's place in the spitting rain and found the front door propped open. A couple of guests were descending the stairs as we entered, speaking to each other in German. Seeing me standing at the foot of the stairs made them pause, bumping into each other, then stare at me as if I were a meteor that had inconveniently crash-landed in front of them. Since it was clear they saw it as my responsibility to get out of their way, I did not, and eventually they slunk past, turning their bodies sideways along the banister, eyes downcast.

I led Jez up the stairs and into the kitchen, which was filled with the grey morning and the smell and sizzle of bacon. The remnants of breakfast were scattered about the dining table: stray morsels of scrambled eggs, crusts of toasts, half-full lipstick-smeared cups of cold coffee. A teenage boy sat in front of a plate of partially nibbled toast coated in peanut butter. He was slouched in the chair, holding a video game in two hands, his thumbs hammering away at the buttons.

At the kitchen sink stood Silas, his back decorated with the bow of a red apron. When he turned around, the front of the apron said REAL MEN BAKE.

"Whoa, morning there, you two!" he said. "How'd you do last night? Murphy treat you well?"

"Yes," I said, "it was fine." We'd seen Murphy, an ancient, hunched man who'd lost most of his teeth, for all of two minutes. He'd given us the key to our room and pointed the way to the door, then announced that breakfast was at eight before disappearing into his own room. "We slept well," I added. Another embellishment for Silas's benefit.

"Great," he said. "We just finished up with the guests. This here's Jason." He clapped the boy's shoulder. Jason kept his eyes on his game. "Say hi, Jason," Silas said. "Christ."

"Hi." His eyes darted up at us for a split second.

"Our son," Silas said, shaking his head. "Most of the time we like him." He scrubbed the boy's hair.

Our son. The words rang in my ears. He must have been seventeen or eighteen years old, I thought.

As if he'd read my mind, Silas said, "Just turned eighteen on Tuesday."

"I'm hungry," Jez said, scanning the abandoned plates on the table.

"We'll get some food in a minute," I said to her. My head was spinning. *Our son.* Eighteen years old. He couldn't be Mutti's son. When Mutti left fifteen years ago, I'd been twenty-one. Ricky had been eighteen.

The boy, Jason, was slight and soft looking, with mousy brown hair in fuzzed curls all over his head. He had none of the burliness of his father. He wore a black T-shirt that was far too large, the sleeves draping down to his elbows.

"I've got some extra bacon here if she wants," Silas said. "She looks like a carnivore to me." He pointed a pair of greasy tongs at Jez, his smile as wide and toothy as a cartoon.

Jez nodded, her tongue jiggling out of her mouth. Silas cleared a spot for us next to Jason.

"What about Regina?" he said. "Bacon? Or I can whip you up some toast?"

My stomach was still sour from the day before, and the thought of putting bacon in it was making me want to retch.

"I'm fine, thank you," I said, sitting anyway.

"Your mom's at work," Silas said.

Jason still showed no reaction, his eyes fixed on his game. Did he know I was Mutti's daughter, I wondered. Did he call her Mom? I peered around the room.

"Oh, sorry," he said. "Not here. Her other job. She works at the lock shop on Thursdays and Saturdays."

A job is a job is a job. How like Mutti not to be satisfied with only one job for eight years. Jez held her fork upright, her teeth pulling chunks from the strip of bacon speared on its tines.

"But," Silas went on, "we talked about it last night and we're having you two over for dinner tonight. No ifs, ands, or buts."

"Oh," I said, "but—"

"Nuh-uh," he interrupted. "I said no buts. We're having lasagna. My spesh-ee-al-ity. Right, Jay?"

"Yup," said Jason.

"This bacon is positively scrumptious," Jez announced, spearing another strip. Silas laughed so loudly and heartily that I jumped a little in my chair. He would make a perfect Santa Claus, I thought, complete with the beard, the laugh, the way his belly stuck out under the red apron. Mutti's men had usually been of the opposite variety: wiry and weaselly, with eyes that seemed to be in a dozen places at once.

"Where's the lock shop?" I said.

21

"IS HE REALLY MY GRANDPA?" Jez asked as we walked up the street toward the city centre.

"No," I said. "Your papa's papa lives far away. On the other side of the country." I pictured Clint baring his hairy chest at the pool, hands on hips, and was glad that he was thousands of miles away. But then as I tried to recall the features of his face, they suddenly became Silas's, and I had to squeeze my eyes shut to blank the image from my mind.

I'd imagined the lock shop tucked away in a dark alley, but it was just up the main road in the middle of town, in plain sight: Carl's Lock Shop. The sidewalk leading up to the shop appeared to be gated off for some kind of construction, so Jez and I walked on the opposite side of the road. As we neared, I made out the words on a hand-painted sign that hung in the window: *Prince Rupert's Other Museum*.

"What happened?" Jez said as we trotted across the street. We could see more clearly now through the yellow fencing that surrounded the lot next to the lock shop: rubble, huge mounds of it, the destruction so total and bald-faced that it was hard to imagine how a building had once been made of it.

"Some kind of demolition," I said. "It looks like they might be taking down an old building to make way for something new."

"There was a fire," Jez said. She stopped at the fence and hooked her fingers in the grate.

"I think you might be right," I said. I clearly could not temper the violence of the sight. Great beams of blackened, splintered wood and bent metal stuck out of the pile, wedged among chunks of concrete, loose bricks, and shards of glass. It was as though the building had been turned inside out and shredded by some savage, fiery machine. Jez and I stood there for a minute or two, examining the site, and I knew that our brains were momentarily in sync, flashing through memories of the fire on the highway. The flames swallowing branches, whole trees, spitting embers and filling the sky with smoke thick enough to chew.

We stood together for a while, taking it all in. Curiously, the lock shop appeared to have escaped the fire quite unscathed, only its brick facade scorched in a band along its side like a rim of black hair.

"My papa said Oma was very sick," Jez eventually said. "She didn't look very sick."

"She isn't," I said. "Not really. Your papa is … a bit confused, that's all."

My eye caught something in the rubble: a woman's dress, its blue sequins still glittering in a few unsullied patches. For the briefest of moments I thought I saw an arm inside a sleeve, the shape of a body lying broken under a cairn of bricks, but my mind quickly righted to reality. It was not a dress at all, but rather the shiny, melted carcass of a sheet of plastic.

"She'll help us," I said. "Mothers always know what to do."

Jez peered up at me as if to gauge my conviction in this callow statement. "My mummy said she didn't know what to do," she said.

"She did, did she," I said.

Jez nodded. "She said she couldn't help me anymore."

Tears were forming in my eyes now, shivering my vision. I blinked them away. "I think that's awful," I said. "And wrong."

Jez shrugged. "I think it's true," she said.

A little bell on the door of the lock shop announced our arrival, though it hardly seemed necessary. The shop was small—small enough that any customers who entered would come immediately face to face with the shopkeeper at the till. In our case, we could barely make room for the door to close behind us since a customer was already standing at the glass case that served as a counter, drumming his fingers on top. Mutti was fiddling with the key cutting machine in the back corner, and I could not tell if she had noticed us or not. The machine whirred and then began to whine and shriek as it did its job. Behind her, across the entire length of the wall, hung uncut keys—thousands of keys in all shapes and sizes, gold, brass, and silver, each one dangling from a little hook stuck into a giant pegboard that had been affixed to the wall. I'd never seen so many keys at once in my entire life, and I admit that the effect of them glinting together like stars against the black pegboard was rather beautiful.

The rest of the shop, however, was chock-full of dulled and dust-laden things. Old things, antiques, you might say, though much of it did not look to be of any value. Having no place to stand at the front as we waited for Mutti, Jez and I began to wander through the narrow aisle that carved its way through the collection. Shelves and glass cases were jammed into every available space, and packed into each was an assortment of trinkets and knick-knacks. It was a dizzying sight for the eyes, particularly since I was so concerned with not bumping into the stacks and piles flanking us on all sides that my head was rolling all over the place to keep track of all my limbs and bulges. Every so often I had to freeze in place to absorb the assault of images. Here, a collection of toy cars and trucks skirting a miniature Bick's pickle truck, an assortment of ceramic doorknobs, feathered fishing flies, glass soda bottles—green, clear, brown—tarnished silver spoons, pocket watches, a sword hung in its scabbard. There, commemorative teacups decorated with the gilt-framed faces of Queen Elizabeth and Charles and Diana, two-dollar bills gone flannel soft, cigar boxes, pin-up girlie calendars, dented Zippo lighters, smoking pipes, whistles, and porcelain Disney figurines—Mickey, Donald, Tinker Bell. In one of the corners stood a shelf filled top to bottom with old cameras, their black lenses clustered together in the dim like giant spiders' eyes.

It occurred to me that not a single thing in sight would exist in nature.

Jez plucked a rabid-looking stuffed rat out of a fishbowl and touched its crooked teeth with the tip of her finger. While its fur was clearly synthetic, the teeth looked quite real—hard as bone, ivory-yellow, and pointed. "Can I have this?" she whispered, as though we really were in a museum.

"We'll see," I whispered back.

The bell rang again, and the door opened and whacked shut. A faint electric buzz filled the silence.

"How did you know I was here?" Mutti's voice called out. I could not see her face because it was behind a spinning case of jackknives.

"Silas told us," I said. I moved through the aisle, sucking in my gut so as not to snag anything. The customer was gone, and Mutti stood behind the case, her hands pressed flat to the glass.

"I mean," she said, "how did you know I was living here? In this place."

"Your letter," I said. "I kept it."

Mutti shook her head. "I thought you might have moved. I should have known."

I stood in front of her, the glass case between us. Mutti's hands were knobbly, the skin loose and papery over the bones, the nails bitten down. Beneath them, peeking up through the grimy glass, lay a collection of old war medals and brass bullets standing on end, all lined up in neat rows.

"I don't know what I'm doing," I said to her hands.

"With what?" she said. "What do you mean?"

"With anything." Jez came up beside me then, and I could feel her small hand slide into mine, which was enough to make the tears begin gushing from my eyes once again. I was pitiful in that moment—how stupid, how utterly useless it was to cry here and now, like a baby, at the sight of my mother. I rammed the crook of my elbow into my face to stop it from happening.

Mutti bustled out from behind the counter, but it was not to me she came. She bent down and said to Jez, "My good friend Liberty runs the bookstore next door. Can I take you there for a few minutes?"

I assumed Jez nodded, because they quickly went to the door, me with my arm still pressed into my eyes and the bell ringing again as they left. In the few moments of solitude, I managed to collect myself. My eyes were bleary now, the keys on the wall shimmering like a gold and silver tapestry.

Mutti returned. That incessant bell tinkling. "I know about the girl," she announced.

"Know what?" I said.

"What she did," Mutti said. "You have no business bringing her here."

"She's not dangerous," I said, and my voice came out like a bark, much louder and more forceful than I'd intended.

"How do you know, Regina? You're not her mother. This is not— some kind of game."

"What would you have me do, then?"

"Bring her back."

I shook my head. "They don't understand her," I said.

"And you do?" Mutti shot back.

"They think she doesn't feel anything, but she does. She feels more deeply than anyone. It's more than they could ever comprehend, it's so much it can't even fit inside her." I was raving, I knew, the words spooling out of me like ribbons. "They'll ruin her," I went on, shouting now. "They'll hollow her out until she's empty. Nothing. Like some kind of hideous *thing*—as if she doesn't have a brain, a heart, like anyone else. Some *thing* they can hide away until everyone forgets. She's only a god-damn child. She deserves to be loved. Real love."

Mutti let out a sigh so loud and long I felt the wind of it on my face. "You can't erase it," she said. "Bedenke das Ende."

"I love her more," I said.

Mutti folded her arms, as though her point had been proven. "You think you're saving her," she declared. "But this is all selfish. Whatever fantasy you are imagining—it won't happen. Things will only get worse for you."

"I don't care about me," I snapped.

"Then do it for her. Bring her back to Richard. Back to her mother. She needs her mother."

"That's a bit rich coming from you, no?" I said.

Mutti did not look wounded, as I'd hoped. She pressed her lips together. Her hands set themselves firmly on her hips. "You're more of a child than that little girl is," she said. "Now please leave. I'm working."

We arrived for dinner at seven o'clock. It wasn't until Silas greeted us with open, expectant hands that I realized I should have brought something—flowers, perhaps, or wine? But it would have seemed absurd to bring a gift, an act of playing along with the charade that we were welcome, which I was not prepared to do. Jez had brought the stuffed rat. I wasn't entirely sure if Mutti had allowed her to keep it or if Jez had taken it without her knowledge. Either way, I was glad for its hideous face to be peeking out from under her arm, aiming its beady eyes at Mutti and her surrogate family.

"Did you get a chance to see the sights?" Silas asked. We stood with him in the kitchen while Mutti and Jason were setting the table.

"What sights would those be?" I said.

Silas chuckled, then stopped himself when my face stayed stoic. "Well, you know, most people like to walk the waterfront a bit, visit some shops, check out the museum. Some nice hikes around here too."

I looked down at myself, at the green Crocs I wore on my feet and the wrinkled hem of my unwashed dress, which must have betrayed how farcical I thought the idea that I'd come here to hike, because Silas went to the oven to check his lasagna without waiting for me to respond. What had Mutti told him, I wondered. Was he as clueless about what had happened earlier—as ignorant about everything, really—as he appeared? He put me in mind of a sloth, not because he was slow or lazy but because he always seemed so cheerful despite being left out of the loop, as if for him, living was as simple as eating, sleeping, and watching.

"Does she drink milk?" Mutti asked me as she set glasses down by each plate.

"I don't know," I said. "But you can ask her."

Mutti glared at me, then fetched a carton of milk from the fridge and set it on the table.

Having finished his task, Jason pulled a shiny silver cellphone out of his back pocket as he sank into a chair at the table. His thumbs began poking at the screen.

"Jay, do you mind?" Silas said. "We just talked about this."

Jason rolled his eyes and put the phone back into his pocket.

"Have a seat wherever you like," Silas said. "Dinner's not too far away. Jason, tell them about your award."

Another roll of the eyes. "Dad, it's not a big deal."

"Silver in the National Robotics Challenge," Silas said, raising his fists in the air. "He built a combat bot. From scratch. I'd call that a big deal."

"Well. Silver, that is impressive," I said, though I had no idea what a combat bot was. I imagined a little tin robot jerking fists clad in red boxing gloves.

Jason's face was almost pained in his effort to suppress his smile. He blushed pink.

"Where's your medal?" Silas asked. "Show 'em your medal, Jay."

"Naw," Jason said. "I don't even know where it is now."

Silas ducked into another room and came out dangling the medal from its blue ribbon. Jez and I looked. Engraved into the shiny disc was a picture of a person and a robot reaching their hands out toward one another in a gesture of longing. Because it was all in silver, the person appeared to be made of metal also—a more advanced robot, sophisticated enough to convincingly mimic a real person. It gave me a bit of a chill to think of robots seeking touch, affection.

"Can I see your robot?" Jez asked.

"Uh, sorry," Jason said. "It's back at my dorm."

"He's studying electrical engineering down in Vancouver," Silas told us. "On full scholarship."

"All right, enough, Sy," Mutti said. "You're embarrassing him."

"Sorry," Silas said. "Proud dad here. Well, we're both proud."

Mutti turned away. "Are we all ready?" she said, opening the oven door and peeking inside. "It looks brown enough to me."

We settled around the table, Jez and I opposite to Mutti, while the steaming lasagna cooled in the centre of the table. When Silas began to dish it out, the layers oozed red juices into the foil pan.

"She's a little runny," Silas said, "but it's the taste that counts, right?"

"It smells delicious, my dear," said Mutti. She laid a hand on Silas's shoulder but drew it back when she saw me looking.

"Haven't had lasagna in a while," Silas said. "It's Jason's favourite. A treat for his visit. When's the last time, Jay? Was it your graduation?"

"Yeah, I think so," Jason said, holding up his plate. Silas slopped a gigantic heap in the middle, the weight of it making the plate knock against the table. Silas must have seen my eyes bulge at the portion.

"Hungry man," he said. "You think this is a lot, you shoulda seen how much he ate the last time." I had a hard time believing it, the boy was so skinny.

"We had that giant cake that night too," Silas went on. "In the shape of one of those graduation caps. Fanciest cake I've ever seen. It even had gold leaf on it. But Jay was so full of lasagna he couldn't even take another bite!"

I couldn't help but think of Ricky's graduation. That evening, after the ceremony, Ricky had gone for a walk to 7-Eleven and had come back with a stray dog. The way the dog barked was like an old man hacking. It was a mutt of some sort, rusty brown all over, with a pit-bull's broad jaw and wide-set, piggy eyes.

"The poor thing was whining outside the store," Ricky said, scrubbing the dog all over its flea-bitten coat. "No one cared. Everyone was just walking past him."

"He might have diseases, though," I said to Ricky.

"Yeah," he said, continuing his scrubbing anyway.

I'm partial to animals, of course, but truth be told, I was afraid of this one. It was skittish yet full of wild glee, like a hyena. It seemed to have instantly fallen in love with Ricky. And Ricky was already returning that love with gusto, giving him an endless loop of "good boy, good boy," never seeming to tire of the dog's tongue all over his face, even cooking up a whole tray of ground beef for his supper that evening. Clint asked to take Ricky out for a celebratory steak dinner at the Keg and Ricky declined, insisting he had to stay home to take care of the dog.

It seemed wrong to let the occasion of Ricky's graduation pass with so little fanfare. I wanted to give Ricky a gift. Something other than the green tie I'd gotten on sale, which turned out not to match his suit after all. I wanted to give him something that acknowledged how difficult it had been for him to graduate from school with his mother gone, with no clear future ahead of him. If she'd still been around, perhaps he would've made plans to go to university. Ricky was bright—his grades were always far better than mine—and he used to talk about becoming an architect one day. But that did not seem like a possibility when it was just the two of us.

I wanted to tell him, somehow, that he was good. Not like the mutt on whom he was showering praise, who'd done nothing at all to deserve it. But, as always, I struggled to find the words. Finally, just as he began plodding up the stairs to go to bed, the dog bouncing at his heels, I said, "Ricky. Mutti would be proud of you."

"No, she wouldn't," was all he said.

In the morning, I woke to find the screen at the back door torn. Ricky had left the sliding glass door halfway open, for fresh air, he'd said. The dog had escaped sometime in the night.

I didn't wake Ricky. I was worried he would be heartbroken, and I wouldn't be able to bear the look on his face. But when he saw what had happened, he didn't seem upset at all. He walked to the screen door and slid it open, and it wasn't until he'd done so that I saw what the dog had left there, on our back porch: a pile of shit. It was perfectly formed and glistening, coiled up on itself like a cobra.

We never saw the dog again. Ricky took a plastic grocery bag from under the sink and picked up the mess with a quick sweep of his hand, then took it straight out to the bin, avoiding my pitying gaze.

In the end, that was all that Ricky had been gifted on the night of his graduation: a pile of shit and yet another absence.

Now, watching Jason look on impatiently as his father portioned slippery squares of lasagna onto all of our plates, I pictured what Jason had been given: the graduation cake shaped like a mortarboard cap, with layers stacked five, six, seven high, glittering in gold leaf, so shiny that the smiles of all his adoring friends and family were reflected in it. Mutti's too.

"Save room for dessert this time," Mutti said quietly to Jason.

"She made strawberry rhubarb pie," Silas said. "Another one of Jay's favourites." I'd never known Mutti to bake. Not even cookies. Baking was an occupation for featherbrained housewives, she'd always said.

"I like pie too," said Jez.

"I don't doubt it, little lady," Silas said.

We began eating, making the customary polite murmurs of satisfaction. The lasagna was meaty and sweet, and flecks of cottage cheese swam in the runny sauce pooling on my plate. Jason ate with his fork sticking out of his fist, hunched over his plate, shovelling mouthfuls. If he were Ricky when we were young, Mutti would have smacked him upside the head and called him a barbarian at the sight of such behaviour. Instead, she poured Jason a glass of milk and set it in front of him. I poured one for Jez, and she looked at it like she'd never encountered milk before. She took a tiny sip and licked her lips.

"So, you two," Silas said. "You're still living … where is it, Medicine Hat?"

"Drumheller," I said, my voice nearly a growl. His obliviousness was beginning to prickle me. The whole thing was—their little family unit of three, the lasagna dinner like some kind of wholesome family tradition, their coddling of Jason and his spoiled toleration of it, and Jez and me outsiders to it all, strangers.

"Right," Silas said. "Where the dinosaurs roamed."

"Mutti—Sheila—brought us up there," I went on. "Me and Ricky. Twenty years you lived there, wasn't it?" I said to Mutti, forking a big bite into my mouth.

Mutti nodded, chewing a mouthful of her own. She was looking down at the table. Something heavy was in the silence among the three of them, Jason's eyes darting from Silas to Mutti.

"Look," Silas said, eyeing Mutti. "We don't really talk that much about the past. It's hard for your mom. There's a lot of … trauma there for her."

"Oh," I said. "I see. Trauma, you say." I laid down my fork. A fizzy feeling was rising up through my body, as if thousands of tiny, sharp-edged bubbles were floating up from my gut and collecting inside the cavities of my head. I breathed in through my nose and the air felt hot.

"It's all right, Silas," Mutti said. Her little embarrassed smile made me want to grab a fistful of lasagna and smush it all over her face. Instead, I spoke. Calmly, my voice humming like a lullaby.

"Where is your mother, Jason?" I said. "Do you have a mother?"

Jason opened his mouth, but nothing came out. He looked at Mutti. She shook her head at him.

"Is it her?" I said, pointing to Mutti. "Is she your mother? Funny, she used to be mine."

"Okay," Silas said, standing, his chair skidding on the floor. "Let's not do this now—"

"Do this?" I said. "What am I doing? Telling the truth? Do you even know the truth? Do you know what she did? That she nearly killed a man?"

"What is going on," Jason said.

"Stop, Regina," Mutti said. "You can be angry. But please, not here."

"Your mother here," I said to Jason, "abandoned her children. Her real children. My brother, Ricky? He had no one when he was your age. His mother could've been buried in a ditch for all he knew."

"Come on now," Silas hollered. His voice boomed, all of us flinching at the force of it. "You were a grown woman," Silas said. "She did everything she could for you."

"She disappeared," I shot back. "Into thin air. Poof. Nothing for twelve years. I thought she was dead."

"It's not like you made it easy on her," Silas said.

"Stop it, Silas," Mutti yelled.

"Suffocating her like that. Refusing to make any goddamn thing of yourself."

"You don't know anything," I said.

"I don't care. Your mother's done her penance, okay? When Jason's mother died? I don't know what I would've done if I hadn't met her. Jason was only two years old, for god sakes. She picked up the pieces. She saved us. She's been a loving, devoted mother. For almost fifteen years now. The rest doesn't matter anymore. She's put all that behind her."

But she hadn't. I had seen that immediately, since the moment we'd found her the day before. I could see it in the way age had tugged down her mouth, the way her body seemed poised to fold in on itself, the way her eyes had apologized every time she revealed glimpses of the ease of her everyday life. This artificial life, which she used as a veil over the old. And now, in the way she was clasping her hands, pressing them tightly beneath her chin, her eyes squeezed shut. Guilt plagued her—an incurable infection, eating away at her insides.

There was a sound then: a splat, thick and juicy. Jez was holding her plate by the edge, tilted down at the floor. Her lasagna a pile of red and brown chunks on the hardwood. We all stared at her. Her face was calm and flat. There was a bit of red sauce smeared under her lips.

"This is crazy," Jason said, holding his head in his hands.

"It's okay, Jay," Silas said. "They're leaving."

I stood. "Does she ask you to hit her?" I said to Silas.

No one spoke. Jez stood too, at my side.

"Does she ask you to hurt her?" My voice wobbled, not quite mine. "Does she still like to be punished? Strangled?"

Jason began to cry. Mutti let out a sob and lunged at him, wrapping him up in her arms.

"You can leave now," Silas said.

22

"YOU'RE IN TROUBLE, REGINA."

"I know," I said to Ricky. I sat on the end of the bed in our room at Murphy's, in the dark. Jez lay next to me, her whole body, even her head, under the quilt, sleeping—or at least pretending to be.

"You should've come back when I said. Do you have any idea how much time I've spent driving around? I went all the way up past High Level, for Christ's sake. Carla's losing her mind."

"I'm sorry," I said.

"She's going to call the police, Regina. I can't keep talking her down."

"Tell her we're coming home."

Silence. He was trying to decide whether or not to believe me. Even I wasn't quite sure whether to believe me.

"When?"

"Tomorrow. We're catching the train in the morning. It will take us a couple of days."

"Train? Where the hell are you?"

"Ricky," I said. "I found her."

Another silence. Then a sigh. How it dropped, like an unravelling, said more than words. "Put Jez on the phone," he said.

She poked her head out from the quilt folds as soon as Ricky said her name. "Hi, Papa," she chirped into the phone, as if it were just an ordinary day. My ears were clearly not as sharp as hers, as I could only hear vague mumblings coming from the other end. Jez listened, nodding her head. "Uh-huh," she said.

We'd had a bath together when we'd arrived back at our B & B. The tub, an oversized dusty-rose Jacuzzi, seemed made for us; when I sank myself into the water, making it rise nearly to the brim, there was a perfect pocket of space for Jez's body between my legs. I used a ceramic mug that I'd found under the sink to pour water over her hair and then shampooed it clean, scrubbing my fingertips in little circles over her scalp behind her ears, just like Mutti used to do. Then Jez did the same to me. She even sang a little song as she rinsed it out, but the words sounded to me like nonsense.

"What song is that?" I asked her.

"My mummy sings it," she said. "It's a Chinese song."

How much I did not know. How much life a person of only six could've already lived. There was goodness in her, but not the kind that others could see. She already knew she was not the perfect copy of Carla that Carla still believed was possible. She was afraid, always, of being invisible.

When I got out of the tub, the water level sank below Jez's belly button.

"Do you want to come out?" I asked her, but she said no. She lay back in the water, letting her dark hair float and sway around her head.

I knew it then. The tether—the one I had pictured when Jez first arrived—connecting her to Carla, wrist to wrist, snaking and looping across great distances, was still there. There was nothing I could do to break it. The thought opened a gaping chasm in my stomach. Just like with Mutti, I'd been looking toward something, some possibility of the future, as if it could be blind to everything that had come before. I'd thought I could somehow change it—not change the past, but change the way it held her, open to the air, unafraid, unashamed, rather than closed up in a fist. But I hadn't changed anything. Perhaps I hadn't needed to.

"I know," Jez was saying now into the phone, still nodding. Then, "Yes. Yes, Mummy." There was just enough ambient light coming from the windows to see the white glow of her eyeballs, turning and pointing in my direction. "No," Jez said. "We went to the Arctic. Now we're somewhere else. Oma's here, but they told us to go away."

I took the phone from Jez.

"Everything's fine, Carla," I said.

"Who do you think you are," she said.

"We're coming back. We'll be back by Tuesday. Don't worry." I hung up.

Not a minute later, the phone rang. The trill startled us both; Jez hopped up and flopped a pillow on top of it, muffling the sound.

I went to her and stroked her hair, still wet from the bath. The phone rang and rang. "It's all right," I said. I kissed her right on the crown of her head, pressing my lips into her hair, the smell of candy pears caught in it. Then I lifted the pillow and answered.

"I know where you are," Ricky said. "Please, promise me you'll come home this time. I can't go after you, Regina."

"I promise," I said. "I'm sorry, but Mutti's not coming with us. She's not coming back. Not ever."

Ricky made a strange huffing noise, like something between laughing and sobbing. "You still don't get it, do you?" he said. "I never wanted her to come back."

I was silent. "But," I said, "you told me I should've gone after her."

"Only because I wanted her to pay for what she'd done. Take some goddamn responsibility."

"I'm angry that she left too," I said. "And now, with some replacement family—"

"Stop." Ricky's voice had gone high, on the edge of screaming. "I don't care. I don't want to hear about any of it."

"You're being a baby."

"She was an awful mother, Regina. She messed me up for life."

"Well. That's quite dramatic. Especially for you."

"My god, you sound like her. Didn't it ever dawn on you why I had to move schools? Why I suddenly lost all my friends and never made any new ones after that?"

"Ricky," I said. "I know about the pictures. The pictures of you. Naked. I saw them."

I could feel his shame in the silence, as though it were seeping through the phone.

"Then you must know that Mutti plastered them all over the school," Ricky said. "Everyone saw them. Kids, teachers, the principal. Can you imagine what that does to a fifteen-year-old kid?"

"What are you talking about?" I said. My vision went sideways for a moment, as if the whole earth had suddenly swerved. "Robin did that," I said, my words slowing. "Robin put up the pictures."

"Robin? Jesus, Regina, are you thick? Why in god's name would Robin do it? Mutti wanted to punish me—for what? Having a relationship with a girl? Having a secret? Who knows. That's just how she was. How she always was with me."

"You're wrong," I said.

"You know who told me it was her?" Ricky said. "That guy. Leon."

"No," I said. "He was lying. He must have been lying, he was always a snake—"

"This is what I mean," Ricky said. "You have an amazing ability to delude yourself. Just like her. I'm not the enemy here, Regina. Neither is Carla. We're people who know right from wrong, that's all."

I tried to sleep. I piled my clothes on top of myself, all the feather-stuffed pillows, but I could not shake the sensation that my body was slowly dissolving. Pieces of me sloughing off in little white flecks and floating away. I had to put my foot on the ground to anchor myself, which felt better, so I swivelled round and put the other down too. It was as if my body were willing me to walk. Somewhere. Anywhere. I looked at the clock: 2:43 a.m.

As I crept out the door, I heard the bed covers toss. "I'm coming," Jez said, crawling out and sticking her feet into her boots.

As much as I'd hoped never to see Sheila's at Cow Bay again, I had a note that I needed to leave for Mutti. It said: *What is the worst thing I could have done? Now think about how I chose not to do it.* I folded it twice and slipped it into the mail slot in the front door.

We walked up the deserted road. It was not raining but the street was still wet, shining under the lights. The briny smell of sea was strong in the air.

"We can't stay," I said to Jez. "We have to go back."

"Yeah," she said. "What will happen when we get there?"

"I'm not sure," I said. "Bad things for me, perhaps. But you will be all right. You'll be back with your parents. They miss you very much."

"I'll protect you," Jez said.

"Okay," I said. "Thank you."

"You know what my papa said? He said, 'as big as a million suns.' That's how big he loves me."

"That's very big," I said.

"Yup," she said. "So big it'll never burn out."

"Hmm," I said. "I like that." So Ricky hadn't forgotten he was a poet. "I feel that way too. For you."

"Me too," Jez said.

We came upon the burned-out lot next to Carl's Lock Shop, the mounds of rubble in the dark making the silhouette of a spiked dragon.

"Look," Jez said. There was a gap in the construction fence. A chain looped around the top with an open padlock dangling off of it. Jez pushed the fence, widening the gap. We stepped through.

The place had a ghostly feeling. It still smelled of burnt wood and plastic. Though all was still, the piled remnants seemed precarious under the shroud of darkness, as if they could at any moment collapse even further, a sinkhole swallowing them into the earth. I wondered how long ago the fire had happened. It couldn't have been long— perhaps a few days. There were people somewhere nearby who were still in a state of shock, unable to understand what they had lost. All of it, the things that had once mattered so much, only meaningless scraps now, destined for some landfill at the edge of town.

Jez picked up a chunk of concrete large as her head.

"Careful," I said.

She slung it under her arm and carried it back through the gap in the fence. I was surprised her little arms had such strength. She dropped it on the sidewalk in front of the lock shop.

"There," she said.

I knew what she meant. I did not hesitate. Up it came, into my hands and high above my head. It sailed through the air, and the crack and shower of shattering glass echoed in the street. I expected an alarm of some sort to sound, but none did.

We both marched back over to the lot. Jez grabbed a brick in each hand and I hoisted another chunk of concrete, this one so heavy I had to hang it between my legs and waddle it over to the shop. It blasted out most of the remaining glass in the window and landed with a thud on the hardwood floor. Jez's bricks arced over it and smashed in the dark. A sound like a slot machine—a million coins showering. Next I chose a beam of splintered wood. I tossed it, javelin style, through the window, and it smacked into a shelf inside, sending glass and porcelain figurines scattering like confetti. Jez swung a hunk of metal between her legs, lobbing it up high and hitting an old mantel clock square in the face, knocking it from its perch.

Strangely, I felt nothing. Nothing at all as we fetched more and more rubble and hurled it at the shop. No seething anger, no despair or desperation, not even release. It was happening, a plain fact, as if it were inevitable as rain.

I saw Mutti then, as she had stood before me in the lock shop, an immovable mountain. How had she seemed so warm and soft, so much like home, in my memories? All the time we'd spent together in the badlands hunting for traces of worlds we couldn't know, Ricky always somewhere else—where?

I moved faster now, retrieving armfuls of wood, plastic, rebar, brick—whatever I could wrench free from the wreckage—and flinging it at the shop. I got hold of a large shard of glass, pointed like a dagger.

"Auntie," Jez cried, taking hold of my wrist. I'd sliced my hand, blood spilling out everywhere. I shook myself free and hurled the glass anyway, along with a spray of blood. Jez sat on the curb and watched.

Now, Mutti's face had become ghoulish: mouth agape, stricken eyes, like the faces in Renaissance paintings of the Rapture—one among the horde of tortured souls.

"Bedenke das Ende," she had said. *Think of the end.*

"Stop me, then," I said aloud.

But no one did. I continued my rampage, moving back and forth from lot to shop like a machine, the measured rhythm of my steps between the tumbles and crashes of rubble making a kind of riotous song. It must have been only minutes, but it felt eternal. Inside the shop, beyond the smashed windows, the rubble was piling up, reforming its amorphous mound.

It was Jez who finally stopped me. She took my hand, and blood slicked from mine to hers, but she held fast. "Okay," she said. And then it was done.

EXPOSE

Wind and rain slowly erode the layers of sediment over time,
eventually returning the fossil to the surface.

SHE REMEMBERS EVERYTHING.

Her dad's silence, even heavier than normal. His jaw tensing as the Buick went deeper into the valley. She tries to imagine what his state of mind would have been: abandoned by his wife just as he was by his mother, afraid of his own daughter, unsure of what kind of future there was for them. The world closing in on him, tighter and tighter. But for her, the journey had felt like the opposite. A kind of opening. The landscape feels comforting to her now, just like it did back then. The hills like giant, ancient sandcastles, their edges soft against the sky. A picture out of focus. Nothing like the starkness of Arizona—those hot reds and greens, the sun penetrating everything with its orange glow.

They are driving the highway along Michichi Creek, but this time it's Jez at the wheel. Fourteen years haven't changed the place. It's a perfect copy of her memory, but shrunken down to a smaller scale. Of course, she knows it's really her who's grown larger. But even Auntie Reg, who'd had the pull of a planet to her six-year-old self, seems smaller now. Shrunken down to the realm of reality.

Regina sits in the passenger seat, stealing glances at Jez's face every now and then, no doubt taking stock of which pieces time has changed and which it hasn't. Jez tries to picture herself from the outside, which features stand out most. The row of silver hoops that hang from the shell of her right ear. The fishbone scar along her jawline. The slight upturn of her nose, like her mom's. They way her eyes look older than they should, which she tries to cover with thick black eyeliner.

They haven't said all that much to each other yet. Over the years they've written dozens of letters. Jez has told her aunt things that she's never told anyone else. But talking is different from writing. Neither of them has ever been much for talking. Talking never seemed necessary when they were together.

For now, they have settled into the silence, listening to the wind pulsing through Jez's open window, making a rhythm with the spinning tires. The sound of it, with Auntie Reg sitting next to her, makes her think of trains. As a kid, around eight or nine years old, she used to dream about a train. The same dream over and over. Riding through endless tunnels of darkness, flashes of light illuminating sleeping bodies. She was the only one awake. Each flash showed her something new. A sliver of eye peeking through the lids. A pair of crossed legs in red pants. A boy's head laid in a lap. Pictures frozen in time, like photographs.

She tried to wake Auntie Reg, but she wouldn't move. She was hunched over in her seat, the top of her head pressing the tray table on the seat in front. Pinned there, it seemed. Jez tried to shake her and found her arm hard, like a lump of clay. It wouldn't even move from its position when Jez pushed on it; it was stiff, anchored in place. Jez pushed harder, pushed on Auntie Reg's whole body, leaning all her weight into it, trying to dislodge it, trying to see Auntie Reg's face, but it was shrouded in a tangled net of hair that was stiff too, like straw.

Jez looked for help, searching the aisles in the darkness, trying to shake the bodies awake, screaming to wake them. But all she could see were the pictures that the flashes had already shown her. A sliver of eye. Crossed legs. A boy's head.

"I'm fine," Jez says to Regina now, without really knowing why. A way of affirming her thoughts, maybe. She's glad to see Regina smile.

They pull into the deserted parking lot. No tourists are here today; it's October, a day like a harbinger of winter, blindingly bright and cold. Even from across the highway they can see the coating of frost on the hoodoos, glistening under the naked, white sun.

They head toward the trail like they have a mission. Maybe Jez does; when she'd arrived last night she'd asked if they could come back here, but she didn't say why. The reasons don't make much sense, even to her. To find out if what she remembers is accurate. To separate what's real from what might be imagined. The wind blows from the west, a drone in Jez's ears. She pulls her hood out from beneath her jean jacket and buries her head in it like burrowing into a cave. Regina doesn't seem bothered. The hem of her dress slashes against her bare shins.

They climb the steps, their boots clanging on the metal grate. Regina stops at each landing to massage her knees. At the lookout they take a break, reading the signage as they are meant to do, taking in the view of the winding river and the rim of buttes on the horizon. Jez takes out her phone and snaps a few photos. A wide view of the coulee, a white layer of rock cutting the landscape cleanly in half. Four hoodoos standing together, backlit, casting pillars of shadow on the bentonite. Looking down on the swirled cap of one hoodoo. Rills combing down a slope. A close-up on a bulge of another slope where a single finger has carved *I was here* into the crust.

"So?" Regina says. "Is it how you remember?"

"I think so. The feeling is the same."

Regina waits for her to go on.

"Surreal," she continues. "Like being on the moon."

Regina smiles. "When I was a girl I used to pretend I was on the moon. When Mutti and I would go fossil hunting in Horseshoe Canyon. She used to ask me to walk behind her. I had to stay back, ten steps behind at least. If I got too close she'd speed ahead. She said she couldn't breathe, she needed air. It didn't make any sense to me. I imagined we were on the moon, we were running out of oxygen. I made a little game of it, like I was an astronaut. Sometimes Mutti got so far away I couldn't see her anymore."

Jez says nothing. She isn't sure whether to respond. Whether there's more to the story. But there isn't. "That's sad," she finally says.

"I suppose it is," Regina says.

"Did you ever go back?" Jez asks. "After we saw her in Prince Rupert?"

"No. I thought about it. But no."

"Probably for the best," Jez says.

Regina nods. "What will you do now?" she says.

Jez shrugs. "Get a job, I guess."

"Here?" Regina says. Hopeful, like a little kid.

"I don't have a work visa." Jez says it like an apology.

"Maybe you could get one?"

"Well. It's complicated."

"I see. Will you go back to the theme park then?"

"Nah. I didn't like that much." She sees Regina's chin drop slightly and realizes she might have interpreted Jez's job choice as following in her aunt's footsteps. But it had only been a waypoint, a way of making some money for a car and a road trip. "All it was was pressing a button all day," she explains. "Cleaning up kids' puke."

Regina laughs.

"I think I might want to go back to school," Jez offers. "College." It's the first time she's told this to anyone. The worry that saying it aloud might set up expectations she's not sure she can meet has kept her from telling her dad. "But I don't know how I'll pay for it," she says.

"I can give you the money," Regina says.

"You don't have any money," Jez says.

Regina sighs. "This is true."

"Student loans, I guess."

"What will you study?"

"I don't know." She does, but she's embarrassed to say. The girl who grew up surrounded by psychologists now wants to become one herself. The way it invites tidy assumptions—her life was changed, and now she wants to help others—reeks of the kind of inspirational bullshit that was constantly served up to her in juvie. She knows that Regina too would have had her fill of that even though she'd only been in minimum security for fourteen months.

"I'll find the money," Regina says.

They finish walking the loop quickly. They both know without saying it that they will keep walking, step over the low fence and make their own path between the sagebrush, just as they did all those years ago. Something had happened that day. A sudden difference, like another set of eyes had been switched on, though Jez had been too young at the time to really understand it. They had walked, searching for fossils, their shoes not even making footprints on the crusted earth, and in the end it had been just about the walking. At first, she'd been thrilled by the idea of doing something her mother would not approve of, something against the rules. Something bad, with Auntie Reg as her accomplice. That familiar rush of rebellion that rose up in her like hunger. What could she do next, she would think to herself, that her mom could not brush away, that her dad could not pretend had never happened, while they kept calling her their sweet, innocent, perfect little girl? But after a while, walking and walking with no destination, the urge had dissolved. A feeling of lightness came over her; she felt like she might float away. It was nice. No one was telling her where to go, how to be, and that felt good. She wasn't anxious. The tightness she carried around with her always, which she hadn't even noticed until then, had loosened. It was like she was filling her own skin for the first time, like being blown up from the inside with cool, fresh air. And when she'd pressed her hand into the mud and Regina had made her own handprint next to hers, the thumbs joined, she had seen the bird they made and thought immediately of the bird she and Adam had trapped in the cage with his pet rat. Making the bird in the mud was like a memorial, a way to leave the memory behind and imagine something new.

And they had found a fossil after all. Sort of. Jez had kept it, brought it back to Phoenix and hid it in her closet so her mom wouldn't know. She was glad, in the end, that Regina hadn't thrown it. It was heavy and jagged, nearly as big as her head at the time; Jez remembers that she had been surprised she could even carry it. She'd dropped it there, right in front of the lock shop. She knew what Auntie Reg would do. What she wanted to do. Jez had wanted it too. She'd even imagined it, how it would all play out, Auntie Reg hurling the thing at the shop with all her might, shattering the window, shards of glass fireworking in the shine of the street lights. The satisfaction of that shatter would have been like a drug for them both, and they would need more, and by then it would already have been too late to stop. She'd imagined how it would all go, every detail, she and Auntie Reg smashing whatever they could, all the baubles and trinkets and stupid junk that no one wanted anyway, until the shop was nothing but rubble. An echo of the lot next door.

But Auntie Reg had done nothing. She hadn't thrown the chunk of concrete. Instead, she left it sitting on the ground, just looking at it.

"Well," she eventually said. "That's it, isn't it?"

"What?" Jez said.

"It's our fossil."

"That?" Jez said. "It's ugly."

"It can be ugly," Regina said. "Nothing wrong with that."

"But what kind of animal was it?"

"I don't know," Regina said. "Perhaps it never was an animal. But maybe it's all right if we don't know. The important thing is that it was something, once. And now it's changed into something else. It can be whatever we want now."

"A new dinosaur egg," Jez said.

"Yes. Of course." Regina picked it up and cradled it under her arm, sitting its weight on her hip. "Are you ready?" she said to Jez.

They had not run away. They had walked. They'd let the quiet take over, thickening with each step they took, back in the direction they'd come from.

Returns. It seems like Jez's whole life has been a series of returns. Returning to her parents, returning to Phoenix, returning to juvie, again and again, returning here. Even now, just as she's thinking about this, she and Regina come up against a steep slope marred with tall grasses, and they are forced to turn back. She had planned to leave tomorrow, but it feels like something has been left hanging. Like she needs to give something to Regina. A way to fill in the gap of time wedged between them.

As they near the parking lot, Jez says, "I haven't seen my mom in a long time either."

"Oh?" Regina says, as if she doesn't already know. "She must miss you."

"I doubt it," Jez says. "The last time I saw her—two years ago now, I think—she took me out for ice cream. As if everything was okay, like we were just some normal mother and daughter and she wasn't wishing I was someone else the whole time. And this guy was with us, her new boyfriend, I guess. He was wearing a bowtie and a blue blazer. A real estate agent, I think. Really white teeth, and this awful fake smile."

Regina chuckles.

"Probably the most unlike my dad you can imagine," Jez says.

"It sounds that way."

"But she seemed happy, I guess."

"That's good," Regina says, almost like a question.

"Yeah."

They climb into the car and Jez starts the engine. "She got mint ice cream," she says. "It got all over her lips, like lipstick, but somehow she didn't notice. I'm sure she would have been mortified if she knew. But it was nice that she could just enjoy herself, for once. Be in the moment. That's the image I have in my head when I think of her now. Happy, with green lips."

It begins to rain as the car picks up speed on the highway. Lightly at first, and then in big, fat drops that hammer the windshield and stream across the windows. The wipers go back and forth, erasing the watery blur with each stroke.

"It's a good memory," Regina says. "Let it stay that way."

All of a sudden, by some magical shift in the atmosphere, the rain turns to snow. The hammering stops, the flakes falling weightlessly like tiny dancing ghosts.

23

I ONCE BELIEVED I had the power to forget. That a memory for which I had no use could be extracted, sliced out with clinical precision and sealed away in a jar, where it would simply wither away. It was an act of getting rid of the excess, that was all. But it seems I have no power to choose after all. Each memory is its own animal, and it will keep living and growing whether you nurture it or not. It will become what it needs to be. And when it finally returns, you might not even recognize it as your own.

Two days earlier, as Jez and I were packing our suitcases, readying for the long train ride ahead, this one returned to me out of nowhere: When I was eight years old, I had a dime-sized scab on my left knee that I was desperate to be rid of. I picked at the thing, scraping bits off the edge, exposing the pink skin beneath, little dots of fresh blood blooming and scabbing over again. I recalled the look of the wound— how it refused to heal properly, how the scabs had become a mottled collection, layering atop one another like miniature hamburger patties. Mutti swatted my hand away each time she caught me picking at the scab. "Alles zu seiner Zeit," she would say. *Everything in its own time.*

One of her favourite sayings, which often led into a lecture about the insignificance of a few minutes, a few hours, days, years, even a lifetime.

"There are rocks beneath your feet that have lived for billions of years," she would say. She would describe how the rocks just stayed there, in one place, getting buried deeper and deeper as time went on. They'd stayed, without a care, while the earth slowly swallowed them, while the remnants of countless plants and animals that lived and died were layered on top of them. Whole eras had come and gone at the surface above. And humans—the earliest forms of human beings like us—had only walked that surface for about two million years. A tiny sliver of that time. The word *sliver* made me imagine my own body as the time scale of the earth and humans as a mere sliver in the tip of my finger.

One week is not a long time, to be sure. But a week is enough.

In the week that Jez and I had been gone, the road had been the only constant. Now, moving in this way—surging forward at a hundred kilometres an hour—had become as natural as breathing. We'd hardly stopped since we'd found the car back in Jasper. There it was, parked in the Safeway lot just as we'd left it, save for the ripened stench inside. I collected the sun-baked mess of wood chips and droppings, filling two plastic grocery bags, which Jez dumped out onto the base of a bare young sapling at the edge of the parking lot. We stood for a moment, giving a silent send-off to the last remnants of Waldo, before setting off back on the 11, but this time headed east instead of west. And now, after four unbroken hours of driving beneath the wide open sky, we were nearly there. At the end but also back at the beginning.

"There," I said, pointing at the sandy buttes rising out of the earth ahead. "The badlands."

Jez sat forward, watching the landscape wrap around us. "Why's it called badlands?" she asked.

That memory was clear as glass: Mutti and me at Horseshoe Canyon, wearing our matching red kerchiefs on our heads. Mutti had scolded me for spilling some of our water on the parched sand, so dry that the little puddle could only skate over it. "There's a reason they call this the badlands, you know," she'd said.

"I believe it comes from a French saying," I said to Jez. "Mutti—your oma—once told me. It means something like 'land that is difficult to traverse.'"

Jez furrowed her brow.

"Traverse means to move across. Travel." Mutti had explained that the early French explorers had used the name when they arrived here, in the New World, when the land was wild and alien. "Quite a truthful name, isn't it?" she had said. As a child I hadn't really understood. I suppose my nascent, unworldly brain could not grasp how a land could be bad, and how the place I'd grown up in—the only place I knew—could be seen as treacherous. How the steep bentonite slopes and deep canyons, the punishing, dry heat in the summer, the sub-zero temperatures in the winter, the sheer exposure, the unceasing desolation, could be harsh enough to be unbearable. To me, it was just the way things were.

But now I recalled that I did learn, many years later, that Mutti had been mistaken. We had an information plaque about it installed at Fossil Land, and it turned out the name didn't really belong to the French explorers to begin with. There were already people living here, of course. The Indigenous people. This had been the badlands to them, in their own language, for hundreds or perhaps even thousands of years already.

"Actually," I attempted to explain to Jez, "the name 'badlands' was given by the first people to discover this land. Long before Europeans. There were no cars then. They travelled from the plains on foot. Just walking. It was all flat, flat as far as the eye could see, until they came here."

Jez's eyes wandered over the hills. I was creating a scene in both of our minds as I spoke. It was a scene of my own invention, to be sure, but facts did not seem so important in the moment.

"Imagine," I went on, "how cruel this land would have seemed to someone who had never known anything like it before."

"Yeah," she said. We were silent for a while as we descended into the valley. The hills loomed like sentries, their scrubby faces brittled by an entire summer's worth of heat. Jez turned her head left and right, taking it all in. "But after a while," she said, "they changed their minds. They saw it wasn't really bad."

I nodded. "You must be right."

"Are you sad that your mummy's not here?" she said.

"Not anymore," I said. And it was true. I rolled down my window and let in the wind, opening my mouth wide, as if I could eat the crisp autumn air like an apple. Jez did the same, and there we both were, our hair whipping around and our mouths stretching wide, wide as they could go. I thought about the nights we'd spent in the same bed, learning each other's breathing, dreaming in tandem. I thought about the things no one else would ever know: the smell of Waldo's soiled wood chips on the car upholstery; the colour of the bruise on Jez's cheek, how the shade of purple turned slightly greener each day; Sal's face contorted by fear, the crack of rock on skull; the crust of the snowpack where Earl lay entombed. I thought about Ricky and Carla, waiting, planning a future for Jez. With or without me. Perhaps the police would be there. How relieved they would all be.

You can't erase it. Bedenke das Ende. I understood now that Mutti had been trying to tell me something not about me, but about herself. She was telling me not to do what she had done.

Yes, I thought. *Think of the end.*

We would pull up to the house. Ricky would run out, but Carla would not. We'd see her eyes, black and piercing, through the sheer curtains of the window. Jez would fling open her door, grin, and jump into her father's arms, and his tears would drip into her hair. Carla would come out onto the porch with her cellphone against her ear, her eyes trained on me, vicious as a panther's. "Here we go," I would say. I would sit under the oak, combing the cool grass with my fingers, and wait.

But for now, there was only the road. Me and Jez, following the route that was set before us. This was living—letting all that had come before fall away, like shedding a long-dead skin. You could look at the shape of it afterward, a mirror to your own, knowing that even though it was no longer a part of you, it was still real. It would not disappear.

"Welcome to Dinosaur Country." I read the sign aloud as we passed, as if it were all new. I could not be certain I'd ever truly been here before.

ACKNOWLEDGMENTS

BAD LAND JOURNEYS through territories in Alberta and British Columbia that I was privileged to visit while writing, several of which I have close personal ties to. Having grown up in Alberta, I feel an unshakable connection to the prairies, the Rocky Mountains, and the badlands, and, since settling in the Okanagan Valley over a decade ago, the beautiful and varied landscapes of British Columbia have become equally close to my heart. However, I wish to acknowledge that I am and have always been a guest on these lands, which continue to suffer the violent repercussions of colonialism. The lands portrayed in this book are on Treaty 6 and 7 territories, as well as unceded territory—traditional gathering places since time immemorial for many diverse Indigenous Peoples, including the Blackfoot/Niitsítapi, Stoney, Cree, Tsuut'ina, Métis, Secwépemc, Lheidli T'enneh, Wet'suwet'en, and Tsimshian people. My home in Kelowna is on the unceded territory of the Syilx/Okanagan people. I am thankful and humbled to live, travel, and write among you.

I am indebted to Alix Hawley and Adam Lewis Schroeder—friends, brilliant novelists, and shrewd editors, from whom I have learned so much and who helped to steer this novel from the very beginning. Thank you to my friends and colleagues at Okanagan College, especially Sean Johnston and Jake Kennedy, for many enlivening conversations about writing craft and great books. Thanks also to Shelley Wood for helpful advice on beginnings and endings.

I am grateful for the time, space, and financial aid I was given to write this novel, which I owe in large part to Okanagan College and the Banff Centre for Arts and Creativity. Spending five weeks at the Banff Centre was like winning the lottery; every day I felt not only incredibly fortunate to be immersed in the spectacular mountain setting among so many talented artists, but also more confident in the worth of my work as a writer. My sincerest thanks to Dionne Brand and Linda Spalding, whose mentorship was invaluable in the early stages of writing.

Thank you to my agents, Samantha Haywood and Marilyn Biderman, for devoting so much time and energy to helping me make this book the best it could possibly be, and for championing it through thick and thin. And to the team at Arsenal Pulp Press—Brian, Catharine, JC, Cynara, Erin, and Jaz—I am in awe of the fantastic work you do and honoured to have had the opportunity to collaborate with you once again. Special thanks to Catharine for being the very best kind of editor and to Jaz for the striking cover design (and all the brilliant variations that were part of its creation). And to my dear friend, Chyla Cardinal, thank you for your expert design advice and for sleuthing out the gorgeous photograph that ended up on this book's cover.

Many thanks to my family, Chi-Fui Chong, Vanessa Chong, Justin Krogman, Alex Lye, Aaron Saunders, Kelly Krogman, and the Eggens, Collinses, and Pulvermachers, for your unwavering support. I owe an exceptional debt to my mother, Bettina Krogman, and my oma, Magdalena Estel, for inspiring many of the Germanisms in this book and, far more importantly, for being such beacons of strength to your children, grandchildren, and great-grandchildren.

And finally, thank you to Andrew and Josephine. As big as a million suns.